## Advance praise for Frank Anthony Polito and *Renovated to Death*!

"A fast, fun read—with bonus renovating tips!"
—Laura Levine, author of *Murder Gets a Makeover*

"The fabulous and fun Domestic Partners in Crime in this wildly entertaining new home makeover murder mystery don't cut corners on the laughs or suspense with suspects coming out of the woodwork! You'll want to both love it and list it as your favorite new cozy series!"
—Lee Hollis, author of *Death of an Ice Cream Scooper*

"The real estate market is hot and so is Frank Anthony Polito's debut mystery, *Renovated to Death*. If you're addicted to HGTV, if you've dreamed of flipping a house, or even if your DIY skills are limited to changing a lightbulb, you'll enjoy this trip to Pleasant Woods— where no one's ever been murdered, until now!"
—Leslie Meier, author of *Easter Bonnet Murder*

Books by Frank Anthony Polito

BAND FAGS!

DRAMA QUEERS!

REMEMBERING CHRISTMAS

RENOVATED TO DEATH

Published by Kensington Publishing Corp.

# Renovated to Death

## FRANK ANTHONY POLITO

KENSINGTON PUBLISHING CORP.
www.kensingtonbooks.com

KENSINGTON BOOKS are published by

Kensington Publishing Corp.
119 West 40th Street
New York, NY 10018

ISBN: 978-1-4967-3559-1 (ebook)

ISBN: 978-1-4967-3558-4

First Kensington Trade Paperback Printing: June 2022

10 9 8 7 6 5 4 3 2 1

Printed in the United States of America

*To Paula Reedy*

*Love,*
*Mr. Polito*

# Chapter 1

The handsome older man looked deep into my eyes. "So, what's it feel like being famous?" Clearly, he was flirting.

I blushed and took a sip of sauvignon blanc, my favorite. "Well, I'm hardly famous."

"You're on a TV show. And you've written all those best-selling books!"

I blushed again. "They're not *all* best sellers."

Being the cohost of a popular home renovation program had indeed given my sales figures a boost. But along with a rigorous production schedule came little time for other creative outlets, like penning the next Great American YA mystery novel.

The handsome older man gave my hand a paternal pat. "You're a modest young boy. I'm a big fan of your writing."

"That's very kind," I said, draining my wineglass. "But I'm hardly a boy."

The handsome older man grinned. "Okay, I'm fifty. How old are you?"

"The same age Jesus was when he died," I replied coyly before coming clean. "I'll be thirty-four in November."

"Really? You don't look a day over twenty-seven."

Like a lot of gay millennial men, I suffered from self-inflicted Peter Pan Syndrome. My first name was, in fact, *Peter*, so it made perfect sense.

Inside, I did feel like a man in his early-late twenties. Outside, my behavior and personal style often reflected as much. I had a preference for pullovers, and wore size small everything, purchased online, of course, because who had time to go shopping?

The handsome older man looked to his left. "This one's a keeper."

We weren't alone. This wasn't a date; it was a dinner party. We were only two of a half-dozen guests in attendance.

The handsome *younger* man sitting opposite me shrugged. "Almost five years I've been stuck with this one. Huh, Pete?" My life partner, who also happened to be my reality TV show cohost, winked at me.

JP Broadway, star of screens both big and small, was by far the most beautiful man I'd ever set my eyes on. *Tall, dark, and sexy* didn't begin to describe him. At thirty-five, dressed in a blue polo that hugged his baseball biceps and made his bright eyes pop, he still looked gorgeous.

"Five years!" A crass voice chimed in from the head of the antique oak dining table. "And you're still not married? Better do it before you guys turn forty. You wanna look good in your wedding photo." Our host, Bob, raised a glass of red wine in a jovial toast. "To PJ and JP. *Mazel tov!*"

PJ and JP.

Yes, it could be confusing.

Growing up, I'd always been called *Peter* by family and friends. When I first met JP, for some reason, he took a liking to calling me *Pete*. Then, when I turned from unpaid playwright to published author, *PJ Penwell* sprang to life—the *J* standing for *James*, after my father.

As a lapsed Catholic, JP didn't care much for being called

*John Paul.* When he joined the actors' union, he officially became known by his first two initials. Shortly after we started dating, he landed a gig on the highest-rated cop drama of the day, *Brooklyn Beat.* I couldn't ask my brand-new boyfriend to adopt a brand-new stage moniker, just because my publisher felt that *PJ* on a dust jacket would sell more books.

"Thanks, Bob," I said graciously to the only straight guy out of six seated around the table.

Bob turned his attention back to the handsome older man beside me. He snickered like a cartoon character. "So, Tommy . . . where's your boy toy tonight?" And he wondered why, on more than one occasion, people had mistaken him for a member of the pink team?

"Hell if I know," Tom Cash replied, rolling his dark eyes. "Think he's mad at me."

"Uh-oh. Tell Fairway Bob what you did wrong."

Perhaps it was because he preferred the company of men who loved other men? Perhaps it was because he was the proud proprietor of an antique shop? Or perhaps it was because, at the ripe old age of fifty, Bob Kravitz still found himself a bachelor?

Being his neighbors for the past nine months, JP and I did our best not to hold his heterosexuality against him. In private, we referred to Bob as a *hetmo,* our preferred pet name for hetero guys who could easily pass for homo. Back in the day, in New York, folks would use the term *metrosexual.* Same diff, only less mainstream.

Bob's real name, of course, was Robert. On social media, he was known to everyone as *Fairway Bob,* after the street on which he lived, and where JP and I also resided, in the sleepy Detroit suburb of Pleasant Woods.

Situated between upscale Royal Heights to the north and modest Fernridge to the south, a mere fifteen hundred residents made their home here. On the west side of Woodward

Avenue, the main thoroughfare that bisected the community, lavish dwellings rested on oversized lots belonging to the upper middle class. The east side—affectionately dubbed *Peasant Woods*—gave way to smaller properties whose owners, while still well-off, earned far smaller incomes.

It was here, on the first block of Fairway Lane, that we'd found ourselves, sitting in Bob Kravitz's beautiful Arts and Crafts style bungalow. The charming house, located at number 3, had been a favorite of ours since moving in next door. We admired the low-pitched roof and great porch, supported by two pillars on either side and a half column in the center. The avocado-colored cedar shake siding and exposed rafter tails contributed to the overall classic character.

The interior was a Craftsman aficionado's dream come true! Dark quarter-sawn oak trimmed the windows and doorways, while tall wainscot panels covered the dining room walls, complete with a wide plate rail running along the top. On the white oak floors lay the finest of floral-patterned William Morris wool rugs, right out of a Frank Lloyd Wright catalogue.

The vintage furnishings—mostly Mission in style—came direct from the business that Fairway Bob operated, a vintage furniture store called Somewhere in Time, after a favorite movie filmed at the Grand Hotel on Mackinac Island. Stained glass table lamps and pendant chandeliers gave off an amber glow, making the home feel extra warm and cozy, particularly on evenings spent in good company.

"What did *I* do wrong?" Tom Cash wondered aloud, in response to Bob's inquiry about his young boyfriend's whereabouts. "A big fat nothing." He held up his large hand in innocence before blushing with guilt. "Okay, maybe I flirted a little with a cutie-pie on Lads4Dads?"

Tom took out his cell phone and opened the gay dating app. "Oh, look." He tapped a thick finger to the screen and swiped. "There he is now! Hunter27. Only point-five miles away."

From where he sat, opposite Fairway Bob and directly to Tom Cash's left, Campbell Sellers took notice of the fancy mobile device. "Is that the new iPhone?"

"Only the best for my brother." The comment, directed at Tom, came from his identically handsome—and equally gay—twin, Terry. He sat across the table, to JP's right, sulking into his lemon-lime LaCroix, totally sober.

Both men were similarly dressed, in dark hoodies and athletic wear that showed off their fit physiques. Other than the opposing ball caps they sported, the men came off as carbon copies. Tom's was blue with a gold *M* for Michigan and Terry's white with a green *S* for State.

"Got mine the other day." Cam, as I'd called him since freshman year at Madison Park High School, reached into the linen jacket he wore and pulled out his own brand-new smartphone, similar to the one Tom Cash held in his not-so-little hand.

As the top Realtor around town, Campbell Sellers had to keep abreast of all the current hi-tech trends. The guy sold more houses than any other real estate agent in Metro Detroit.

"Look at you, being all professional," I said, complimenting Cam on his new purchase. "Hey, can I see it?"

Cam handed me the shiny gadget. "Careful. All my contacts are in that thing. I lose it, I'm up the creek."

It felt so much lighter than the phone I'd been lugging around for as long as I could remember. The pristine glass glistened like a sheet of ice. "We need a couple of these," I told JP, jealous of my longtime best friend's latest find. "Tell Ursula to get us a pair for next season, okay?"

"Why do I need to tell her?" JP clapped back. "She's your producer, too."

"But she's *your* best friend. She gave you your own TV

show. She'll get you a couple new phones if you ask her, I'm sure."

JP shook his head, not wanting to rehash this familiar conversation.

It was almost as old as our relationship, and oh-so typical: the single straight woman, pining away for the unavailable gay man. Not that I didn't love Ursula. Without her, there'd be no *Domestic Partners* on Home Design TV.

Ursula knew we'd been talking about moving to Michigan, where my aging parents and sister still lived. As part of her brilliant pitch to the network, the premise for the show involved a handy gay couple who purchase an old house and complete the renovations over the course of a ten-episode arc, all the while bickering back and forth—albeit affectionately—and providing some requisite eye candy for HDTV's 1.1 million viewers, mostly women and gay men.

From the living room, above the natural fireplace, the mantel clock struck nine.

Terry, the other handsome gay twin, tossed his cloth napkin aside and abruptly stood up. "Sorry guys, I gotta go."

"Come on, Ter," Tom groaned. "You can't take off before we seal the deal with these TV dudes, okay?"

Judging by his dominant disposition, I deemed Tom the alpha of the duo.

Terry sank back into his seat. The old wood chair crackled beneath his solid frame. "Right. The deal."

From his lackluster tone, I got the impression that Terry Cash wasn't nearly as eager as his identical sibling to be taking part in this negotiation.

"So, what do you guys say?" Tom Cash slyly looked my way, then over at JP. "Wanna do this with me and my brother or not?"

I glanced at JP across the table, giving him silent permission to speak on our behalf.

"We're definitely interested," my partner assured the handsome older man. "Aren't we, Pete?"

"For sure. But we need to see what you're offering before we can make up our minds." I couldn't help but feel anxious, becoming involved with these equally handsome strangers.

As a young gay man, I'd befriended my fair share of attractive older gay guys. The relationships had always begun out of some mutual interest: a fascinating film we'd both enjoyed, a memorable experience at the same expensive restaurant, a page-turning novel neither one of us could put down.

Despite my upfront declaration of domestic partnerdom, the mature man would inevitably cross the line and say, or God forbid, do something totally inappropriate. His unwelcome advances would cause me to feel totally uncomfortable. But being the polite person my parents raised, I'd feign feeling flattered in order to not cause him embarrassment.

In the end, I'd pretty much have to ghost the guy, hoping he'd get the hint and just go away. This would cause me to feel as if I'd done something wrong, when all I'd wanted all along was to be a decent human being.

The Cash brothers were another story altogether. Two older gay men meant double the odds for lascivious lechery. Alas, JP and I had no other choice. We both desperately needed to get in bed with these guys.

*Figuratively, not literally.*

"Awesome!" Tom drained his after-dinner drink—bourbon, my favorite. "Swing by the house in the morning. I'll give you the grand tour. How's ten o'clock?"

"Actually, we've got a previous appointment," JP said, politely declining Tom's invitation.

Cam raised a suspicious eyebrow. "What appointment would that be?" Suddenly, he gasped in horror. "You guys aren't adopting a baby, are you?"

"God, no!" I swallowed my last bite of apple crumble, trying not to choke at Cam's question. "But close."

"We're adopting a dog," JP clarified for everyone's benefit, sounding super excited. "Well, we're meeting a dog that we're hoping to adopt."

"OMG!" Cam cheered in approval. "I wanna see a picture!"

Now that the pending new puppy was out of the bag, I couldn't resist being braggadocios.

I pulled out my phone, opened the photo stream, and found an image that I'd saved off the dog rescue's website. "His name is Clyde," I humbly bragged, flashing the pic at everyone sitting around the table—JP included, who'd seen it at least a hundred times since I'd first discovered the adorable image on the Adopt-a-Pet app a few weeks ago.

The reluctant subject was a tiny white doggie with brown brindle markings on the right side of his face and in a half moon-shaped patch over his left almond-shaped eye. His head tilted to one side, ever so slightly, as he stared sadly into the camera. He had the stubbiest little legs and the tiniest pink toenails I ever did see.

We were both madly in puppy love, JP and me, with Mr. Clyde Barker, as we'd planned to christen him on his official adoption papers.

Cam squealed at the sight of the little dog, all bundled up in a tiny red puffy coat. "I love his little jacket!"

"Oh!" Fairway Bob gushed as he gazed at our would-be pup's picture. "He looks so sad. You boys better bring Mr. Clyde home!"

"Fingers crossed," said JP, doing just that. "We're meeting him at the pet store in the morning."

Cam ripped the phone right out of my hand, the better to see Clyde's picture. "What's the dog-rescue group called?"

"Home FurEver," I answered, appreciative of the name's

clever wordplay, being a writer. "They're based down in De-troit."

Cam's eyes lit up at my reply. "That's where I got my Snoop! Feel free to list me as a reference, you guys."

"Good to know. We will for sure," JP promised.

Cam sucked down the rest of his chardonnay and promptly poured another. "Your morning sounds a lot more fun than mine. I'm hosting yet another open house, up in Royal Heights. Eleven to three. On a Saturday! If you can believe it."

I wondered why Cam sounded so inconvenienced by this particular home showing. "Don't you host all your open houses on weekends?"

"I do. But I'd much rather be at a pet store, playing with all the cute puppies."

"Don't let Snoop hear you say that," JP teased. "He might not approve of another dog's scent on his person."

"Definitely not. Snoop does *not* like being cheated on," Cam quipped.

At last, Tom Cash joined in our conversation. Casually, he crossed his legs at the ankle as he offered us some select words of wisdom: "Be sure to mention you're famous. Tell the dog-rescue woman you'll talk up her group on your TV show, if she lets you adopt . . . what's the dog's name, Clive?"

"Clyde," JP corrected. "He's got a sister named Bonnie."

"Of course he does," Fairway Bob said dryly.

Tom sat up straight in his chair, eager to get back to dis-cussing business. "Speaking of your TV show . . ."

"Right!" I said, remembering the reason why Fairway Bob had invited us all to his home on that midsummer eve-ning, after he'd offered to make the introductions and play the mediator.

"Why don't you guys come by the house when you're done with your dog adoption appointment?" Tom Cash sug-gested, bound and determined to sway us. "You'll have a look around. We can discuss which projects you might work on . . . sound good?"

"*Or . . .*" Cam drunkenly drawled. "We could go over and check things out now."

"I don't know," I said, realizing we'd better wrap up the evening.

JP and I were hoping to catch the latest episode of our favorite Friday night political program, before drifting off to beddie-bye, where we would dream of the day we'd finally bring our little Clyde home with us.

"I'm down if you guys are," Tom Cash decided. "A moonlight tour of a spooky old Tudor Revival . . . too bad it's not Devil's Night."

"Come on!" Cam said, offering up his encouraging approval. "It'll be fun!" He snatched his fancy new phone from where I'd left it on the table and started for Fairway Bob's front door. "I wanna take some pictures."

"No posting online, okay?" Tom warned Cam, the social media maven. "I don't wanna see any photos on Facebook. Or Instagram. Or Twitter." He stood up purposefully and turned to address his twin. "Let's go, Ter."

Like sheep, brother Terry, my partner JP, and I followed Tom Cash toward the front door.

Or were we more like lambs . . . being led to slaughter?

# Chapter 2

Fairway Bob's stellar matchmaking skills had no doubt impressed him.

"I just knew you guys would hit it off! When I found out you lost the new property for your TV show," he explained, beaming brightly, "I immediately thought of Tom and Terry's parents' place, sitting vacant across the street."

"And we're glad you did!" I let out an overly dramatic breath. "Ursula would pitch a fit if she found out we didn't have a house to renovate for season two."

JP placed a hand on Bob's sloping shoulder and gave it a gentle squeeze. "Sure you don't wanna join us?"

"No! Been there, seen it before. Besides, I'd rather stay home and play with my Willie." Bob clapped his hands together and gave a quick whistle through his recently whitened teeth. "Here, boy!"

A large black Lab perked up from where he lay under the pedestal table. The dog got to all fours and trotted over to his master, Fairway Bob, tail happily wagging to and fro.

Reaching down, I patted Willie's big head. "Good boy, good boy!"

I couldn't wait until JP and I owned our own dog—or

two—something we'd been planning since moving to Michigan almost a year earlier. Fingers crossed, it would happen
sooner than later.

"Terry, wanna meet for brunch in the morning?" Bob suggested, before waving us goodbye. "Ten o'clock at Chianti."

Terry carefully considered Bob's invitation. "I won't get
home from work till after two tonight. By the time I go to
bed, it'll be closer to three . . ."

"So, let's make it eleven," Bob decided. "Terry needs all
the beauty sleep he can get," he joked to the rest of us guys as
he ushered us outside.

We started down the steps of the bungalow's brick porch
in a single file line, like school kids off on a nighttime field
trip.

JP turned to Terry, who'd barely said a word the entire
dinner party. "How long has your folks' house been empty?"

Before Terry could answer, his twin Tom replied: "Oh, a
good twenty years."

"Twenty-*five*," Terry corrected, shooting his brother the
evil eye.

The *click* of a Zippo lighter put an end to the dispute as
Tom lit a cigarette. While the pack he'd pulled it from featured the words *natural* and *organic*, it still surprised me, in this
day and age, to see a man in such great physical shape smoking. But Tom had been drinking all evening. Maybe he only
partook in the bad habit when he'd been under the influence
of alcohol? Regardless, I wasn't about to criticize the behavior
of a man I'd only just met.

"Your parents both passed?" I asked Terry Cash, hoping
I wasn't being too personal. But really, who was I kidding?
Fairway Bob had already filled in both me and JP on the entire Cash family history. Still, I chose to play dumb, out of
respect for the deceased.

Terry nodded. "They were *killed*."

The man definitely had a way of telling it like it was.

"Oh, my God," JP gasped, showing off his skills as an actor. He'd heard the exact same account from Bob that I had, when he'd offered to arrange our meeting with the Cash brothers.

"Snowmobiling accident, up near Traverse City," Tom elaborated. "They were celebrating their wedding anniversary." He dragged hard on his cigarette before continuing his sad story. "Dad was driving, Mom riding behind him. Hit an icy patch, crashed into a telephone pole."

Tom tilted his head back, filling the awkward pause that hung in the night air with a blue-gray plume of smoke. Suddenly, from across the street, we heard a hoarse cry: *"Heeey!"*

An elderly man stood on the small front porch of a canary yellow Cape Cod, circa 1920. He wore a short-sleeved button-down shirt of a similar color, along with matching plaid golf pants. Well into his eighties, he stumbled down the concrete steps and stomped his way across the freshly cut lawn of his home at 6 Fairway Lane.

"Oh, God," Tom Cash muttered. "Here comes Mr. Hank." Evidently he wasn't the least bit delighted to run into his family's former neighbor.

Hank Richards hobbled from the humble sidewalk out into the empty street. Beneath the light of the old-fashioned lamppost, he waited, arms akimbo, to accost the five of us. The waning full moon peeked through puffy clouds as old Hank began to rip into twins Tom and Terry.

"I wanna talk to you boys!" he told the brothers, all but wagging a bony finger in their identically handsome faces. Having observed the Cash twins come up in the house next door, it was clear that Hank Richards still viewed the full-grown men as a pair of prepubescent kids.

"Well, hello, Mr. Hank," Tom said, feigning politeness. Quickly, he crushed out his cigarette, like a schoolboy caught in the act of being bad on the playground. "What would you like to talk to us about?"

Old Hank pointed toward the abandoned 1929 Tudor Revival, with its decorative half-timbering and cream-colored stucco exterior. The slate shingles that covered the steeply pitched gables were all worn and weathered from many a harsh Michigan winter. Copper gutters ripped away from the fascia, brought down by heavy ice that had formed time and again, the result of insufficient insulation. Paint cracked and peeled around windowpanes; dried mortar broke off in chunks between crumbling brick.

The structure—as a whole—was a far cry from condemnation, yet utterly uninhabitable in its present condition. With patience and the right care, the old home could painstakingly be brought back to its former glory. A few fresh coats of semigloss to the interior, a complete renovation of both the kitchen and second-floor bath, a professional refinishing of the white oak floors and dark wood trim throughout, and . . .

*Voilà!*

All would appear as it once had, on the day the happily married couple, Larry and Linda Cash, first moved into the historic house located at 4 Fairway Lane.

On the opposite side, at number 2, a two-story Queen Anne, circa 1898, bustled with Friday evening activity. The first floor housed a popular upscale wine pub/restaurant called Chianti, where Fairway Bob had mentioned he would be meeting Terry Cash for brunch the very next morning at eleven a.m. The owners, Andrew and Brianna Kim, a lovely husband and wife couple in their forties, acted as co-managers and lived on the second level above the establishment.

From our master bedroom window, JP and I had the most picturesque view of late-Victorian era architecture. A charming turret sprang up from Chianti's second floor, supported by a corbel and capped off with a slate-tiled conical rooftop. Through a circular stained glass window, Brianna Kim would wave to us each morning as she sipped cappuccino and took in the local landscape from her private sanctuary.

Both these homes—the Tudor Revival and the Queen Anne—were typical of the ones found throughout much of Pleasant Woods. All were of a certain aesthetic, built with the utmost attention to detail, and no two alike. These factors were a definite part of the appeal that drew me and JP to PW when we began the search for our Forever Home.

Back out front of the canary Cape Cod, Hank Richards continued with his tirade . . .

"When are you guys gonna take care of that yard? It's out of control!" he complained. "I'm sick and tired of looking at that mess. I tell you, I'm gonna burn the place down . . . with *you* in it!"

JP and I grimaced in unison, contemplating what, exactly, we'd gotten ourselves into.

Tom Cash chuckled through gritted Chiclet teeth. "Don't threaten me, old man."

"Just look at all those weeds!" Mr. Hank spat, his one-track mind still focused on the eyesore that was the Cash family's former home.

He did have a point.

The lawn at 4 Fairway Lane was indeed a bit unruly, the tall grass wild with weeds. The overgrown high hedges that flanked the wide front porch, with its storybook entryway, obstructed the diamond-patterned lead glass windows on either side. Stunning they were, but barely visible to passersby.

"I know, I know," Tom said, attempting to sound sincere. "I'm sorry, Mr. Hank. I've been busy."

Old Hank wasn't buying Tom Cash's mediocre excuse. "Running around with that twenty-year-old? All you're doing these days! Hennie and me seen you over at the pool in that ridiculous Speedo. You're with him up at The Depot, breakfast, lunch, and dinner."

Tom Cash bit his tongue. "Kyle is almost twenty-*nine*! And we went out to eat last night down in Corktown."

"Well, he's still too young for you! When are you gonna find a guy your own age, huh? First that bartender boy, Donny, now this new kid."

"No disrespect, Mr. Hank," Tom began, "and not that it's any of your business," he added. "That bartender boy is over thirty years old. And his name is *Danny*."

Old Hank shook his balding head. I'd only known the man nine months, and already I could tell that he strongly disapproved of Tom Cash's lifestyle.

Not because Tom was gay.

Pleasant Woods was an accepting and tolerant community, another part of the reason that JP and I chose to make it our new home. According to the most recent census, the neighborhood boasted the seventh-highest rate of same-sex couples in the nation and received top marks, annually, from the Human Rights Campaign.

"What can I say?" Tom Cash shrugged his broad shoulders. "I like 'em younger. Always have, always will . . . till the day I die."

Tom's brother, Terry, stood listening in silence. With the toe end of a size sixteen tennis shoe, the hulk of a man kicked at a crack in the pavement.

"Mr. Hank," my best friend Campbell Sellers interjected, clearing his throat. He'd lived on the same block as Hank and his wife, Hennie, for the past ten years, and the long-wedded couple adored him. "I'm sure Tom's sorry for letting the yard go for so long."

"No, I'm *not* sorry." Tom wasn't having it. "I'm not some

little kid anymore, Mr. Hank. You can't tell me what to do. It's my house—"

"It's your mom and dad's house," old man Hank hissed, his temper escalating.

"No, it belongs to me and my brother." Tom puffed out his chest and folded his big arms across his muscular body for added emphasis.

"Larry and Linda would turn over in their graves if they could see that house right now," Hank Richards muttered. "You boys have let that place fall apart. It's a disgrace! Bringing down everybody on the block's property value."

Mr. Hank huffed, taking a labored breath. "This is a designated historic district we live in. We've got rules here in this neighborhood, you know? I'll file a report with the town council! Won't be very good for you, as a small business owner."

In defiance, Tom Cash lit up another cigarette and practically blew the stinky smoke right into old Hank's craggy old face. "Okay, *sir!*" he spat back, putting an end to the argument. "My lawn service guy is on vacation, so I can't call him," Tom told his former neighbor, taking on a more neighborly tone. "But I'll come by in the morning after breakfast and take care of the yard myself."

"He sure did change his mind," Cam mumbled to me, "once Mr. Hank threatened to destroy his reputation."

Together we watched Tom make a beeline over to the unoccupied house that once belonged to his parents. He punched in the four-digit code on the keypad, disabling the security alarm.

Cigarette dangling from his lower lip, Tom cried: "Welcome to Casa Cash!" He flung open the heavy, custom-made wood front door and gestured for all to enter through its wide arch.

"Tommy, please don't smoke in the house," Terry begged. "Mom and Dad wouldn't like it."

"Jeez, Ter." Tom took a last hit, sucking hard, then tossed the offensive object out the front door onto the overgrown lawn. "I'll pick up the butt in the morning when I'm here cutting the grass."

Once we were all safely indoors, Cam whipped out his fancy new phone. "OMG!" He tapped the camera app, turned on the flash setting, and quickly snapped a few photos.

The house stood eerily quiet, shut up like a proverbial tomb for the past quarter-century.

"Sorry, the power's off," Tom apologized, sensing our discomfort. "Why pay for electric when no one's using it?" He chuckled to himself. "Lemme just open up the drapes and let some light in, so you guys can get a better look-see."

"Crack a window while you're at it," Terry droned, a dour expression befalling his handsome face. He pulled an ancient flip phone from his pocket and glanced at the tiny screen. "Can we hurry this up? It's almost nine-thirty. I gotta get to work."

"Work can wait," Tom said, firmly dismissing his twin.

"Tommy, I'm the doorman," Terry reported, trying to sound important. "I ain't there, people sneak in without paying cover."

"And I own the bar," Tom barked, once again asserting his alpha status over his beta brother.

The business the men had been bickering about was the local gay watering hole down in nearby Fernridge. Well, it wasn't a *gay* bar, per se. Not since millennials, like me and my partner, had come of age during a time when single straight women could have fun with their queer male friends without the hassle of being hit on by a barrage of douchey frat boys. But it was the first gay-friendly tavern I'd ever been to, back when I first turned twenty-one, almost thirteen years ago.

Simply called Shout!, the bar had been in operation for nearly twenty-five years. In its heyday, I'd heard tell, it had been the go-to hot spot for Metro Detroit's most fabulous gays: a place to see and be seen by anyone who was anybody. By the time Cam and I were legally allowed to set foot inside, a tarnish had befallen the once celebrated establishment. No longer were the weekends packed to the rafters, the dance floor filled to capacity with a sea of gyrating gymbos. The weeknights were even more disappointing.

On return trips to visit family over the holidays, JP and I would often meet up with Cam for drinks there, purely in the name of nostalgia. But those visits had become few and far between as the clientele had gotten older, married, or both, and spent more time elsewhere.

Sadly, there was nothing *gay* about an empty gay bar that wasn't technically such.

Fortunately, for the sake of the community, the business had undergone a recent renaissance. To celebrate its upcoming twenty-fifth anniversary in style, Tom Cash had taken it upon himself to fully remodel the entertainment venue, to the tune of five hundred thousand dollars.

From what we'd heard, the investment had indeed paid off. The crowds were starting to return in full swing, in part thanks to Harmony House, a legend on the Detroit drag circuit, who emceed the weekend karaoke show she had single-handedly made famous.

Since moving to the neighborhood, JP and I, shamefully, had not paid a visit to Shout! 2.0. Supposedly, they threw an awesome happy hour, where five dollars and fifty cents could get a couple guys a couple domestic light beers. In New York City, a single cocktail would cost double that price! Unfortunately, our hectic schedule shooting a TV show had kept us from taking in the fun.

Now, with our hiatus soon concluding, we were running

out of opportunity. But, by the time ten o'clock on a Friday night rolled round, we were usually too exhausted to even think about heading out anywhere.

"That drag queen can be a real pain," Terry Cash complained to his brother. "If I ain't there to help her—"

"Shut up, already!" Tom ordered. "No one wants to hear it, Ter. *Jeez.*"

Terry licked his wounds as Tom strolled over to the front windows that faced onto Fairway Lane. He pulled a dangling cord, and a pair of dingy curtains parted with a rusty squeak, allowing the almost full moon outside to faintly shine in. Still, it was too dark to sense any sort of specific interior detail.

"I'll grab a flashlight from the basement," Tom offered. "Be right back."

Narrowing my eyes, I strained to get a better look at the time capsule surrounding us. The cream-colored plaster walls of the living and dining rooms were cracked in more places that I could count. The trim around the doors, windows, and baseboards had all been painted a putrid brown color, hiding any hint of natural grain.

Anyone who knew anything realized the proper procedure for refinishing woodwork involved stripping the boards bare, sanding them down multiple times using various grits of sandpaper, then completely restaining and polyurethaning everything thrice.

The process was time-consuming and tedious. The results, exquisite if well executed.

Why anybody in their right mind would ever paint over woodwork was totally beyond me! Ask any *Domestic Partners* premiere season viewer; this was one of my many on-air mantras.

"Look, Pete . . ." JP nudged me softly and pointed a finger upward.

Tilting my head back, I just about lost it.

Yes, there were exposed beams running the entire length of the coffered ceiling, but someone had totally destroyed the integrity of the décor by hastily painting over them. I prayed the crime had occurred post–1978, when the guilty culprit would most likely have applied a latex-based pigment, as opposed to the old-fashioned oil variety. Talk about a pain in the butt to deal with! And if the paint in question contained lead . . .

Forget about ever getting it off.

"Okay, I'm here!" Tom returned with an industrial-sized silver flashlight that he aimed about the room as he spoke. "So, nothing's been changed. What you see now is exactly the way it was twenty years ago when Mom and Dad died."

"Twenty-*five*," Terry said, correcting his brother for the second time that evening.

JP rubbed his hands together in the awkward silence. "Okay! Can we take a look at the rest of the house?"

"Sure thing!" Tom graciously pointed the light toward the back wall and ushered us onward.

Just off the dining area, the kitchen was actually a decent size for a house from the period. Unlike with the grand designs of the current day, an early twentieth-century homemaker found herself in need of far less space to prepare her family meals, as she was often the only person occupying the room while she cooked. In the homes from this time, there were no such things as expansive prep islands, double ovens, or fancy pot-filler faucets. Counter space, if any, was a highly sought-after—and severely lacking—commodity.

A flash from Cam's fancy new smartphone filled the small room with light. "OMG! I love that sink!"

Behind me, he propped open an old-fashioned wood swinging door, reminiscent of the one at my grandmother's house up in Royal Heights, God rest her sweet soul.

The wide single basin was of a deep style, what we'd call

*farmhouse* by today's standard, fabricated from porcelain enameled cast iron, with a pair of legs in front that had been intentionally shaped to resemble those of ornate furniture.

While the kitchen of the Cash family home was well beyond outdated, I had to marvel at the original cabinetry lining the wall on either side of the massive sink. Though not abundant in terms of storage, the solid wood construction outrivaled anything currently available from the so-called big box stores.

"I don't think I've ever seen an entirely original 1920s kitchen," I mused aloud.

Even the one at my grandmother's house, God rest her sweet soul, had been slightly updated, with the addition of a first-floor powder room built in the former food pantry.

"Dad wanted to remodel," brother Terry remarked, inching into the small space to join us. "But Mom insisted everything be left the way it was when they first bought the house. They were only the second owners, and she was all about keeping the original integrity. Mom was a sentimental woman, for sure."

These were probably the most words Terry Cash had spoken at one time, since we'd first made his acquaintance back at Fairway Bob's house over dinner.

Something told me there was more to this man than what we'd seen on the surface.

# Chapter 3

Tears formed in Terry Cash's eyes as he spoke of his dead parents' memory.

"When did your folks move in here?" I wondered aloud, there in the dark of his family's former home, attempting to lighten the mood.

"Gosh, Pete. Like well over fifty years ago." Terry sighed, a man who'd just realized he was past his prime.

"So, they're not responsible for this lovely linoleum?" JP joked, taking note of the inexpensive 1940s tile flooring that had been all the rage.

"Nah. Pretty sure it was already here when my folks bought the house. But Mom loved it, so it stayed."

"Well, it's definitely gotta *go*," Cam declared, disgusted. "You think there's hardwood underneath? That would be awesome!"

Like a photog at a fashion shoot, Cam sent the room ablaze with a burst of flashes from his phone. Clearly, he'd already put on his Realtor hat and was thinking ahead to making a sale, even though JP and I had yet to accept the offer to tackle the renovation.

"I wouldn't touch nothing, if I had my druthers," Terry started to say. Then . . .

Twin Tom stepped through the narrow doorway into the kitchen, and Terry fell radio silent.

"So, what do you think, huh?" Tom asked, his big voice booming as he waved the flashlight back and forth. "This room's a disaster, right? Needs a total overhaul. I say gut it, put in a brand spankin' new *everything*. What I'd do if I were you dudes."

I couldn't have disagreed more.

Off the top of my head, I would have advised leaving much of the kitchen in its current state. Update the appliances, for sure, but I wouldn't have recommended tearing out everything and starting fresh.

It wasn't my or JP's aesthetic, as team *Domestic Partners*, to go crazy and start knocking down walls or turning intentionally small rooms into larger ones. We both had an affinity for old houses and the problems that come with them. We considered ourselves *restorers*—not remodelers.

The main reason why we'd agreed to host an HDTV home rehab show, when Ursula had first come to us with the idea, was because we wanted to help save the historic homes of Detroit and its outlying areas. So many had already succumbed to the wrecking balls and bulldozers.

It also didn't hurt that the network had offered to pay us a sizable sum of money. The cash would certainly come in handy as a supplement to our main sources of income. Not to mention the national exposure that could give both our writing and acting careers an extra push.

JP hadn't worked much since his TV cop series had shuttered. His most recent job was a supporting role in the second national tour of a third-rate musical that had no business ever seeing the light of his namesake Broadway. I, personally, hadn't done any real writing since a spec script I'd penned for an up-and-coming young producer in Hollywood failed to get any traction in the traditional market. So much for the brilliance of a modern-day take on a classic high school rom-com featuring a transgender female protagonist!

Neither JP nor I launched into our *remodel versus renovate* spiel. Something told us that it would have totally fallen on deaf ears, as far as Tom Cash was concerned, had we tried explaining the differences between the two schools of design thought.

"We could definitely make some updates to the kitchen," I heard JP tell both Tom and Terry, drawing me out of my inner monologue.

"What about the bathroom?" I said, changing the subject to another topic of popular home renovation projects.

Terry pointed toward the ceiling. "Upstairs."

"Only one in the whole place," his brother Tom added. "Sucked growing up with a single toilet for four people. But what can you do? Nineteen-twenties house for ya!"

"It's pretty typical," Cam said, providing his professional assessment. "Most of the homes I sell around here are the exact same way. People either deal or they take a downstairs coat closet and turn it into a half bath. Easy enough update."

*But then what do you do with all your winter jackets?*

"Let's go up and take a look around," JP suggested, getting the home tour back on track.

"No problem. Lemme show you." Tom led us out of the kitchen and pointed in the direction of a magnificent—but also putridly brown-painted—solid oak staircase. The carved balusters, alone, were works of craftsmanship.

"Up the steps and around the corner to the right," Terry instructed us.

"Just be careful on your way," Tom advised. "Stairs are kinda janky, okay?"

Gingerly, I placed my hand on the banister. It gave a little under my grasp as I began my ascent. The treads beneath my feet creaked with each tentative step that I took.

"Watch out! There's a loose board near the top!" Tom called as JP trailed close behind.

Cam paid extra attention as he trotted up the rickety old staircase after us. "Guys, wait for me!"

Like the kitchen we'd just inspected, the second-floor bath retained much of its original character: clawfoot tub, pedestal sink, subway tile. All were white, utilitarian, and sanitary, in keeping with the germ-conscious concerns of the remote past.

One-inch white hexagonal terrazzo tiles, accented by a patterned mosaic black border, made up the flooring. One of the most interesting features we found was the cast-iron two-piece toilet, manufactured in 1923 by the Kohler company. It had seen better days, for certain, but made for quite a unique artifact.

"Awesome!" Cam cheered as he took in the period details with his camera phone. "Too bad I could never sell this property in its current condition." Disappointed, he slipped the device into his back pocket.

"Maybe we *should* come by in the morning?" I said, echoing Tom Cash's original suggestion. "When we can see things better, in the light of day."

While a drunken escapade in the dark was proving adventurous, it didn't make for the best barometer in gauging how much renovation the house would actually need.

"Probably a good idea," JP agreed. "Pete, let's go talk to Tom and Terry. We'll come up with a time for us to drop by tomorrow."

"I wanna talk to them too!" Cam followed us back down the narrow hallway. "I need to make sure they hire me to sell this house. Gonna be worth a fortune once you guys fix it up on television for all the gays to see."

We came upon the rickety old staircase, like a death trap waiting to snag its next victim.

"Careful on the steps," I reminded the guys. "I'd hate for anyone to trip and fall and break their neck."

Having a lawsuit on their hands would *not* be the best way for the HDTV network to kick off the sophomore season of their newest home renovation program.

Less than two seconds later, Campbell Sellers almost killed himself.

"OMG!" Cam's right hand grasped frantically for the carved wood banister. The heel of his left foot slipped on the loose stair tread, throwing his center of gravity totally off-kilter.

Thankfully, he was able to regain his balance and land backward on his bum, instead of lurching forward and falling headfirst down the steps, landing flat on his face at the bottom of the rickety old staircase.

The entire incident lasted all of five seconds. JP and I both did our best not to bust up laughing at the sheer physical comedy of the situation.

"Not funny, you guys! I almost died," Cam whined, his pride wounded more than his corporal body. "Ooh! I'm a little tipsy from all that booze we had at Bob's."

"What did I just get through saying?" I whispered, so as not to alert either Tom or Terry Cash to the fact that my best friend since freshman year of high school almost became a casualty while on their private property.

"Guess Tom wasn't joking," JP teased, but only slightly. "He said that step was dangerous."

"Make sure you guys fix it first thing." Cam picked himself up and dramatically dusted himself off. "No one's gonna buy a house that's a safety hazard."

Upon our return to the main floor, we caught the twin

brothers in the midst of what sounded like a minor disagreement . . .

"Tommy," Terry said discreetly, "I thought we decided
we're gonna leave the house alone."

"And I thought we decided it's time to let it go. What
do we need it for? We already got a place to live, over on the
west side."

JP, Cam, and I held back, tucked behind the wide archway that divided the lower level of the home into two almost
equal halves. I hated to eavesdrop. Or at least have it look like
we were intentionally listening to what was clearly a familial
dispute.

"But Mom and Dad . . ."

While we couldn't see the expression on his face at the
moment, there was a definite sound of sorrow in Terry Cash's
tone.

"They're *dead*, Ter," Tom said, matter-of-fact. "They're
not coming back. This house is nothing but a harsh reminder."

Terry sniffled, as if to say he'd heard his brother, loud and
clear.

Peering at JP and Cam from our hiding spot, I sent a tele-
pathic message, wondering what we should do next.

Cam quickly nodded, like he had things all figured out. I
could tell he was still drunk from one too many after-dinner
drinks, as if his recent near-death experience on the rickety
old staircase wasn't already evidence enough.

Cam began walking in place, stomping his feet on the
creaky floor, just loudly enough for the brothers to hear from
where they stood on the opposite side of the plaster. He called,
totally stilted, at the top of his voice: "Gee, I wonder what
happened to Tom and Terry!"

Taking that as my cue to continue, I led us around the
corner. As soon as I saw the twins, I play-acted at being sur-

prised. "Hey, guys!" The Intro to Drama class that I took in college, at Wayne State down in Detroit, came in handy whenever we had to reenact a real-life scenario on our TV show, and/or in times like these when I didn't want someone thinking I'd intentionally been spying on them.

"Bathroom's in pretty bad shape, huh?" Tom said as soon as we arrived, getting right back to business.

"We've seen worse. The one in our house when Cam first showed us the place . . ." I shuddered at the memory of the pink-painted mess that was the clawfoot tub, the wall-mounted sink, and the porcelain commode.

"Overall, the property's in pretty good condition, guys," JP confidently announced. "Which is good for us, in terms of what projects we can feasibly conquer over a ten-episode arc."

Tom grinned, his eyes wide. "So, we got a deal then?" He reached out a manly hand and held it aloft in midair.

JP checked my reaction before accepting, brow raised in anticipation.

"I love the house," I said, finally making up my mind. "Let's save it."

Plus, it wasn't like we could afford to be choosy. We still needed a property to renovate, after the owners of the one we'd thought we were going to tackle had backed out on us, last minute.

Due to the overwhelming success of season one of our show, the HDTV network execs bumped up the taping schedule of season two. Instead of shooting in the fall like we'd done before, we'd been slotted to begin filming in just a little over two weeks.

As my mother always said: *Beggars can't be choosers.*

"We've got a deal," JP told Tom, taking hold of his large paw.

As I copied the gesture, the handsome older man's big

hand held onto mine, a bit longer than I deemed customary. Tom Cash was indeed a flirt, albeit one with super soft skin. His palm against my own felt as smooth as a baby's bottom.

"Awesome!" Seeing dollar signs, Cam silently calculated his commission from facilitating the future sale of the home.

Out of the corner of my eye, I caught a glimpse of Terry Cash's reaction to the exchange he'd just witnessed. Physically, he looked so much like his twin, Tom . . .

But clearly, Terry was *not* sharing the same emotion of excitement at that moment.

# Chapter 4

Campbell Sellers wasn't quite ready to call it a night.

Before we all went along on our separate ways, he had a deal of his own to seal with Mr. Thomas Cash. "You haven't hired a Realtor to sell your parents' place yet, have you?"

The effects of the alcohol he'd consumed earlier hadn't completely worn off, so Cam's speech was still a bit slurred. Fortunately, he only lived three doors down from where we stood outside, smack-dab in the middle of Fairway Lane, preparing to bid our farewells. I said a silent prayer that he wouldn't need to be escorted home and tucked safely into his king-size bed, alongside his nine-month-old American Staffordshire terrier, Snoop.

Terry Cash had just ridden off in his car, an older model SUV that paled in comparison to the brand-new version his brother Tom had been about to drive away in . . .

Until Cam stopped him dead in his tracks.

"You do know who the number one real estate agent in Metro Detroit is, don't you?" Cam asked coyly, blatantly tooting his own horn.

He wasn't exaggerating.

Having sold two homes per month, on average, for the

past five years, Cam had an annual salary adding up to mid-six figures easily. On more than one occasion, he'd slapped a SOLD sign out front of a property that had never even made its way onto the MLS, along with the eye-catching caption on the online profile: *Listed, Pending, Same day!*

Cam had even helped me and JP find our current home, a 1924 Craftsman Colonial whose previous owner had passed away right before we started looking to buy. Talk about a lucky break! Well, for us. Not for the dead old man, Mr. Voisin.

"I do. I've seen the signs," Tom answered, playing along with his drunk friend, "on the benches at all the bus stops and even a few billboards. That would be the one and only Campbell Sellers."

*"Ding-ding-ding!"* Cam cried out like a bell, the kind that alerts a game show contestant who's just correctly answered the million-dollar question.

Tom lit another cigarette, his third in the past half hour, as he broke the news as gently as possible. "Unfortunately, I've already promised the listing to someone else."

The dopey grin that had graced Cam's face since he'd finished his fourth glass of chardonnay over at Fairway Bob's place quickly turned itself upside down. He stuck a finger in his ear and gave it a quick rattle, as if he were cleaning out the worst buildup of earwax.

"Sorry, don't think I heard you . . ." Cam placed a cupped hand behind his ear and leaned toward Tom. "Sounded like you said you wanted to shoot yourself in the foot. Because that's exactly what you'd be doing if you allow an inferior Realtor to sell your beloved family home."

The time was fast approaching ten o'clock. We knew that we should excuse ourselves at that moment, before things between Cam and Tom Cash either got weird, heated, or both. Yet for some strange reason, we couldn't walk away.

"Cam, come on," I said calmly. "It's getting late. You've had a lot to drink. Don't put poor Tom on the spot like this."

Cam gasped in horror. "Poor Tom! What about poor *moi*?"

"Dude, I'm sorry," Tom Cash apologized. "I wanted to help a friend out, so I told them they could help me and my brother sell the house. You know how it is? Nothing personal. I promise."

Cam took a step back. He put a palm flat against his chest, fingers splayed, taking offense. "A friend?" He shook his head slowly. "How long have we known each other? I thought we were friends."

Tom clapped a firm hand on Cam's shoulder. "Dude, we are."

Cam sloughed off the big man's touch, almost knocking the lit cigarette from between Tom's lips. Like Dr. Jekyll, he instantaneously morphed into Mr. Hyde. "Get your paw off-a me! Clearly, I'm *not* your friend." He spun around and faced the opposite direction, addressing JP. "Could you please pull out the knife that's protruding from between my shoulder blades?"

Tom snickered, mildly amused by the dramatics. "Maybe Cam should be the actor," he joked, turning to me. "Instead of your husband."

"We're not married," I informed the handsome older man.

"Not yet," JP added, more for my benefit as far as I was concerned.

It was a small bone of contention between us, our not being lawfully wedded, and I'd been wondering when, exactly, we might make it official—as was my mother.

These past three years, she'd been planning my and JP's nuptials, since the day my sister up and eloped to Las Vegas with her then-fiancé, Mason Parker. Long before Pamela hopped on the plane at Metro Airport and headed west, Mom had been looking forward to her big debut as Mother of the Bride. But my now-brother-in-law couldn't bear the concept of having all eyes fixed on him, as he waited at the altar while my father walked his only daughter down the aisle. God forbid he toss a garter to a mob of drunken bachelors or dance the cupid shuffle at the reception! According to Pam, Mason begged her to put the kibosh on the formal ceremony, in favor of an intimate fête at the world-famous Chapel of Love, officiated by an ordained Elvis impersonator.

All of this broke our mother's heart, but the saving grace arrived when I called from New York and announced that JP had finally proposed, just shy of two years after our first date. Mom realized that, thanks to Marriage Equality, her gayby boy could also reap the rewards of a ridiculously expensive wedding—the bill footed by his father, of course—to which she could finally wear the *haute couture* gown gathering dust in her closet.

"My bad," Tom Cash said, sounding more like one of my teenage readers than a fifty-year-old.

I chuckled at the mistaken assumption that JP and I were one of those couples who filed a joint tax return. "No worries."

"You've been together five years, right?" Tom said, not because he was genuinely curious to learn the tale of *How PJ Met JP*. It seemed more like he was trying to avert the attention that Cam had placed upon him in any other direction than his own.

"*Almost* five years," JP quickly corrected.

"Did you guys meet in the Big Apple?"

Not wanting to be rude by informing Tom that nobody who lived in New York referred to the city by that silly nickname, I went for a more respectful response instead: "We did."

Tom grinned. "On which app?"

For the first time since making the man's acquaintance, I noticed the slightest gap between his two front teeth. Normally, I'd consider this a flaw, but on Tom Cash it made him even more attractive. I stopped to wonder, for a moment, did his twin possess the same imperfection?

"I acted in a play Pete wrote for an off-off-Broadway LGBT play festival," JP clarified, now contributing to the conversation.

I could sense that my partner felt awkward, so I attempted to lighten the mood. "Long before they tagged on the Q, the I, and the A."

Cam didn't appreciate my wry sense of humor one bit. "If you guys are finished with your trip down memory lane, can we please get back to the matter at hand?"

Oh, how I wished I could click my heels together and find myself no-place-like-home! The last thing I felt like watching was my best friend square off in the middle of our block with his former boyfriend.

Yes, they had been *lovers*, Campbell Sellers and Tom Cash.

No, it wasn't a secret affair.

But it had been something that Cam desperately hoped to forget.

Ten years ago, Tom had been a real catch. At forty, he operated his own business, lived in a big house on Pleasant Woods's west side, and drove a brand-new BMW. He took care of himself, working out five times a week in the community center, and the results were apparent. For a man his age, Tom Cash had an awesome body! Sure, he did smoke occasionally—cigarettes only—but nobody was perfect, and Cam could overlook this fact.

He regularly attended the theatre and the cinema. He spent a good amount of time taking in professional sporting events. All the Detroit teams, except for football. Tom had suffered one too many disappointments to count himself a

Lions fan. Instead, his heart belonged to his alma mater, the Michigan Wolverines. Hence the blue and gold cap he wore proudly, more often than not.

Campbell Sellers had heard the stories about the type of men that Tom Cash preferred to go out with. Once he'd found himself fitting the mold, Cam wasted no time in making his move on the handsome older man.

It was a known fact within the gay community that Tom had a thing for guys in their early-late twenties. They weren't young enough to be deemed inappropriate, but they were still in their sexual prime. Funny thing, while Tom himself may have aged as the months passed by, his taste in boys would forever remain the same. In fact, the last three guys that Tom Cash had dated—Campbell Sellers included—had all been exactly twenty-seven years old when the romance had first begun.

Ultimately, the end of Cam and Tom's relationship came as a result of one incident alone: Cam's *thirtieth* birthday. No longer did he fit Tom's preferred boyfriend age range. Soon, Cam had discovered himself replaced by a slightly younger guy, a bartender named Danny, who'd been hired by Tom to mix cocktails at Shout!

For Cam, it had been no easy feat to remain devoted to the same man for almost three years solid. But he'd given it his best shot. Never once did he stray, tempted as he might have been. After things with Tom Cash unfortunately failed, Campbell Sellers insisted on accepting a sad but simple truth: He just didn't have time for love in his life.

Now, standing before the one who'd gotten away, Cam intentionally chose to harden his heart. Otherwise, one look from Tom and he'd melt into a puddle on the pavement.

"My very livelihood is at stake here," Cam continued, laying it on thick. "Do you know how hard it is to sell a house? Especially in this economy! But if my ex-boyfriend won't even give me the opportunity . . . I guess I can always eat ramen for dinner."

*Talk about being a total Drama Queer!*

I mean, Cam had a point, for sure. He was *the* Realtor in the area. Anytime anyone had a home they wanted to sell, all they had to do was give Campbell Sellers a call or shoot him a text. He had a digital contact list of prospective buyers saved in his phone, all vying to purchase a piece of Pleasant Woods, at whatever price.

With the entirety of the neighborhood totaling a half-mile square, available property was hard-pressed to come by. On average, at any given moment, there were fewer than a dozen homes on the market and all the accompanying mobile apps. Once folks were fortunate enough to find their way into The Woods, never did they wish to depart.

"Seriously, dude?" Tom sneered. "You don't *need* the listing. I know for a fact you sold three houses just last week. Two of them up in Royal Heights, both for over half a mil."

Cam knew he was caught. He did his best to backpedal, to downplay his act of desperation. "So, what's your point?" he said simply, before switching tactics, in search of a way to turn Tom against his competition. Whoever it might have been. "The least you could do is tell me who you promised the listing. I seriously doubt he's nearly as good an agent as I am. Or has the kind of connections I've got."

"*She* just got her Real-a-tor's license," Tom said, in answer to Cam's query. "I told her I'd help her out."

Cam rolled his eyes. "What's her name? And the word is *Realtor.* Two syllables."

Tom crushed out his cigarette on the bottom of his shoe, choosing to ignore Cam's correction. "Cheri Maison."

Cam's jaw just about hit the pavement. "You gave my listing to a *lesbian*?" He gawked in awe at Tom's revelation.

"You got a problem with Cheri?" Tom thrust his dimpled chin forward in defiance.

"To be honest, I do. Cheri Maison is a total newbie. She hasn't sold a single house. *Ever.*"

"That's why I'm giving her the listing for mine. Duh! So she can finally make her first sale."

"And what if she doesn't? Homes get listed all the time, Tom. With the wrong agent's name on the sign out front, they can sit there—unsold—for months and months and months."

"Uh, this is Pleasant Woods. A house hits the market, it sells in like a week, if not less. And nine times out of ten, it goes for above the asking price. *Way* above."

"Just because we live in one of the prime spots in the Detroit area, doesn't mean your house is going to sell itself," Cam said. "It doesn't work that way, Tom. A good Realtor is a self-motivated entrepreneur, with the tenacity to pursue every lead, and the hustle to aggressively market your property in order to score you the highest possible price."

"Have you met Cheri Maison? She worked in marketing for like fifteen years. Ask Andrew and Brianna Kim! She busted her butt making Chianti one of the most lucrative businesses in this neighborhood. You see the crowd down there right now?"

Unconsciously, JP and I focused our attention toward 2 Fairway Lane, directly across from our own Craftsman Colonial at number 1. The first floor of the late-Victorian-era house was indeed jumping. It had been since well before we'd arrived at Fairway Bob's place for dinner.

Cam nibbled his lower lip thoughtfully before continuing to offer Tom Cash his expert advice. "Marketing a restaurant is not the same as selling a home. Selling a home isn't just about busting your butt. It's about being smart and doing whatever it takes to close the deal."

Tom smirked. "Not very smart of you to come for me the way you are right now."

"I'm not coming for you," Cam assured his comrade, tone softening. "I'm trying to help you, Tom. If you put *my* name on a sign, in the middle of your front lawn, people will see it and pay attention. You put Cheri Maison's name on it . . . well, I can't guarantee you'll receive the same results."

"While I appreciate your professional opinion, it's a chance I'm willing to take."

Cam couldn't believe what he was hearing. It was high time he finally put his foot down and lay everything on the line, no holding back. "Do you have any idea how it will look? I sell every single house here in Pleasant Woods. *Every* house! If you don't allow me the courtesy of listing yours, what kind of signal would that send to our friends and neighbors? It's like you're basically saying you don't trust me. And if Tom Cash, owner of one of the most popular nighttime establishments in the area, doesn't trust Campbell Sellers, then why should anybody else in the community?"

"So, this is all about *you*?" Tom shook his head. "Instead of giving somebody new a shot, you want me to go with the old tried and true?"

Cam recoiled, insulted beyond belief. "Are you saying I'm old?"

"No. I'm saying you're a jackass," Tom coolly replied. "Don't think I wanna work with someone who only thinks of themselves. Sorry, Cam. I'm sticking with Cheri."

Cam scoffed. "Good luck! You're gonna need it." He turned on his heels and marched up the sidewalk, toward the boxy-shaped Prairie-style Four Square that loomed like an urban fortress under the cloak of the night sky.

When he reached the two-car drive, Cam did a brusque about-face. "So help me, Thomas Alton Cash . . . if you damage my impeccable reputation . . ." Cam stood his ground, firing off a threat at the top of his voice, for everyone in the vicinity to overhear: "I will *murder* you!"

With that, Campbell Sellers, Realtor Extraordinaire, strutted up the cobblestone walkway leading to the wide wood porch of his historic home at 11 Fairway Lane.

With a forceful slam of the front door behind him, he disappeared inside.

# Chapter 5

Terry Cash pulled his old car into the public parking structure.

The dashboard clock blinked a digital warning: *10:20 p.m.* By the time he'd made the climb to the third deck, found an open spot, made it back down to the ground floor, then walked around the block, Terry knew it would be well past half past the hour.

At that point, karaoke would have already started. Its host, Ms. Harmony House, was sure to let Terry have it as soon as he stepped onto the premises. He was the doorman, after all. He was supposed to be outside manning the *door*, checking IDs, and collecting cover charges, all the while keeping the Friday night riffraff out of Shout!

It was only a matter of time before the hordes of heteros would arrive in Fernridge *en masse* with their bachelorette parties and single guys looking to pick up bridesmaids. Since word had gotten round regarding the spectacle that was Drag Queen Queeraoke, more and more straight folk began finding their way to the nightspot with the rainbow flag flying proudly out front—the very bar that Terry Cash had spent the better part of the past twenty-plus years slaving away in, while his proprietor brother Tom reaped the rewards: moncy, power, and the handsome young men who flocked in regularly, impressed by an older man with both money and power.

Terry Cash may have physically resembled his twin, but that's where the identical line had been drawn. He possessed neither money nor power, and he'd been made well aware of the fact on more than one occasion, by more than one handsome young man.

On the tippy-top floor, Terry parked his SUV at the far end. He didn't mind walking the distance back to the one single staircase located on the opposite side. Only lazy people used the elevator, and the Midwest was loaded with them!

He checked his watch as he prepared to make his descent: *10:25 p.m.*

Terry took the concrete steps two at a time, round and round until he landed safely at the bottom. No sooner was he on solid ground that his cell phone vibrated. He reached into the pocket of his track pants, removed the ancient device, and flipped it open. On the tiny screen, he found a message from Danny the bartender: *Where r u?*

He didn't bother responding.

For one thing, Terry hated modern technology, hence his holding onto the flip phone he'd received as a fortieth birthday present from his twin, Tom. Secondly, texting on a flip phone took forever. Last of all, he was running behind schedule. Taking time to text the bartender back would only make Terry later.

He flipped the phone shut with an audible *snap* and returned it to his pocket before stepping up his pace.

"Everything okay?" Danny called out the second that Terry appeared through the door.

Sure enough, Shout! was jam-packed with the usual Friday night regulars. Terry had to give the drag queen host credit. She could really draw in a crowd. Before his brother had come up with the idea to construct a cabaret space, the bar had been on the verge of bankruptcy. In order to save the dying business, Terry had to put his foot down and dissuade Tom from taking on a loan from some rather unsavory associates.

Terry called back over the loud music that blasted from the sound system: "All good!"

On any given work night, he arrived no later than 9:30. Part of his evening duties included helping the legendary Detroit drag performer, Ms. Harmony House, set up for the so-called *show.* Terry could never figure out why the drag queen host referred to the twice-weekly event as such a thing. The very act of karaoke involved nothing but a bunch of drunks getting up in front of an equally drunken crowd and making drunken fools of themselves.

Terry had given up drinking when he'd hit the big 5-0— and never did he sing. Despite being a failed professional, Stephen Savage-Singer, aka Harmony, considered himself a star. Karaoke was his way of shining brightly in front of a live, captive audience.

Sporting her usual '90s-inspired emcee attire and long beaded braids, a look she referred to as *Fly Girl couture,* the African American beauty took to the stage. "All right, all right!" She daintily held the silver microphone, taking care not to muss her manicured fake nails as she greeted her adoring fans. "Welcome to another edition of Drag Queen Queeraoke. I'm Harmony House, your hostess every Friday and Saturday night from ten-thirty till one-thirty." She shot a dirty look across the bar toward Terry Cash. "I do apologize for the late curtain this evening . . ."

With that, she launched into her opening number.

Terry had never been a fan of hip-hop. He had no idea the name of the song that Harmony always sang first—something about chasing waterfalls—so he couldn't compare her performance to that of the original. As a rule, he did his best to tune out the drag queen hostess whenever she took a turn, since she'd always chosen similar selections in keeping with her signature style.

Upon concluding her premiere performance, Ms. Harmony reached into her cleavage and retrieved a slip of paper. "Next up, we have jacQ with a capital Q!" she read, pronouncing the *nom de plume* of the next performer as if it were, in fact, French: *Jacques*.

Terry rolled his eyes at the pretentiousness of it all, wondering why people couldn't just go by the names listed on their driver's licenses. He'd known the guy making his way up to the microphone for years. His name was plain old boring *Jack*. Back in the day, Terry had found the guy to be a total cutie. Now he just seemed pathetic, hanging out with a crowd of gays who were barely born when he and Terry were still students at Fernridge High.

The *faux français* singer wore a faded Detroit Tigers T-shirt and navy Old English D baseball hat. His short stature and boyish looks made him appear far younger than his fast-approaching fifty years. As the low bass of the selection he'd chosen began to boom, jacQ with a capital Q declared: "This song is older than all of you!"

Terry begged to differ. He recognized the tune from when he was a teenager. Personally, he preferred the English version they played on WHYT over the foreign language one. At least he could understand the lyrics. He squeezed his way through the throng, all bellied up to order a Bell's Oberon or have Danny whip up one of the specialty cocktails he was known around town for fixing.

"I texted Tom, looking for you . . ." The self-proclaimed mixologist poured a cranberry-colored concoction into a stem glass, then slid it over to an awaiting customer. "We lost out on almost an hour of cover charges. Tom's gonna be pissed."

Terry stepped behind the bar momentarily to grab the

stool he liked to sit on while he worked the door, if business ever got slow. "You lemme worry about my brother, okay?" If it wasn't for Tom wanting to meet with the fancy New York City gays from that ridiculous reality show, Terry wouldn't have been tardy for the Drag Queen Queeraoke party.

Sure, they were both good-looking guys. He didn't mind having the opportunity to admire them from a distance, across Fairway Bob's dinner table. Still, Terry resented the so-called Domestic Partners coming in with their grand plans, intent on erasing the memory of his dead parents by turning their old home into something new.

"Whatever. As long as you're here now." Before returning to his work, Danny gave the handsome older man a firm pat on the shoulder and allowed his hand to linger.

Terry gazed at the younger guy with the flippy dark hair, sparkling blue eyes, and pouty pink lips. He wondered what Danny had ever seen in his twin. Tom could be a real jerk, more often than not. If Danny had been Terry's boyfriend, Terry would never have dropped the guy just because he'd turned *thirty*. The fact that Danny continued to work for Tom, even after he'd broken Danny's heart by dropping him for an even younger guy—the aptly named Kyle *Young*—showed what a good man Danny Murphy was, deep down. Or maybe he just needed a job and knew he couldn't do much else with his life, so he sucked it up and stuck it out at Shout!?

Either way, it made Terry happy to have Danny around.

"I'll be out front," he said, feeling himself blush.

In passing, Terry smiled at the cute young boy standing on the opposite side of the counter, the one that Danny had just served the cranberry cocktail. Surprisingly, the cute young boy smiled back.

"Hey, CashMan," he said, all but batting his eyes as he sipped his adult beverage. "Remember me? Hunter27. You chatted me up on Lads4Dads."

Of course, the cute young boy assumed Terry was Tom. It could be the only explanation as to why he was being so forward. Cute young boys took no interest in the doorman. No matter how handsome or fit he might be, Terry Cash felt awkward around most people. He wasn't active on social media, where most guys he knew would go to hook up.

Terry let out a sigh. "Sorry, kid . . . you're barking up the wrong daddy. I'm the twin brother."

"Oh," Hunter27 said, disappointed at striking out. "Well, is Tommy here?"

"Not to my knowledge. Why don't you hit him up online? If he ain't at work, that's where you'll usually find him." Terry took hold of the metal stool and headed toward the front entrance.

En route, he could hear the audience growing restless, the din of their chatter increasing as it bounced off the high tin ceilings. Folks sitting at four-top tables in front of the stage barely paid attention to the singer, jacQ, clutching the mic stand like a wannabe rock star. The poor guy! He did his best, belting out the '80s pop tune—in the original German, no less—a song about some *luftballons* floating across the *horizont*.

Holding the stool out in front of him with his two large hands, Terry leaned his massive back against the heavy door. He gave it a firm shove. The hinges creaked as the portal swung open, releasing the doorman out onto the deserted sidewalk.

The street sat deathly quiet, off the beaten path of the major thoroughfare. Over on Main, storefront shops, vintage boutiques, and DIY art studios that drew customers in by offering wine along with their classes gave the city the aura of an Anytown, USA, straight out of an old time-y movie. The picturesque square, complete with whitewashed gazebo and concave band shell, added to the feeling of pure Americana.

Terry loved the old-fashionedness of Fernridge and his

own home of Pleasant Woods. Neighboring towns like Royal Heights and Madison Park, however, were starting to see an influx of young couples moving south from the distant northern suburbs. Places like Clarkstown, Orion Oaks, and Bloomington Hills were no longer desirable for folks to raise families.

Unlike their parents before them, the millennial set actually wanted to live close to Detroit, yet they still craved the safety of suburbia. If it meant tearing down the older historic homes and erecting mammoth facsimiles that swallowed up every bit of the lots on which they were constructed, leaving little open land to grow any grass and provide a backyard for children to play in, well then, so be it.

Terry Cash despised these people.

This was all the more reason why he now resented his brother, after giving the *Domestic Partners* guys permission to swoop in and destroy the only memories he had left of their dead parents.

Unlike most children, whose simple duty was to settle the estate, the brothers had made a solemn pact: The men, who as twins tended to be of one mind, had agreed to leave everything untouched, frozen in time, a testament to the lives that were once lived behind those very walls.

The Mission-style furniture in both the dining and living rooms remained in place, like pieces on display in a Henry Ford Museum diorama. The upstairs master bedroom, where Mom and Dad had slept many a night by each other's side, projected the illusion of a couple off on vacation, one day soon to return, save for the layer of dust that coated the quilted comforter pulled up tightly over the queen-size bed.

The brothers—Terry and Tom—had found themselves in complete and utter agreement: The house that had once belonged to their parents, along with all its contents, was never to be sold or, God forbid, torn down.

At least not during their lifetimes, while either of the two men still drew breath.

Tom might have originally suggested that they offer Larry and Linda's old house as a grand gesture, to help out the TV stars after they'd found themselves without a property to renovate on their show. But Terry could tell that his brother had an ulterior motive: Once the author and his actor boyfriend turned the vacant Tudor Revival into something new and totally unrecognizable—all in the name of reality television—Terry's twin would surely want to sell their parents' place and pocket a considerable profit.

Terry refused to allow any of these awful things to happen. He made a silent vow to put a stop to the changes that were being proposed for 4 Fairway Lane . . .

At whatever cost.

# Chapter 6

We'd been wondering about the abandoned property located at 4 Fairway Lane.

Since the day Campbell Sellers first suggested we make Pleasant Woods our new residence, we felt the vacant house would be the perfect project for *Domestic Partners* . . . and for our Forever Home.

The 1920s were by far both JP's and my favorite era in American architecture. While we preferred the exposed rafters and triangular peaked dormers of the Arts and Crafts style, the rundown Tudor Revival was still a magnificent structure, a throwback to a period of design the likes of which our country hadn't seen in almost a century. Plus, if we were able to buy the place, fix it up, and move ourselves in after the fact, we'd be living on the exact same street as my very best friend from high school . . .

*How cool would that be?*

Sadly, Cam had regrettably informed us that, despite sitting empty for the past twenty-plus years, the Cash family home was *not* on the market at the time, nor had it ever been. The current owners, a pair of middle-aged gay twin brothers, continued to hold onto the house. In fact, they'd kept it in the

exact same condition as it was last seen by their mother and
father, when they both had died on the exact same day.

In spite of the persistence of Pleasant Woods's premiere
Realtor, with his database of potential, deep-pocketed home-
buyers, the identical siblings had informed Campbell Sellers
that neither had the desire to engage with him in business.
The sentimental value of their childhood home was worth
far more than the potential profit they might fetch from the
highest bidder.

"What do you think made them change their minds?" JP
asked as we strolled across the street toward our Craftsman
Colonial, opposite Chianti, finally wrapping up our Friday
night.

Even at the late hour, happy couples and co-workers gathered outside, on the fabulous wraparound porch of the upscale wine pub and restaurant, for craft cocktails and locally
sourced charcuterie.

"Good question," I said. "That Tom Cash sure is an eager
beaver."

"Right? He seemed to do most of the talking all evening."

"He really wants his family's house featured on national
TV."

"Can you blame him? You know how good the exposure
will be. For both him and his bar. Guess that's why he's the
businessman brother."

I thought of poor Terry Cash, looking so melancholy, earlier in the kitchen. "I feel sorry for the other one."

"He didn't seem too keen on us sweeping in and giving
their parents' old house a makeover."

"Did you see how sad he got, talking about his mom?"

"Poor guy. I could totally sympathize."

"Of course you could," I said, taking hold of my partner's
hand.

To think, JP's own sweet mother had died of breast cancer when he was still just a boy. It killed me to know that I'd never get to meet her; that she wouldn't be a guest at our wedding one day. Nor would JP's father, whom he'd lost five years prior, to a long battle with Alzheimer's.

Hopefully, brother Terry would change his mind once the renovation had been completed and—more importantly—not create any hassles for us as we were trying to get it done.

As we arrived at the front sidewalk leading up to our home, I found myself having to stop for a moment, in order to reflect on the sight.

*Our home.*

Words I'd thought, living in New York City for so long, we'd never hear ourselves utter. Thousands of dollars we'd thrown away over the years on renting an apartment, all the while paying the mortgage on someone else's piece of property. No matter how much we'd invested, financially, we'd never have been able to call the places we'd lived our own. Neither one of us would give back the time we'd spent in pursuit of our artistic endeavors. But now, at this stage in our lives, both JP and I wanted so much more.

"I still can't believe we live here." I sighed, filled with unbridled happiness.

JP echoed my sentiment. "We found ourselves a great house."

Built in 1924, the home at 1 Fairway Lane featured a large screened-in front porch, held up by three sturdy columns. The dormer above formed a wide rectangle, inside of which sat the four windows of two of the second-floor bedrooms, encased by the same white aluminum that sided the upper half. We had a sneaking suspicion that beneath lay original cedar shake shingles and one day vowed to either restore or replace them.

The lower portion of the Craftsman Colonial had been fabricated from fine, red-colored bricks. A bay window jutted out from the western side, providing the formal dining room with a view of the steady stream of traffic humming along Woodward Avenue. As part of the third episode of *Domestic Partners*, JP and I planted a row of six-foot arborvitaes to help buffer some of the noise.

We ascended the steep steps of the side porch, with its own wisteria-covered trellis, just off the driveway that had been newly poured on part six of our TV series.

Entering the house through the original oversized solid wood door, I groaned. "Those stairs climb like a Brooklyn brownstone stoop!"

The glow from a Tiffany-style lamp atop a Mission oak library table, acquired at Fairway Bob's antique shop, welcomed us into the ample-sized copper-colored mudroom.

JP locked up as I plopped down on the Gus Storage Settle by Stickley that we'd won in an online auction. The piece was an Audi replica—not original Gustav or even L. & J.G.—but the cherry bench we'd gotten for a steal. The cost of paying a personal shipper to pick up in Maine and drop off a thousand miles away in the Motor City, however, did make a bit of a dent in our credit union joint checking account.

JP sat beside me on the seat cushion, custom-made by a local upholsterer called Foam 'N' More. We kicked off our sandals, allowing our feet to breathe freely. I glanced up at the handcrafted built-in cabinet that hung from the wall high above.

"It turned out nicely," JP said of my refinishing work. "Looks much better than before."

"Thanks, hon," I replied, happy to receive his approval. "Why they were so janky, I have no idea."

When originally constructed, the wood doors had been

hung crookedly, leaving a gap at the top of the left and a slight overhang on the bottom of the right. Fortunately, I was able to correct the flaws by flipping the panels, vertically, and reinstalling them on the opposite sides of the cabinet.

"Like I always say," I said, "if you're gonna do something . . ."

JP took pleasure in completing my mantra, while parroting my personal design philosophy: "Do it right!"

"Don't even get me started on the paint splatters."

"Oh, I won't!"

This was a private joke between us and our HDTV viewers, the result of my finding a million tiny flecks of latex speckling the six-inch wood baseboards of every single room in our new house.

After slipping on our slippers, we headed farther into the home through a single French door that I'd also painstakingly stripped, sanded, restained, and varnished in order to restore its original splendor. Comprised of fifteen leaded glass panes, with a vintage brass-plated lever-style handle, the portal into our twelve-by-fourteen dining room gave the entryway a sense of sheer elegance.

JP pushed the mother-of-pearl dimmer switch button we'd found on a reproduction hardware website. The stained glass chandelier hanging over our circa 1910 quarter-sawn oak Tobey dining table lit up the nine-foot ceiling. When we'd first inspected the property, we discovered the plaster medallion that had once hung, slightly off-center, had somehow gone missing. So during the on-screen rehab, we made sure to install a replacement.

"Do you want a snack or should we just watch our show?" I could feel a tiny pang of hunger, but not what I'd call *starvation* by any means.

"We can skip the snack," JP said seductively, "and even

skip the show." He made his way around the circular table, another online find from an antique dealer in eastern Pennsylvania, over to where I stood near the bay window.

A matching sideboard with hammered brass hardware sat tucked into a corner between the kitchen door and living room arch.

"Why, Mr. Broadway," I said, doing my best Southern belle impression, "whatever are you insinuating?"

JP wrapped his big arms around me and nuzzled the nape of my neck. "Oh, nothing."

While the window seat cushion was wide enough for two grown men to cuddle up on, we chose to prolong the romance a bit longer . . . and headed upstairs.

JP led me by the hand through our living area, past the Pewabic tile fireplace, past a second leaded glass French door similar in style to the one off the mudroom—only wider—and up the staircase to our home's second story. The walnut-stained wood steps almost perfectly matched the trim surrounding the windows and doors of the first floor. In total, there were fourteen and four, respectively, all of which we'd refinished with the assistance of a small team of local contractors.

"Give me one sec to freshen up," I told my partner as we reached the top floor.

JP headed up the narrow hallway to begin *shutting down the house*, a term we'd use to describe the nightly duty of lowering the shades and closing the blinds that covered the upstairs windows. The bright yellow sunroom at the back had seven alone! The other three rooms—guest, master bed, and home office—boasted two windows apiece, bringing a grand total in the entire house to thirty. Thankfully, JP was a considerate man and took on the seasonal responsibility of washing them. What that guy could do with an aerosol can of glass cleaner and a few sheets of old newspaper!

Slipping into the bathroom, I pulled the white-painted wood door shut behind me, leaving it open a slight crack. The bath, along with the kitchen, were the only two rooms in the house that we'd actually fully remodeled as part of the recent renovation. Before we'd even purchased, a pipe burst, resulting in drastic second-floor water damage. As much as we would have preferred to keep the finished design as close to the original as possible, after careful consideration we concluded that reconfiguring the layouts and updating the interiors would make the most sense, while giving us the best return on our investment.

I turned on the left tap of the his–and–his double sinks we'd installed, with the help of a professional plumber, and let the water run. For a moment, I contemplated taking a cool shower. The humidity still hung in the air outside and, to be honest, I wasn't feeling my freshest. A bubble bath for two could have made for a romantic nightcap, if only we hadn't opted to forgo installing a tub when we redid the room. As a gay couple with no plans to one day have children—and who rarely had time for the luxury of a long soak—we felt the need to restore an antique clawfoot less of a necessity than some of our other more important improvements.

JP popped his head through the partially open door and smiled at me, reaching for my hand. "Ready?"

Slowly, we walked across the hallway to our bedroom. We both realized that we needed to take advantage of being alone together in the silence.

Soon enough, there'd be a third presence in our lives each and every night for the next dozen-plus years . . . hopefully longer.

# Chapter 7

The lanky blond boy stumbled up the sidewalk.

Beneath the warm glow of the streetlights, he focused his fuzzy gaze on the blur of storefront windows in search of the one displaying the rainbow flag, the universal symbol for Gay Pride.

"You okay, Kyle?"

Hearing a familiar voice say his name, he halted in his tracks. At last he'd found his destination. It wasn't his first stop of the night.

"Oh, it's *you*," Kyle sneered. He sidled up to the handsome older man working the front door at Shout!

"Sorry to disappoint."

Kyle glanced down at his phone, opened to the Lads4Dads hookup app. "Is he here?" The words caught slightly in his throat. He definitely needed a stiff drink to quench his dry mouth and calm his shaky nerves.

"Tommy?" Terry Cash shrugged his broad shoulders. "Not yet. Have yourself some fun till he gets here."

Kyle quickly concealed the image on his phone screen: a cute twink in the arms of an older daddy type. "What's that supposed to mean?" He didn't appreciate what Terry had just insinuated about his fidelity to his boyfriend.

The doorman stared down at the pavement. "Nothing. Forget it."

"Well, do you know where he is?" While Kyle was quick to ask the question, a part of him didn't want to know the answer.

"We were at a dinner party earlier. I left to come up here; Tommy stuck around for a bit. He'll be by a little later."

Kyle slipped his thumb and two fingers into his shirtfront pocket and removed a bent cigarette from a crushed flip-top box. Terry adroitly retrieved the disposable lighter he always carried on him and casually lit the young man's smoke.

Kyle gestured with the hand prop held stiffly between his fingers. "Want one?" He wasn't a real smoker. He'd only picked up the habit to impress his sugar daddy, Tom Cash.

"No, thanks." Terry put up a large paw in protest. "Turned fifty, I quit."

Kyle couldn't imagine ever being that old. "Well, if you see Tom, tell him I wanna talk to him."

Terry touched the brim of his Michigan State ball cap and gave a friendly salute. "Will do." He opened the door, allowing his boss/brother's drunk boyfriend to slip past without paying the five-dollar cover charge.

Kyle strolled confidently into Shout! He knew the guy who'd been hitting on his daddy was somewhere inside the bar. The dimly lit room made it difficult to see who, exactly, chose to spend their Friday night attending Drag Queen Queeraoke. But Kyle was both bound and determined. According to Lads4Dads, Hunter27 stood a mere twenty-odd feet away. Unless he was sitting down at a table in the cabaret room.

Kyle pulled up the younger boy's profile on his phone to

get a clearer picture of the guy who'd been trying to steal his man. Or at least get busy with him. He stumbled over to the bar area, giving total attitude to the bartender on duty as he ordered. "I'll take a bourbon, neat."

From where he stood on the opposite side of the counter, Danny winced at the smell of liquor on Kyle's breath. "How many is that tonight?"

Kyle shook his blond head, fuzzy from more cocktails than he could count. "Just pour the drink and don't ask questions."

Danny grabbed a clean glass from the back of the bar. He filled it with water from the soda gun and slid it Kyle's way. "Start with this. We'll see about some bourbon once you've sobered up."

Kyle didn't want the damn water. Nor did he want some loser bartender monitoring his alcohol intake. He pushed the glass aside, spilling its contents in the process. Cubes of ice leapt over the rim and bounced across the bar top.

Danny wiped up the mess with a rag. He looked past Kyle to the Asian American man and woman waiting in line behind him. "What can I get you guys?"

"I'm not done!" Kyle declared as he cut in front of the older, presumably straight couple.

"It's okay, Danny," the man assured the bartender, taking a step back.

The woman gave the man a look that said she felt sorry for the drunk boy, but they'd best stay out of the kid's way.

Kyle carried on, raising his voice over the roar of the karaoke background music. "I want my drink. Bourbon, neat. *Now.*"

"And I want you the hell outta my bar," Danny said, polite as punch so as not to be accused of being disrespectful to a customer.

"Your bar?" Kyle scoffed. "Last I checked, you just worked here." He turned to the older couple, breathing booze in both their faces. "You know who owns this place, don't you? My boyfriend."

The bartender casually leaned against the bar top, the better to get up in Kyle's flush face. "He was *my* boyfriend first. Till *you* stole him from me."

Kyle was in no mood to argue with the help. Not tonight. Every time he ran into the guy, Danny had to rub the facts in Kyle's face: How, right before Danny had turned thirty, Kyle conveniently came along, and pretty soon after, Tom Cash broke it off with him.

As far as Kyle was concerned, Danny Murphy was just a bitter old queen, washed up at the age of thirty-one, without a boyfriend and nothing to speak of but his job. The same job he'd had since he dropped out of college over ten years ago. Danny might call himself a *mixologist*, but he was just a stupid bartender, plain and simple.

Danny slammed down a rocks glass in front of Kyle and filled it with brown liquid from a bottle. "Here's your damn drink. Enjoy!"

Kyle took a sip off the top. The warm liquor burned the back of his throat. He didn't thank Danny for his hospitality. Nor did he bother paying the man. Kyle Young's money was no good at this bar. Not since he'd started dating the boss, over a year and a half ago.

Sadly, something in the pit of Kyle's soul told him that his free-drinking days were numbered. If Tom had broken up with Danny the bartender, all because he'd turned *thirty*, what would happen to Kyle once the major birthday milestone had befallen him? He'd heard the stories about Tom's reputation for dating guys in their early-late twenties, and then dropping them once they'd gotten too old for his liking. What would stop Tom from doing the exact same thing to him when Kyle hit the big 3-0?

At that moment, the thought of Tom leaving him made

Kyle go mad. A burning rage began to boil in his belly. He couldn't control the horrific images that flooded his mind: A *younger* boy sharing Tom's bed, a *younger* boy here in this very bar, while Kyle watched from a distance as Tom showered the *younger* boy with the same affection he'd once shown him.

But unlike Danny the bartender and the many guys before him, Kyle refused to allow Tom to leave him. In fact, he'd do anything to keep the handsome older man from walking away.

It was right then and there, in a dimly lit corner during Drag Queen Queeraoke, that Kyle Young came to a drastic conclusion: *If he couldn't have Tom Cash, no one would.*

He needed to find Hunter27 immediately so that he could settle the score between them. No way was Kyle losing everything, all because of some younger guy on a stupid hookup app.

He returned to the bar area, where he spoke to the Asian American couple whom he'd been rude to moments before, albeit much friendlier this time. "Do you guys know Tom Cash?"

The man and woman had both ordered their drinks from Danny—a Manhattan for him, a boulevardier for her—and were chatting quietly amongst themselves when Kyle had approached. The woman, cute with her short dark hair and denim overalls, stood a few inches taller than the man dressed in lightweight joggers and a jersey.

*Was he Chinese or Korean?*

Whatever Far Eastern country the muscular man's ancestors had come to America from, it didn't matter. The guy was hot! Skin the color of gold; hair as dark as ink. His emerald eyes sparkled; his perfect smile glowed bright white beneath the bar lights.

If only he were a little older and, presumably, not *heterosexual.* And if Kyle himself were single and not already hopelessly in love with an older gentleman who, at that very moment, might be off somewhere cheating on him with another, *younger*, boy.

The woman smiled at Kyle in recognition. "We know Tom."

Kyle stared hard at the woman and her companion. Or was he her boyfriend? It was hard to actually tell who, in this gay-friendly establishment, played for the pink team and who was simply slumming because, well, drag queens made everything more fun!

"Kyle, it's us," the woman said, a hand upon her ample bosom. "Brianna and Andrew Kim . . . from Chianti, the wine pub in Pleasant Woods?"

Kyle was too messed up to make the connection, and too distressed to care if he might offend. Still, he pretended to recognize the couple, in case they were indeed important. "Sorry, I've had a bit to drink. If you see Tom, do me a favor? Tell him I'm looking for him."

"We will," Andrew promised. "And if you see Tom, tell him we'd like to know what's going on with the house."

"We saw him talking with those *Domestic Partners* guys earlier," Brianna explained, after sensing Kyle's confusion over her husband's statement. "Out on the street. Are they remodeling the Tudor Revival for their TV show?"

Kyle shook his head, too full of his own anxiety to worry himself with Married People Problems. "I really don't know . . . and I really don't care."

Every time he and Tom ran into the Kims, they made sure to mention how much they wanted to buy Tom's parents' old place so they could demo it and put in a parking lot for their restaurant.

Kyle pushed his way past Andrew and his annoying wife and headed toward the front of the bar. He didn't mean to be rude, but he was in no mood. As far as Kyle was concerned,

Andrew and Brianna Kim needed to learn the old adage: *When you're dead, lie down.*

On stage, the drag queen known as Harmony House strutted up to the microphone, nearly knocking Kyle Young out of her way in passing. "All right, all right!" She knew very well that the drunk kid was the boss's latest boy toy, but she had a karaoke show to host and needed to hustle.

"Once again we're at the top of the rotation," Ms. Harmony told her minions, each one anxiously awaiting their next shot in the spotlight. "If you're only just arriving, pick out a song, grab a slip of paper, fill it out. I promise I'll get you up here as soon as humanly possible." She paused for a beat, her bright eyes twinkling in the colored stage lights. "Of course, anybody who truly knows me knows I'm *not* a human being. Just ask my husband, Evan. He's got the bite marks to prove it."

As Harmony bared her fangs and struck her best vampire pose, Kyle perched himself at a high-top table and consulted his phone screen. He scanned the room, in search of the elusive Hunter27, now approximately a few yards away.

The bar had gotten considerably crowded in the short time since Kyle's arrival. The longer he sipped his drink, the more difficult it became for him to clearly observe his surroundings.

Kyle obnoxiously shoved his phone in the face of a person standing nearby: a young man around his own age, tall, with curly hair the color of copper and a pair of rather nice legs, shown off by a pair of rather short shorts. "Do you know this guy?"

Any other time, Kyle might have flirted or at least made small talk. The copper-haired boy, from what Kyle could tell in his current state of intoxication, was cute enough. But far too young for his taste. Plus, he wasn't there to make new friends. Kyle needed to find Hunter27—fast!—and take down the little piece of trash.

The copper-haired boy with the rather nice legs giggled like a girl. "Oh, my God!" He slurped up the remainder of his sloe gin fizz through a plastic stir-straw. "I totally know him. He's right over there!" The copper-haired boy flailed his arms wildly, like one of those inflatable air-dancers posted in front of a mobile phone store in order to attract new customers. He screamed out: *"Hunty!"*

This was all the information that Kyle needed.

Fueled by adrenaline and alcohol, he made a beeline across the bar. Kyle took hold of the back of his enemy's hoodie and jerked the younger boy around to confront him. "Yo, Hunter! Leave my man alone, got it?"

Clearly confused, the younger boy had no idea who Kyle was or the crime of which he'd been accused. "Excuse me?"

"You heard what I said. Chat with my boyfriend again and I'll kick your—"

"I don't know your boyfriend," Hunter27 promised, carefully backing away from his potential assailant.

"Don't play dumb! You met him on Lads4Dads. Hot salt-and-pepper, fifty, super fit."

Hunter stared down the nose of his nondescript face. "Honey. I meet a lot of hot daddies. Tell me the name of yours. I might know him. I might not."

Kyle flashed his phone, open to a picture of himself and Tom Cash, taken while on vacation in South Florida. "His screen name is CashMan . . . and he owns this bar."

In the photo, the daddy-son couple posed for the camera, poolside at an all-inclusive gay-owned Key West resort, both men bronzed from a week of fun in the sun.

"Oh, him!" Hunter grinned. "Yeah, I know Tommy. But we only chatted like twice. And he slid into my DMs first, I swear. Nothing happened between us. Seriously."

"First off, his name is *Tom*," Kyle said, correcting the younger boy. "And second, I don't care."

Judging by his hurt tone, Kyle clearly *did* care. Otherwise, he wouldn't have confronted a total stranger in the middle of a crowded bar the way he had done. "Tom and me have been together going on two years. What we've got is real. I love him. And he loves me. And . . ." Tears started to fill his eyes as Kyle began to doubt his own affirmations.

Hunter placed a forgiving hand upon his shoulder. "I'm sorry. But like I said, your man chatted *me* up. You should be talking to him."

The younger boy was right. Kyle knew that he needed to speak to Tom personally, in order to save his relationship, before it was too late and everything fell apart.

If Tom were to leave him, like Kyle suspected he might, he knew that he couldn't handle it. Kyle knew, deep down, he was no better off than poor Danny the bartender. Yes, he drove an expensive, current-model car. He shopped exclusively at the upscale Somerset Collection, where he'd amassed a wardrobe comprised of pieces from the trendiest designers. But apart from his good looks—that he knew all too well would one day fade—the rest of Kyle's possessions had resulted directly from his relationship with Tom Cash. Without the generosity of his sugar daddy, Kyle Young would have nothing to call his own.

Still, Kyle knew in his heart that he didn't *need* Tom Cash. He *wanted* Tom Cash. And contrary to what anyone might have thought or said behind his back, Kyle Young *loved* Tom Cash . . .

But could he really trust the guy?

# Chapter 8

We pulled into the parking lot around 9:45, dressed to impress in the new summer shorts we'd chosen to wear for the special occasion.

Mine were navy, a polyester non-wrinkle blend, and JP's the same, but in maroon. Our collared shirts were both button-down, in complementary colored cotton. Some might say we looked too matchy-matchy. For us, dressing alike—not identical—was how we designated ourselves to the outside world as being a committed couple.

JP drove; I sat shotgun. Typically, we weren't early risers, but neither one of us had gotten much sleep the night before. The anticipation we'd both felt far outweighed the need for rest.

"I can't believe we're here!" I cried as JP maneuvered our crystal black SUV into a tight spot just outside the entrance to the pet store.

Having lived in New York for as long as we did, we'd both gotten used to walking. The old story I always told everyone was that, growing up, my dad would hop into his car and *drive* ten houses to the corner just to mail a letter.

"Let's try not to make a scene," JP suggested, as if causing a commotion in public was my modus operandi.

We stepped through the sliding doors. The rush of air conditioning, along with a distinct smell that I would come to describe as simply *Pet Supplies Plus*, washed over us like a pungent wave.

"Where is he, where is he?" I wondered, scanning the surroundings like a submarine periscope. Of course, I was behaving exactly as my partner had moments ago advised me against.

I couldn't help it. I hadn't owned my own dog since I'd been ten years old, when I unapologetically begged my dad to let me bring home a black-and-white shepherd-collie mix puppy from our neighbor's house down the block. I called her Lucky, and I promised to love her and walk her and—more importantly—pick up her poop each and every day, with no complaints.

Sadly, as I grew into a young adult, placing my friends before all other relationships, my poor little pet soon found herself more the family's dog than mine.

Truthfully, it was my mother who had become Lucky's primary person. Mom was the one who opened the can of food each morning, let her out into the yard, cleaned up her messes, and carted her to all the necessary vet appointments . . . including the very final. Just six short weeks after I'd headed off to forge my way in the world as a writer, on a cold winter morning back home in Michigan, my poor little Lucky left us forever.

All these years later, I couldn't help but feel that I'd somehow let her down. I disappeared, lured away by the bright lights of the big city, not giving the slightest consideration as to whether my little girl might even notice that I was gone; if she could no longer sense my presence in the house; if she might actually miss me.

In retrospect, I didn't deserve her. This beautiful pup, my poor little Lucky, had loved me unconditionally all her days.

We grew up together, a boy and his dog, and selfishly I abandoned her. Was it the tumor in her belly that finally took her, or did she die of a broken heart?

In my defense, the twenty-four-year-old me hadn't realized that a dog's life is short.

At almost fifteen, Lucky was an old girl. Her eyes had grown cloudy, her hearing no longer sharp. She had difficulty moving about, up the stairs or down. The thick fur that had once kept her warm had worn away in patches, leaving her skin raw and irritated.

Gone was the playful puppy I'd placed inside a wicker basket, attached to the handlebars of my sister's bicycle, and drove around our block on the first day we'd spent together. I honestly believed, in my naïve mind, that the next time I returned home for a visit, I would see my little Lucky asleep beneath our kitchen table, the way I'd always found her every other time I'd ever left.

I was wrong.

Right then and there, in the middle of the Madison Park pet shop, mere blocks from where I'd grown up and my own little Lucky was born, I made myself a promise: If the Powers that Be would bless us and allow me and my partner to bring into our lives this handsome creature called Clyde, I would never take another dog for granted.

"OMG!" JP shrieked like a banshee, wildly gesticulating in the direction of a makeshift kennel assembled in the corner of the store. "There he is!"

*So much for not making a scene.*

A dozen wire cages were filled with doggies of various sizes, shapes, and breeds, yapping excitedly, eager to please the hordes of humans who might rescue them from a life of permanent fosterhood.

"I don't see him!" I cried, too anxious to even utter Clyde's name aloud.

"He's over there in the crate"—JP pointed—"with the two little chihuahuas."

Sure enough, across from where we'd been standing, the chunky little beagle-bull lay sprawled out on his freckled belly. The expression on Clyde's sad puppy face spoke volumes. In his short seven months on the planet, he'd already attended one too many of these so-called adoption events.

"OMG!" I said, echoing JP's earlier outburst.

He looked so tiny lying there, so quiet. His two cellmates, Lilo and Stitch, bounced about, leaping back and forth, climbing one on top of the other, showing off for their weekend visitors. Clearly, Mr. Clyde was having none of their antics. In response to the hubbub, he let out a heavy sigh and shut tight his almond-shaped eyes.

"Let's say hello," JP said eagerly, ever the go-getter.

We crossed the floor a few steps, over to where the beautiful pup lay sound asleep. Up close, his dense snow-colored coat gleamed shiny and bright under the fluorescents.

We both beamed at the sheer sight of him.

Intentionally, I held myself back a bit. A part of me wanted to rush in and give Clyde all the love that I'd felt since first seeing his on-screen image, bundled up in the little red puffy coat. Another part feared that if I got too close, if I opened myself up and allowed myself to feel too deeply for this dog, should things not work out in our favor . . .

Well, I'd be nothing short of devastated.

Still, I couldn't resist taking out my mobile device and snapping a quick digital puppy pic. Immediately, I texted it to Cam, along with a message: *Just look at our handsome boy!*

"Good morning!" a cheerful voice greeted us from behind, startling both me and JP.

We turned to see an older woman, around fifty, maybe? A plum-colored, oversized T-shirt covered her curvy figure, with the logo of the rescue organization stretched across her buxom bosom. The woman's hair was wild and dyed red, worn in an updo that framed her pretty face.

"I'm Margot. Are you gentlemen interested in adopting?"

Trying not to visibly blanch, I shot a silent glance toward my partner. I had this theory that the term *gentlemen*, when directed toward us specifically, was code for *gays*. Why not just refer to us as *guys*, same as any other Michigander?

JP turned his attention to Margot, the dog-rescue woman. We'd seen her picture online, so we knew right off that she was the one we'd need to impress—read: kiss up to—in order to have our adoption application approved.

"We're very interested." JP flashed his killer smile, in hopes of winning over Margot with his charm.

"Awesome! Is there a particular pupper you have in mind?"

"There is," I cut in, feigning full confidence when really I felt terrified. "His name is Clyde."

"Our beagle-bull? Clyde is very popular this morning!"

"Is he?" JP said, his optimism suddenly waning. "We can see why. He's a beautiful little guy."

"He's special for sure," Margot declared, the proud foster dog mommy.

"Can you tell us a little more about him?" I asked, not that we needed to know anything else. We were already sold! But I wanted to make sure to show enough of an interest, in order to put our best feet forward.

"Well, his mama, Freckles, is a fifteen-pound beagle," Margot elaborated, as if she'd memorized Clyde's bio and could recite it by rote. "His dad, I've been told, is a Staffordshire bull terrier—they're one of the smallest members of the bully family. We've gotten quite a few applications for him today already. But you're more than welcome to throw your hats in the ring, if you'd like."

This was *not* the response that we'd wanted to hear.

While JP got started with the paperwork, I took on the

task of smooth-talking the woman in charge. I hated having to do it, and it showed the instant that I opened my mouth. "What a great turnout!" Casually, I glanced around at our dog-adoption competition. "I grew up in Madison Park. This store wasn't around back then."

"Nope. It's only been here a year."

*So much for my attempt at making a personal connection!*

"Ah. Well, we just moved to Michigan nine months ago. From New York." I added *City* to indicate just how special we were, unlike the other prospective adopters who'd not ventured out into the great wide world the way both JP and I had done.

"Never been to New York. Way too crowded. And too dirty."

*Strike two!*

At that moment, I remembered what Cam had said about rescuing his dog, Snoop, from Margot's group. As I prepared myself to name-drop, I felt the rude interruption of a firm hand upon my forearm.

"Pardon us?"

Two fortyish ladies with wispy short haircuts stood by my side. Both proudly sported the same violet HOME FUREVER T-shirt as Margot, leading me to conclude that they were either super fans of the rescue or basic volunteers.

"You're that guy from that new HDTV show!" the blonder of the two women announced.

Her strident Michigan accent reminded me of my Aunt Nancy, God rest her sweet soul.

Episodes of *Domestic Partners* had only recently started airing, so I was still getting used to being recognized in public. Admittedly, I hadn't given it much thought when I'd first signed on to do the show. For me, my goal wasn't to achieve reality TV celebrity status. I was not—nor did I strive to become—a real housewife or a New Jersey Shore stereotype.

But I wasn't about to lie to the ladies.

"I am that guy from that show," I whispered, so as not to draw further attention toward myself.

"Oh, my Gahd!" the women screamed at the top of their Midwestern lungs.

Unfortunately, our cover had been blown. JP looked up from the clipboard he'd been holding, pen to paper, and turned toward the sound of the high-pitched screeches.

"It's the other one!" the darker-haired woman shrieked. She grabbed hold of her cohort, alerting her to JP's presence in the pet shop.

More screams erupted from the women in purple, causing quite the ruckus.

"Ladies!" Margot obviously disapproved of their public display of emotions. "What's with all the excitement?"

"These guys are on that new home rehab TV show!" the blonder woman wailed.

"Oh, yeah?" Margot sloughed off the comment, as if she couldn't care less. "Well, I'm fostering six pups at any given moment. Doesn't leave much time for watching television."

Feeling the odds stacked against us, I was just about ready to throw in the towel. Then I recalled the sage advice given to us the evening prior by one Mr. Tom Cash: *Be sure to mention you're famous.*

"It's called *Domestic Partners*," I explained. "On HDTV. My partner and I do historic home renovations. It's a very popular program," I added, only slightly exaggerating while trying not to come off too cocky. "We'd be happy to mention Home FurEver on an episode sometime, once we adopt our puppy . . ."

Intentionally, I'd left the last statement dangling. I hadn't meant it to be a threat of *quid pro quo* or anything as nefarious as bribery. If Margot took my remark as incentive to allow us the honor of bringing Clyde home, all for the sake of our helping to better publicize her dog-rescue organization, well then so be it!

"That's good to know," Margot said with a smile, seeming suddenly interested.

But then . . . the dog-rescue woman did a complete one-eighty!

Helplessly, we watched as Margot permitted a heterosexual couple and their two small children to take *our* Clyde out of his crate—and leave the pet store with him, cradled lovingly in their arms!

JP stared at me across the aisle, eyes glassy.

I swallowed, a lump growing large in my larynx.

All around us, desperate doggies vied for attention . . . yet none could capture our hearts like the one who'd been carried away.

# Chapter 9

We rode home in silence.

Neither JP nor I spoke a word, anxious that our insecurities over what had just happened would bring to fruition our worst fears.

"Cam still hasn't replied to my text," I complained after checking my messages. "I sent him a picture of . . ." My sentence trailed off, but both JP and I knew the exact word that I'd almost uttered.

*Clyde.*

Were the strangers we'd seen at the pet store—the ones who had carried our fur baby away—now the new dog parents of a handsome beagle-bull puppy?

"Cam's at an open house, remember?" JP reminded me.

In my morning angst, I'd completely forgotten that Cam was stuck up in Royal Heights till three o'clock that afternoon, showing off a million-dollar McMansion. A quick glance at the dashboard clock revealed the current hour: *10:55 a.m.*

"Oh, right. He's just about to get started. I'll leave him alone." My stomach grumbled. The oatmeal we'd eaten before our trip to the pet shop had just about run its course.

"Who's hungry?" JP wondered in a playful high-pitched

tone, quoting his actor friend Murray, with whom he'd performed in summer stock, back when they were both fetuses, as Murray liked to put it.

"Should we stop for brunch?" I said, more of a suggestion than an actual question. "Oh, wait. We told Tom Cash we'd come by the Tudor after our appointment."

JP hesitated before replying. "Tom's probably still busy cleaning up the yard. We can swing by after we eat."

The last thing either of us felt like doing, in our current depression, was playing friendly with our potential new business partner.

JP turned the car off Woodward Avenue onto Fairway Lane and pulled into our drive. Across the street, a line had formed in front of Chianti as the brunch crowd spilled down the wood porch steps and onto the sidewalk.

I cringed at the thought of having to wait an hour for eggs Benedict. "You wanna skip it?"

"But I could really use a Bloody Mary after this awful morning." JP was clearly referring to the tragedy we'd encountered with Home FurEver.

I chose not to dwell on it. At least for now. Later, after a few mimosas, I would probably break down and have myself a good cry.

The problem with Chianti was the lack of public parking. Because the restaurant had started out as a private residence, there was no actual lot connected to the property. Thankfully, we owned a two-car garage directly across the road and could tuck our vehicle away inside before heading over for brunch on foot.

"How many?" The woman who greeted us, just inside the recessed doorway of the wine pub, was none other than Chianti co-owner herself, Brianna Kim.

That morning, the Asian American woman wore her

short dark hair slicked back, a black tuxedo shirt, black bow tie, and black pants. A far cry from her usual Bohemian chic style.

"Hey!" Brianna did a double take. "Sorry, I didn't recognize you guys. How are my favorite neighbors?"

"Starving," I answered, refusing to rehash the sad tale of our Saturday morning pet store epic fail.

"You and everybody else," Brianna muttered. She grabbed a pair of menus from the host stand. "I've got a table for you, no problem."

I noticed at least three other parties ahead of us in the tiled entry hall. "Are you sure?" The last thing I wanted to be accused of was using our newfound celebrity to our advantage.

"Of course! I can't make you wait. You guys are famous. Right this way."

Sure enough, as we followed Brianna into the main room—formerly the parlor, when the restaurant was still a private home—a young couple we'd never seen before caught our attention.

"We love your show!" the wispy-haired woman gushed.

The blue streaks in her black hair reminded me of an exotic bird I'd once seen in the atrium at the Detroit Zoo.

"We watch it every week!" The stocky man grinned, even more excited than his date.

A quick check of both their left ring fingers showed no sign of matrimonial commitment. Maybe they were simply just friends?

After thanking them sincerely—and signing our names to a paper napkin—we stepped through what was once the formal dining room into an alcove, on the opposite side.

"Where's Andrew this morning?" JP asked Brianna, faking small talk to mask his disappointment over her hunky restaurateur husband's absence.

"He should be here soon . . ." Brianna navigated our way through the tight space between the row of bistro tables. "He went to an open house up in Royal Heights. Which is why I'm alone, handling all this craziness right now. He promised to get there as soon as it started and be back ASAP."

Brianna halted at an available two-top. She pulled out a cane-back dining chair for me to plop my bottom down into.

"*Merci, madame.*"

"No problem. Hey, I heard you guys are redoing the Tudor Revival next door for your TV show."

"You did?" I adjusted in my seat, a bit surprised. "News sure travels fast on Fairway Lane!"

"Drew and I were up at karaoke last night. We ran into Tom Cash on our way out. He filled us in. Said he'd just come from meeting with you guys . . ."

"It's not a totally done deal," JP confided. "Please don't say anything to anyone just yet."

"No, no, I won't." Brianna locked her lips with an invisible key that she promptly tossed aside. "Java for two?"

"Please!" we both begged, in desperate need of a caffeine fix.

Brianna headed off toward the kitchen, past the exposed brick wall where dozens of Chianti bottles had been hung, signatures scrawled across the straw baskets by the persons who'd emptied them. On the day that we first toured the Pleasant Woods house that would eventually become our home, Cam brought us to dinner at the upscale restaurant, and we'd added our own names to the collection.

"Why would Tom say something about us renovating his parents' old house?" JP hissed at me, once Brianna was safely out of hearing distance.

I could tell from my partner's biting tone that he was a little more than peeved. "I'm sure Tom's just excited. Everyone wants to be on TV." Casually, I perused the menu, even though I already knew exactly what I'd be ordering.

"Well, hopefully he hasn't jinxed us. You know I hate talking about things until they're one-hundred-percent solid."

"I wonder if the property Andrew's looking at is the same one Cam's selling?" I mused, intentionally going off topic.

JP was clearly still in his head, calculating all the things that could go wrong with our impending deal. "Could be . . ."

Glancing up, I noticed our next-door neighbor greeting one of the men we'd dined with the night before. "There's Fairway Bob!" Judging by the Michigan State ball cap that his companion wore, I took the handsome older man to be Terry Cash.

Bob sipped coffee, looking super summery, dressed in a floral print button-down, khaki shorts, and sandals. Terry sat himself and waited for their server. Once again, he wore a dark hoodie and casual athletic wear, as if he were heading to the gym immediately following his meal to burn off the extra calories that came with a side of bacon.

Brianna returned to our tiny table carrying a pair of steaming ceramic mugs. She placed them before us, along with a small silver pitcher full of fresh cream. "Ready to order?"

JP requested the potato latkes with eggs over medium, while I chose *las migas,* adding black beans and avocado to the Mexican mix. Brianna didn't write down our dishes, which always impressed me, as someone who'd been fortunate enough to pursue an artistic career without ever having to work as a waiter.

"You aren't selling the restaurant and moving, are you?" JP asked her, before she could head off again. "You said Andrew's off looking at a house."

"We don't *wanna* . . ." The wine pub co-owner exhaled.

"We love living in Pleasant Woods. But parking for the restaurant is becoming a bit of an issue. We might need to find a better space."

"Oh, no!" I'd heard complaints from friends who'd drive in from afar about having to secure a spot on either Fairway Lane or around the block on Meadowbrook Boulevard. I hadn't realized the fate of Andrew and Brianna's business had been hanging in the balance.

"Before we opened," she continued, "we talked to Tom and Terry about buying the Tudor. Drew thought we could tear it down, put in a parking lot. But the guys wouldn't go for it, so . . ." She shook her head sadly.

"Well, we certainly hope you both stay," JP said sincerely.

The thought of losing the Sunday morning eye candy that was Andrew Kim, I'm sure, had been some cause for his concern.

"Us, too." Brianna lingered a little longer at our table, something clearly on the tip of her tongue that she wanted to spit out.

"Everything okay?" I asked, sensing the woman's discomfort.

Brianna huffed. "When we heard Tom and Terry were letting you guys remodel their parents' old house, it made us so . . . *angry*."

This was not the response I'd expected coming from the typically mild-mannered Brianna Kim.

"We practically begged the Cash brothers to let us buy it," she elaborated, "so we could save the restaurant. But they said they wanted to honor their dead mother and father by keeping the place for themselves. Now that doesn't seem to be the case."

"We're sorry," JP apologized.

"Yeah," I said, unable to think of a more compassionate remark.

"This morning, I had to stop Drew from busting down Tom's front door and telling both him and his brother off," Brianna confessed. "He's worked so hard to get Chianti off the ground. This restaurant is his baby. If he loses it, I don't know what he'll do."

JP and I kept silent, allowing the woman her moment to vent.

"My husband might seem like a sweet man," she said calmly, "but he's got a temper. Especially when he's crossed. He's also a fourth-degree black belt in Taekwondo, so the Cash brothers better watch their backs." Brianna let out a little chuckle to show us that she was teasing.

We joined in on the laughter, albeit nervously, before observing her trot away.

"Did Brianna just make a threat?" JP stared at me in a stupor.

"Sure did sound like it."

"Wow. Well, I'd hate to see Chianti close," JP said, "but I'm happy the Tudor Revival isn't being torn down and turned into a parking lot."

I couldn't have agreed more.

An hour later, as the clock tower struck noon in the neighborhood square, JP and I stood on the sidewalk staring up at 4 Fairway Lane. The vacant property looked far less menacing in daylight than it had on the night before, when we'd been given our initial tour.

Surprisingly, not a single soul could be found within the confines. The mower lay abandoned in the yard, as if the person who'd been using it had gone off somewhere, mid-mow, and would be returning any minute to finish up the job. That person, we both knew, was none other than Tom Cash, a fact supported by the collection of cigarette butts that littered the half-cut lawn.

But where Tom had disappeared to, we were about to find out soon enough.

"He said he'd be here, didn't he?" JP said, agitated. "Do you have Tom's number? We could give him a call."

I felt for my mobile, tucked into my front shorts pocket, warm against my thigh. Scrolling through the contacts, I came across Tom Cash's info and began composing a text, alerting him to the fact that we'd just arrived. Upon finishing, I hit *send* and patiently waited for a reply.

My message went unanswered, same as it had when I'd reached out to my best friend, Campbell Sellers, earlier that same morning.

"What's up with everybody?" I wondered aloud. "It's like no one knows the rules of cell phone etiquette anymore!"

At that precise moment, our neighbors, Evan and Stephen Savage-Singer, appeared in front of 5 Fairway Lane. The legally married couple lived on the opposite side of Bob's bungalow, in a late mid-century modern ranch, the most contemporary house on the block. Evan, a burly bear, grew up in the home that he'd purchased from his mom and dad upon their retirement down south. He was a unique specimen on the gay male spectrum. A Gulf War veteran, father of a trans tween daughter from his first marriage to the girl's mother, Evan had come out later in life, around age thirty, and soon thereafter met Stephen, a househusband by day, entertainer by evening. They'd been together almost twenty years.

"Hey, boys!" Stephen called, waving a well-manicured hand. The other clutched an assortment of shopping bags, branded by the logos of several high-end shops found at the upscale suburban Somerset Collection.

My guess was he'd also purchased the designer tracksuit he sported at the exact same mall.

Stephen's cocoa-colored skin glowed, from a recent spa

treatment, no doubt. Evan, pale-complexioned and the quieter member of the couple, nodded as he stood nearby, unloading even more loot from the back of a classic muscle car.

"Hey!" I called back. "Did you guys happen to see Tom Cash over here this morning?"

"Hmm . . ." Stephen turned to his other half, who was now emptying out the trunk of the sleek midnight-blue Nova. "Baby, did you see Tom Cash?"

Evan slammed the lid shut and joined Stephen on the sidewalk, the underarms of his loose-fitting light-colored polo damp with perspiration. "Did I see Tom Cash when?"

Stephen turned his attention back to JP and me, with a slight shake of his mini dread knots. "All brawn and no brains, my man. But at least he's mine!" He let out a deep belly laugh. "I seen Tom Cat—that's what *I* call him—last night up at Queeraoke."

Stephen paused for a beat, suspiciously observing us. "But who I did *not* see is you boys."

"Sorry," JP apologized, "we couldn't make it. Sometime soon?"

Stephen chided us, playful yet dead serious. "Listen, I know you're famous TV stars and all that. But you been back in Dee-troit for almost an entire year now, and you've not *once* seen my show. Do you realize how unloved that makes a poor girl feel?"

"I know!" I said, totally put on the spot. "We really wanna come check it out."

"Fridays and Saturdays, ten-thirty till one-thirty, down in Fernridge at Shout!" Stephen gave us a little Fly Girl impression to accompany his advertisement. He waved his free hand in the air and gyrated his slim hips, the way I assumed he did as his drag queen alter ego, Harmony House, named for the now-defunct local record store chain.

JP and I both nodded nervously, unable to think of any words that might spare us from Stephen Savage-Singer's guilt trip.

"Good luck finding Tom Cat," Stephen growled. "He's probably off prowling after some young boy. Wouldn't be the first time. Ta!"

Once our neighbors had disappeared into their house with their purchases—safely out of hearing distance—I turned to JP. "We should really check out Drag Queen Queeraoke sometime."

My partner shot me a look, nostrils flaring. "You know how I feel about karaoke . . . and how I feel about drag queens!"

Despite being a fan of our reality show rival, *Top Drag Superstar*, the competition program that ran on a different network in the same time slot as *Domestic Partners*, JP swore up and down that he had an avid phobia of female impersonators.

At first, I thought maybe the way they overexaggerated their makeup evoked in him some deep-seated dread of circus clowns. But he had no problem with Bozo, or Krusty, or the super scary Pennywise, so I scratched that excuse off my proverbial list. Then I worried maybe my partner had a problem with men who wore women's clothing to earn a living. But several of his New York City actor friends dabbled in draggery, so I couldn't possibly label him a dragophobe. What it came down to, I eventually learned, was JP's fear of the unknown.

One never could tell what might come out of a drag performer's mouth once she opened it. The quick wit most queens possessed, coupled with their wry sense of humor—and the way they would shamelessly flirt with him—made my partner feel extremely awkward and embarrassed.

As an actor, JP abhorred the art of improv much in the same manner. Without a script containing written dialogue that he could commit to memory and recite on cue, anything could go amiss. JP Broadway had spent far too many years gaining control over his life, his career, and his image to be made a mockery of by some catty gay man in a dress.

Still, I wasn't about to criticize, and played my role as a supportive partner by skirting the issue. "I can't believe we haven't been back to Shout! since the remodel," I lamented, in an attempt to ward off some of the guilt that I'd felt for not frequenting Tom Cash's bar more frequently.

JP stared down from his high horse. "How different can it possibly be now?"

For whatever reason, my partner had no interest in checking out the local gay bar that wasn't an actual gay bar. NYC had obviously spoiled him when it came to the club scene. No matter how cool or trendy Shout! 2.0 might be, as far as JP Broadway was concerned, it was still a product of Michigan.

"Oh, look!" I said, noticing for the first time a significant detail in our current quest.

It appeared that the exterior portal to the classic Tudor Revival had been left open a tiny crack.

JP stepped forward for closer examination. "Maybe Tom got hot working and went inside to wait for us? Let's go see if we can find him."

We headed up the sidewalk and stepped onto the wide front porch.

"Hello?" I knocked gently on the heavy wood door before slowly pushing it open.

JP called out: "Tom! You in here?"

Sure enough, Tom Cash was indeed inside his family's former home.

Upon passing through the foyer into the larger living area, at last we found the man we'd been looking for that morning.

Sporting his favorite blue and gold U of M ball cap, dressed in the same dark athletic attire he'd worn to Fairway Bob's dinner party the evening before, Tom Cash lay facedown on the floor near the bottom of the rickety old staircase . . .

*Dead.*

# Chapter 10

We inched closer to better inspect the body.

There appeared to be no breathing, no movement whatsoever. But first, we needed to make certain that Tom Cash was, in fact, no longer living.

Like a pair of sleuths out of one of my own mystery novels, we bent down and carefully examined the corpse.

"Don't touch him," JP cautioned. "This could be a crime scene."

Having played a police detective on television, my partner was well aware of the protocol involved when coming across a potential murder victim. He and the rest of the *Brooklyn Beat* cast had received extensive training from professional New York City law enforcement during production.

"What should we do?" I said, worried over the unfathomable situation we'd unexpectedly found ourselves in.

Although I'd published several books dealing with death as a subject, I'd never seen an actual dead person up close, other than at a funeral. Even then, I tended to avoid approaching the casket, whether the deceased was a close relative or not.

JP focused on the spot where Tom Cash lay prone on the worn oak floorboards. "Bodies can begin decomposing quickly." With a wave of his right arm, he motioned for me to keep my distance. "Careful, Pete! Skin and fluids contain potentially infectious blood-borne pathogens."

"Gross!" I was already familiar with these disturbing facts from research I'd done for my past writing projects.

The last thing I planned on doing was touching a dead man, particularly someone I'd had dinner with—and who'd blatantly *flirted* with me—less than twenty-four hours before.

Squeamish, I took two baby steps backward. My left foot stepped down on something, six or so inches in size, relatively flat, composed of hard plastic and glass, maybe? The thing made a crunching noise, then slid out from under my sneaker and across the hardwood, where it lodged beneath a Mission-style tabouret end table resting in the corner.

Startled by the unexpected sound, JP gasped and gaped in the direction the unknown object had traveled. "What was that?"

I took a guess, based on the feeling I'd felt under my foot. "I think maybe it was a cell phone?" Sure enough, when I bent down to retrieve the item, I discovered a rather new-looking mobile device with an unfortunate crack crisscrossing the screen.

"Leave it!" JP warned loudly, just as I was reaching under the table for the damaged electronic gadget.

"It must be Tom's," I said, recalling how impressed I'd been by his iPhone being the latest model. "It looks like the one he had at Fairway Bob's house last night. He pulled it out at the table to check his hookup apps."

"Don't touch it!" JP hissed, morphing into TV police detective mode. "That phone is evidence."

"We need to call 9-1-1," I stammered. "Tell them we found someone. We should probably also mention the cell phone I stepped on," I added, removing my own mobile from my front shorts pocket.

A thought quickly occurred to JP: "Maybe Tom fell down the steps? He kept warning us how unsafe they were. Remember, Cam tripped and almost killed himself?"

I gave my partner's assessment careful consideration. Tom could have easily fallen, spinning head over feet as he came crashing down the staircase, landing at the bottom with a bang. He wore a hoodie. The position he lay in on the floor caused the fabric to bunch up, partially covering the back of his head, making it difficult to conclude if there was any blunt trauma to his neck area or not.

"Let's call the cops," I concluded. "They'll be able to tell if he's actually dead . . . and how he died, if he is."

Within fifteen minutes, a Pleasant Woods police officer showed up on Fairway Lane at the historic Tudor Revival.

"What seems to be the problem?" He didn't recognize me when he arrived at the scene of the would-be crime.

I couldn't say the same about him.

At age forty, Detective Nick Paczki had been a member of the PWPD for close to two decades. Growing up in Madison Park, he dated my sister in high school, when he was a senior and Pamela a sophomore. Eleven years old at the time, I'd thought Nick was super cute, with his dark blond hair, deep blue eyes, and pale Polish American skin. The hair was turning to gray now, the eyes slightly crinkled around the edges. But I'd have recognized the hunky cop anywhere. Even with the fuzzy mustache that now sprouted over his upper lip.

We met him on the sidewalk in front of the vacant house. "There's a man inside," I said. "Pretty sure he's dead."

The expression on Detective Paczki's face betrayed him but a little. "Oh. Well, what makes you guys think that?"

We filled him in on the details of what we'd experienced that morning thus far.

"He doesn't seem to be conscious," JP stated, picking up

his cue from where I'd left off. "We think he fell down some stairs and broke his neck."

The police officer took out a notepad and began scribbling in it with a ballpoint pen. "Go on . . ."

"We also found a phone!" I cried, overly excited by the fact.

We showed the detective the fancy device that we'd discovered. The cop pulled a plastic bag from his pocket and dropped the object inside, taking care not to smudge any prints it might have picked up.

"We'll see what kinda info we can get off this, if any," he assured us. "Check the call history, text messages, all that good stuff. Now, how do you two fellas figure in all this nonsense?"

"Well . . ." I wasn't sure what exactly we should say without our lawyer present.

JP jumped in and took over the reins, speaking on both our behalf. "We were over here last night. Tom warned us about the staircase being unstable."

The policeman nodded. "And what were you guys doing at this house? I've been on this beat a long time. Nobody's lived here in like twenty-five years."

"The owners were showing us around," I explained. "We're doing some rehab work on the property."

Detective Paczki blinked his azure eyes. He stared at me with scrutiny followed by shock. "I know you!"

I blushed, flattered that he finally recognized me. "Yes, you dated my sister."

The cop looked confused. "I did?"

"Pamela Penwell. You went to Madison Park High together. I'm her brother."

The detective did a double take. "You're Peter Penwell! How the heck are you, man?" He enveloped me in a warm hug, with a pair of strong arms, which admittedly took me by surprise.

As it did JP.

By no means was he jealous. He hadn't any reason to be. My partner was as good-looking—if not better—than the beefy officer with the bushy mustache. He just hadn't expected, when he woke up that morning, to see a handsome stranger hugging his boyfriend later in the afternoon. Especially when one of our neighbors lay dead a few feet away, inside a house we'd been hired to renovate on a nationally televised TV show.

The policeman followed us into the Tudor, where we showed him our gruesome discovery.

"He's definitely dead," Detective Paczki determined, after more closely examining Tom Cash. "My guess is he fell down the steps there, broke his neck at the bottom."

Smirking, JP turned to me. "Just like I suspected."

"Do you think Tom fell . . . or do you think maybe he was *pushed*?" I asked, bringing up a scenario I'd considered but had been too afraid to suggest.

Might the popular bar owner's death *not* have been an accident?

Could it have been possible that foul play might have been involved?

Did someone actually kill Tom Cash?

Coming to this conclusion, I felt like TJ Inkster, the teen detective in my *Murder High* series of mystery novels, except for the almost twenty-year age difference. In book one, *Death of a Drama Club Diva,* the Madison Park High senior discovers the school's star thespian lying lifeless on the auditorium stage, one night after rehearsal. When the principal dubs the poor ingénue's death accidental, it's up to TJ and his sidekick, JR Sterling, to uncover the true cause of the girl's demise.

Observing Tom Cash's body lying twisted at the bottom of the staircase caused the wheels of my mystery author's mind to rotate. He seemed like a real charmer when we'd chatted over dinner and drinks the night before. I could just imagine the trail of broken hearts the handsome older man had left behind, all vowing bitter revenge against him in the name of unrequited love.

Of course, maybe I'd watched one too many *Murder, She Baked* movies with my sister the weekend prior, and I had crime on the brain? I realized, in that moment, just how eager I'd been to get back to my mystery novel writing.

Detective Paczki laughed at my proposed theory. "You guys lived in New York, right? I 'member running into Pam a while back. She mentioned you were living there with your partner."

"We did," I affirmed, before realizing I hadn't officially introduced my sister's ex, the hunky policeman, to the hunky actor standing beside me. "Nick, this is him. My partner, JP Broadway."

The policeman reached out for a firm handshake. "JP, hey! I seen you on that Brooklyn cop show before. Good to meet you, buddy."

JP appeared a bit smitten as he held the handsome officer's big hand in his own. "Likewise."

I made a mental note to tease him about this moment, later on.

"As I was saying," Detective Paczki continued, "this isn't New York City. There hasn't been a murder in the hundred years people been living in this town. Hence the name, *Pleasant* Woods."

"No disrespect," I said respectfully. "This is still Detroit." We natives considered anything within a twenty-mile radius of the river as being part of Motown, aka *Murder Capital of the World*.

"Yeah. But it's not Detroit proper. You're smack-dab between Royal Heights and Fernridge, two of the nicest suburbs in the metro area."

"So, you think it was an accident?" JP asked, sounding hopeful.

Raised in Shadyside, Pittsburgh, on the border of East Liberty, JP Broadway was more than familiar with living in a neighborhood deemed as *safe,* juxtaposed against a less-than-desirable one.

"We'll complete a thorough investigation," the detective promised us. "But I do believe we're talking about an unfortunate incident. Pure and simple."

"What happened here?" The voice that anxiously asked this question came from none other than Tom Cash's own twin, Terry.

He stood in the doorway of the home that he and his brother had grown up in, dressed almost identically as the deceased, except for the green and white Spartans cap that he wore. In his large hand, he juggled a set of keys and an ancient-looking flip phone.

Detective Paczki stoically greeted the victim's sibling. "Hey, Ter. Sorry for your loss."

Terry Cash remained calm. His eyes showed no trace of the emotion he might be feeling, if any, as he glanced down at the mirror image of himself, sprawled out lifeless on the hardwood. "I just come from having brunch with Fairway Bob at Chianti. Thought I'd stop by and see if my brother needed a hand cleaning up the yard."

Detective Paczki flipped to a blank page in his notebook. "How about we step outside?"

"Sure thing!" Terry thrust the keys and cell phone into the front pocket of his track pants.

We followed the officer through the front door and around the side of the house. While he seemed confident in his assessment that Tom Cash's death was indeed accidental, Nick Paczki still needed to question his only living family member.

He kept the conversation light, in lieu of the tragic situation. "How was breakfast this morning?"

"Good," Terry said. "Wasn't super hungry. Got the breakfast sandwich."

"You guys ever been to Chianti?" Detective Paczki asked me and JP.

"We go every once in a while," my partner answered. "It's right across the street from our house, so it's super convenient."

"Took my wife when they first opened," the police officer admitted. "Fifteen dollars for an omelet! A bit pricey, for what it is, you ask me."

Terry Cash chuckled. "That's how my brother feels."

An awkward silence hung in the humidity. We all thought twice about Terry's choice of verb tense in describing his brother's aversion to the local wine pub and restaurant.

"That's how my brother *felt*, I should say," Terry said, correcting himself. "He's really gone, huh?"

"Afraid so." The detective held pen to paper, preparing to take the dead man's twin's official statement. "Can I ask you a couple questions?"

Terry Cash stared blankly, as if he had nothing to hide.

"What time did you meet Bob for brunch?"

Terry's handsome face twisted in thought. "I got there a little after eleven. Maybe eleven-fifteen? I was moving kinda slow this morning."

"Can I ask where you were before brunch?"

"Sure. I was at home."

Detective Paczki chewed on the end of his writing instrument. "By yourself?"

Terry looked sideways at the cop. "If you're asking about my love life, Nick, you know I ain't got one."

The policeman jotted down this bit of information on his pad. "You live over on the west side, right?"

"One-one-one-oh-four Borman Avenue. It's Tommy's house, technically." Terry stopped to consider his choice of verb tense again. "It *was* Tommy's house. He bought it after Mom and Dad died. Been living there with him for like twenty years."

"Guess it'll be your house now, huh?" Detective Paczki joked. When he realized that none of us found his humor funny or remotely appropriate, Nick softened his tone. "I'm real sorry about your brother, Ter."

"If it helps," JP said, interrupting the interrogation. "We saw Terry and Bob together this morning at Chianti. Didn't we, Pete?"

I nodded in agreement, backing up my partner's statement.

"You can ask Bob," Terry Cash said, in case the detective had any doubt about his alibi. "We met around eleven and stayed until just before I got here. Bob's a gabber, so I couldn't get outta there any sooner."

"Did you happen to see your brother this morning," the police detective asked Terry, "before you met up with Bob?"

Terry shook his salt-and-pepper head. "I did *not*. When I woke up, Tommy was already gone. He eats breakfast with his boyfriend, Kyle, on Saturday mornings at The Depot. My guess is that's where he was before he came over here to clean up the yard."

Detective Paczki closed his writing tablet and tucked it away. "Got it. I will definitely pay young Kyle a visit," he promised, "just to make sure everything checks out."

"You're sure this was an accident?" Terry asked, even-keeled in his questioning.

While there was no trace of remorse or sadness in his tone, I chalked it up to Terry Cash being in shock over the loss of his twin brother.

"Appears to be that way," Nick Paczki confirmed. "Like

I told the fellas . . ." He gestured to me and JP. "My guess is Tom was alone in the house here. He tripped on the loose stair coming down—maybe going up? Lost his balance and fell, landed at the bottom, broke his neck."

Terry nodded. "If that's your professional opinion, detective, I'm good with it."

And that was that.

Just another Saturday in Pleasant Woods, Michigan. Except, on this particular weekend morning, a perfectly healthy fifty-year-old man had died under mysterious circumstances.

While I had no reason to distrust Nick Paczki's judgment as a law-abiding police detective, I couldn't shake the fact that maybe Tom Cash hadn't tripped and fallen down a rickety old staircase to his unfortunate demise.

Sure, it seemed far-fetched, given the neighborhood in which we all had chosen to make our home. But maybe . . . just maybe . . .

Someone had actually *killed* the man?

# Chapter 11

Somber music played softly as we stepped up to the casket.

I won't say that my partner forced me, but since we were local celebrities of sorts, JP felt it best that we keep up public appearances, in order to avoid suspicion. Especially once the press had gotten word that we'd been the ones to discover Tom Cash's dead body.

Fortunately, the autopsy report had revealed that the fifty-year-old man died from a fatal cervical fracture, while on the premises of his parents' former home, after tumbling down a flight of stairs and hitting the back of his head on the hardwood floor at the bottom. This official finding meant that both JP and I were off the hook as potential murder suspects.

Regardless, all the major media—online and otherwise—began immediate coverage of the death of the gay Metro Detroit businessman, and his connection to the hosts of HDTV's hottest new reality show. Already, we'd received dozens of interview requests from the morning news programs, tabloid journalists, and LGBTQ+ lifestyle bloggers, funneled through our *Domestic Partners* publicist in New York City.

JP loved the attention! Me, not so much.

I did receive some rather good news from my book editor, Sabrina James of Huntington Publishing, in the form of an email, informing me that *Murder High* sales figures had noticeably risen within hours of the terrible tragedy. She also asked, much to my astonishment, when would I be ready to write a new novel? I told her I'd give it some thought and get back to her. There was one thing I'd learned during my stint as a published author: *Writing is hard work!*

First off, a story needed to start with an idea. Some scribes were full of them. For me, they came few and far between. It wasn't as if I'd had writer's block. Once the seed had been planted and the actual writing started, the words would flow rather quickly. But that initial spark, to coin a phrase, could be as elusive as lightning caught in a bottle.

My sources of inspiration stemmed from real-life situations: an event I'd encountered or a tale of which I'd heard tell. Being a novelist, I toiled in a fictitious universe, whether the landscape resembled one based in reality or not. The names I'd always change—to protect the *guilty*—though I was never creative enough that a clever reader couldn't see through my characters into their real-world counterparts, especially if the reader had been acquainted with me personally.

The next step in my creative process was creating a step outline. Chapter by chapter, in chronological order, I mapped out the plot, detail by detail. With four books under my belt, I'd come to the conclusion that each scene needed to fall on a specific calendar date, though I'd rarely make mention in the narrative. Following this tightly woven structure better familiarized me with the order of events that occurred in my story, from its humble beginning through to its muddled middle, until the ultimate bitter end.

More recently, I'd taken to writing on my mobile phone, using Microsoft's Word app. Back in Brooklyn, I'd haul myself and my laptop to the nearest Starbucks where, between the wannabe screenwriters and Williamsburg stroller mommies, finding an empty seat could be a lesson in survival of the fittest. Now, I just kicked back in bed, with JP scrolling through cute pet videos beside me, and typed out a few hundred words with a simple slide of my finger across the digital keyboard. The next morning, I'd open the file on my MacBook, connect the old AirPods, and let the *Read Aloud* feature recite it back to me as I sipped my coffee. By actually hearing the words in my ear, it became more evident if I'd unintentionally repeated a word or a phrase—my pet peeve—than if I were to simply skim the pages using only my sense of sight.

When it came to sharing my work in progress, I rarely ever did so anymore. With my first book, once I finished writing a chapter, I passed it along to my partner for his perusal, before moving onto the next. While I appreciated the honest feedback, I soon realized that my tight schedule simply didn't allow for this added step in the process. I won't say that I needed to crank out the novel, but my deadline had given me less than a year to finish writing the dang thing. The luxury of laboring over each and every adjective wasn't something that I could afford. Ultimately, I learned to trust my own instincts and wait for my editor's opinion on the finished manuscript. In the end, she had final say on what made it into print, and I trusted her completely.

The arrival of Sabrina's recent email message served as a cruel reminder: My last book had gone on sale over a good two years ago. Readers would soon lose interest in TJ Inkster, teen detective, if his creator didn't come up with a new mystery for him to solve—and soon.

"He looks good." JP gazed down on Tom Cash, at rest in his coffin. "Don't you think?"

I couldn't agree less.

With his hair slicked back, the way that Tom's head had been propped up on the silk pillow made him look both unnatural and uncomfortable. Not that he could feel anything anymore. The odd angle could have easily been accounted for as a result of the severing of his spinal column during his fall down the staircase. Still, nothing about the person lying in the solid mahogany wood box resembled the man who, mere days before, had been so flirty and so full of life.

The Tom Cash we'd known briefly was barely recognizable. Not just because he'd been dressed in an expensive suit, as opposed to the casual athletic wear we were used to seeing him sporting. The makeup the mortician had applied was a shade too dark for Tom's skin tone, despite the hours he'd spent at the tanning salon, coupled with a recent trip to Key West in the company of his significant other, Kyle Young.

*Speaking of . . .*

"Where's the bereaved boyfriend?" I wondered, surveying the almost empty funeral home. "Where's everybody else, for that matter?"

"It's a Tuesday morning," JP said, making excuses for why most of Pleasant Woods had chosen to skip out on attending Tom Cash's memorial service. "Unlike us, most people have to work."

He looked handsome in his navy suit and tie, a big difference from the dirty—albeit super sexy—coveralls I was used to seeing JP wearing on most days, while we taped our TV show.

"Well, if *you* were the one in that box," I said, perishing the thought, "no job would keep me from being here right now."

JP took me in his arms and held me tight. He cooed, kissing my cheek and nuzzling my neck. "You sure are sweet."

"I mean it." I felt the sting of tears as I put myself in poor Kyle's place. I could totally imagine what the guy was going through, wherever he may have been.

"He must be devastated," I said, burying my face against

JP's broad chest, resisting the urge to weep. "Can you imagine losing the love of your life at all of twenty-eight?"

"I can't. But not everyone is as lucky as we are."

Taking a step back, I stared into my partner's bright eyes, thankful that I'd still had the ability to perform such a feat. "You don't think Tom was the love of Kyle's life?"

"Pete," JP said, sounding surprisingly condescending given the current circumstance. "I've never even met Kyle— and neither have you. Who's to say if he and Tom Cash were in love? We don't know anything about their personal, private relationship."

"You're right," I said, feeling my bubble burst. "I'm a hopeful romantic."

Really, I just wanted everyone to be happy, the way JP and I were. No matter how much time a person spent with the one they truly loved, it would never be long enough if that love were suddenly taken away.

Fairway Bob, of course, showed up at the service, his peepers puffy from crying. "I can't believe it, you guys. He's gone."

Being his own boss, Bob had given himself the day off from his antique shop, Somewhere in Time, to attend Tom's funeral.

"We were just all together on Friday night," he lamented. "Now this . . ."

The poor guy had been a wreck since Saturday afternoon, after spotting the arrival of the ambulance that would remove his best friend's body from his childhood home at 4 Fairway Lane.

Neither JP nor I knew what, exactly, we should say. We'd only officially met Tom a little more than three days ago. Bob and the dead man's relationship went back almost *thirty years*.

"He's the reason I moved to Pleasant Woods from Ann Arbor," Bob informed us. "We went to Michigan together.

After graduation, Tom told me he was coming back here. I had no intention of returning to the U-P . . ."

"You're from the Upper Peninsula?" JP asked in amazement.

"Don't remind me," Bob replied bitterly. "Escanaba, born and raised."

"Wow."

"Well, Gladstone. But nobody's ever heard of it."

"No kidding?"

"Oh, yah," Bob answered, putting on a genuine Yooper accent, sort of a cross between generic Minnesotan and bad Canadian. "My parents owned a pasty shop."

"Well, I've been wanting to check it out," my partner confessed.

Ever since I'd met him, JP Broadway had a fascination with the fact that the Great Lake State consisted of two parts. But unlike the Dakotas and Carolinas, there was no North or South Michigan. Anything involving the half located beyond the Mackinac Bridge fell under the category of *exotic*.

Fairway Bob rolled his bloodshot eyes. "Do yourself a favor. Don't bother."

I decided to ask him about Kyle Young's whereabouts, mostly out of concern. Also, I found it downright odd that his dead boyfriend's funeral was about to begin, and the guy was not in attendance. "You're pretty tuned in to the goings-on in PW, aren't you?"

Bob beamed, holding his head high. "They don't call me Yenta Yelena for nothing."

"He wants to know where Tom Cash's boyfriend is," JP said, totally reading my mind, while at the same time butting into my personal interaction with our next-door neighbor.

"Don't you mean *ex*-boyfriend?" Bob said, a lilt in his voice and a glimmer in his eye.

JP and I both stared at the straight man, speechless.

"Word on the street is: Tommy and Kyle called it quits. And by the street, I mean, I heard it from Terry."

"Oh, no!" I said sadly, my heart breaking for a man I hadn't even met.

"Oh, yes! It happened the day Tommy died, like right before."

"You're kidding? Poor Kyle!"

"Poor Kyle, not! That boy knew exactly what he was getting himself into when he started dating my best friend. God rest his fickle soul."

"So, they lived together?" JP said. "Tom and his boyfriend."

"They didn't so much *live* together," Fairway Bob explained. "It was more like Kyle moved himself in, early on, and he never left. But that's all changed, I guess. Terry says, as of yesterday, Kyle took his stuff and moved back to his tiny apartment, down in Fernridge."

"I suppose it would be hard for Kyle, living in Tom's house without him there," I said, putting myself in the guy's place.

"Well, it's Terry's house now," Bob told us. "With Tommy gone, he gets everything. The house, the car, the bar . . . you name it."

JP shrugged. "Makes sense, Terry being Tom's only relative and all."

"One would think, but . . ." Bob leaned in closer and lowered his voice. "Now you didn't hear this from me. Let's just say, there wasn't a lot of love lost between the brothers Cash."

"Oh, really?" While I enjoyed good gossip as much as the next gay, I wasn't sure what, exactly, Bob had alluded to here. It seemed as if more story needed to be told, but a funeral wasn't the proper place for salacious chatter, so I let it drop.

Stephen Savage-Singer and his husband, Evan, soon arrived to pay their last respects. The more flamboyant of the pair made a grand entrance, decked out in black designer couture. For some reason, I'd expected to see Stephen dressed from head to toe as his alter ego, Ms. Harmony House.

Alas, he was not.

Stephen greeted us, with kisses on both cheeks, beneath the crystal chandelier that hung in the marble-tiled funeral parlor lobby. "I had to come," the out-of-drag queen said in a hushed whisper. "Tom gave me my job hosting Queeraoke, after he redid the bar. I wouldn't be the star I am today if it weren't for that man. God rest his miserable soul." He sneered in the direction of Tom's body, lying in its casket a few feet away.

I wasn't sure how I should respond, or what else I could add to the conversation for that matter, so I smiled politely. "Were you guys close, outside of work?"

Stephen's nostrils flared like he smelled something foul. What remained of his own natural eyebrows lifted an inch on his high forehead as he regarded me. I couldn't help but wonder how long it took him—or his stylist, no doubt—to tweeze them into shape . . . and how badly did it hurt having them done?

"Girl, you have gotta be joking! While I don't wish to speak ill of the dead, I could hardly stand the guy. In fact, Tom Cash was an A-number one—" Stephen pursed his lips together, intentionally cutting himself off from further self-incrimination. "I'll let you boys complete that sentence on your own. Though, to be honest, I find most people detestable. I do wonder if Tom Cat really fell down that staircase . . . or did somebody up and push him?"

As this had also been my and my partner's alternate theory as to how Tom Cash had died, I felt the need to get Stephen's take on the situation, as someone who'd actually known the alleged victim. "What makes you say that?"

Stephen took a step toward us and lowered his voice when

he spoke. "You didn't hear this from me, but . . . rumor has it, the half a mil Tom used to remodel the bar came from none other than the pink mafia."

"You mean like the gay mob?" JP asked, awestruck. "Does that even exist here?"

Stephen wagged a slender finger in our faces. "Oh, you better believe it! A whole cartel of sleazy characters— homosexuals all of 'em—ruling the mean streets of Motown like gangsters in some old movie."

"Really? I grew up in Metro Detroit," I said, shocked by what we'd just learned. "And I've never heard of such of a thing."

Stephen scoffed, barely able to contain his laughter. "That's because I'm yanking your chains! You white boys are so gullible. A pink mafia bumping people off in Pleasant Woods? But seriously . . . think about it: Where did Tom Cat come up with half a million dollars to redo his bar? He had to get it from someone. And if the time had come to pay that someone back, and Tom Cat didn't have the funds . . . well, you know what they say about double-crossing a gay mafioso?"

I honestly didn't know what they said—whoever *they* might have been—but I ventured it couldn't be good. If Tom Cash had borrowed the money to renovate his business, and he wasn't able to reimburse the lender in a timely manner, his error could have easily led to his untimely demise.

But how could we Domestic Partners prove it?

"Well, I've said my piece," Stephen said, slipping a pair of dark sunglasses on the bridge of his broad nose. "Ta!" With that said, Stephen Savage-Singer strutted into the chapel to take an up close and personal peek at the dead man whom he'd just totally dissed.

Fairway Bob curiously scanned the crowd that wasn't so much of one. "Where's Campbell at?"

I was beginning to wonder the same thing myself. "That's

a good question. He told me he'd be here when I talked to him last night."

JP couldn't resist commenting. "You know how Cam is . . . the guy can't be trusted. He won't even text you back."

"He did text me back," I snapped. "The very next day." I'd had enough of listening to my partner bash my very best friend, ever since I'd sent Cam the picture of Clyde, after our Saturday morning pet store excursion, and he didn't immediately reply.

JP just wouldn't let up. "So, what was his excuse?"

"For your information, something happened to his brand-new phone, and he had to get a replacement."

"With friends like Campbell Sellers . . ." JP shook his head in disapproval.

"Be nice," I said sweetly, intentionally taking the high road. "Cam's a busy guy."

My partner wasn't about to let me off the hook. "And you're not?" While he liked Cam perfectly fine, JP didn't care for the way he took our friendship for granted, more often than not.

Personally, I chalked up Cam's insensitive behavior to the fact that I'd been away living in New York City for so long. He'd simply gotten used to my not being around. Hopefully, now that I was back home, we could make up for lost time.

Neither one of us could believe we were coming up on the twenty-year anniversary of our first meeting, freshman year at Madison Park High. I'd never forget the day Campbell Sellers came limping into fourth-hour Phys Ed, doctor's note in hand, excusing him from any sort of activity that could put a strain on his recently sprained ankle. The lucky dog got to spend the entire period kicked back on the bleachers, foot propped up, watching me and the rest of our classmates huffing and puffing as we ran laps around the gym's perimeter.

The second the bell rang, to my surprise, I caught sight of

Cam sprinting out the double doors and down the hallway. Little did I realize at the time, the guy had mastered the art of forgery and signed his physician's signature to the piece of paper he'd presented to our hunky teacher, Mr. Goodbody.

Later that afternoon, our paths crossed again, this time as two of only five boys in sixth-hour honors choir. Miraculously, when it came time to stand up and sing, Campbell's lower leg injury suddenly healed itself as he rested his full weight on both feet. After class, I couldn't resist calling him out. Sans shame, he confessed to the ruse and swore me to secrecy.

The next day, to keep my silence, Cam met me outside the gymnasium before our class, wielding yet another fake doctor's note . . . this one with *my* name on it. Turns out, according to the convoluted backstory he'd concocted, I'd hurt myself falling off the choir room risers and would need to join Cam on the bleachers for the next two weeks while we both convalesced. At which point, Cam promised he'd come up with another clever scheme to get us out of whatever torture Mr. Goodbody dreamed up for us next. Thankfully, dodgeball had been banned at Madison Park High long before we'd arrived, just in case his brilliant plan fell apart.

For the next four years, Cam and I were pretty much joined at the hip. With both of us being gay, we naturally hit it off. At first, I'd worried that maybe he thought of me as boyfriend material. While I really liked the guy, I just didn't think of him in that way. Quickly, Cam put my concerns to rest by spelling it out—in no uncertain terms—that I was definitely *not* his type: older, taller, and with a totally hot bod; yet another thing that bonded us: our similar taste in boys.

Upon graduation, Cam and I sadly went our separate ways. I stayed in Madison Park with my parents and enrolled at Wayne State down in Detroit, while Cam moved up to

Mount Pleasant to attend Central Michigan. Sure, we saw each other every so often, mostly on Christmas and summer vacations. Then, another four years later, Cam announced he'd be moving back to the area, which was just about the time I'd decided to pack up and head to New York City.

It seemed as if suddenly we were two ships, destined to pass each other by, instead of dropping anchor in the same port. But if there was anything I'd come to learn over the past ten-plus years of mostly being apart, Campbell Sellers would forever remain my very best friend.

"It's like you said," I said to JP, only the slightest bit snippy over his criticizing Cam's recent lack of communication reciprocation. "It's not like I have to work."

"Well, you'll be busy soon enough," JP reminded me. "Once we start taping the show again."

We'd been on hiatus from shooting since early spring. Other than exercising every other day at the community center, making weekly trips to Costco, and stopping for lunch at Starbucks three—maybe four—times a week, my life as of late was a never-ending vacation.

"*If* we start taping the show again."

Inside chapel B of the Scott-Ashley Funeral Home, the man lying silently in peaceful repose served as a cruel reminder: The certainty of our future, as well as that of the nationally televised reality show that we hosted, was more than ever at stake.

"We've gotta find a project for season two," I told JP soberly. "Or we might not even have a show."

At that moment, by the saving grace of a higher power, I felt a firm hand upon my shoulder . . .

"Can I talk to you guys a sec?"

Turning toward the familiar-sounding voice, I gasped, swearing for sure that I was witnessing a ghost. Standing beside us, with his hair slicked back and dressed in an expensive designer suit, the guest of honor himself, Thomas Alton Cash, smiled softly at my partner and me.

"Hey, Terry. Nice to see you," JP said sincerely to the dead man's twin.

Relieved, I let out a sigh, having failed to remember for a moment that a carbon copy of the deceased did exist. He was alive and well, living on the west side of Pleasant Woods in his dearly departed brother's cushy home. Though, at present, he found himself playing host at a funeral for said dead sibling.

"Thanks for coming," Terry Cash greeted us. "It means a lot having you both here."

"It's our pleasure," I said, still trying to catch my breath after the brief shock of forgetting the existence of the identical brother.

"Tom was a good man." While he'd barely met the guy, JP knew this was the kind of comment one made in these types of circumstances.

"I wanted to ask a favor," Terry Cash continued. "If you're still interested in remodeling our folks' old house . . ."

Both my and JP's eyes grew wide. Together, we witnessed the ray of hope that shined through the clouds of doom that, only moments before, had blown in from the west.

"Yes!" I exclaimed, more than grateful for this bit of good news. "We'd very much like to renovate your family's former home on our TV show."

Graciously, Terry grinned, an action we'd not yet seen him perform. As he did so, I noticed that he did share the same slight gap between his two front teeth as his brother, Tom. It made me wonder if their fingerprints also matched. I'd have to do some online research into twins.

The other night, as we'd dined together and toured the house that Terry had grown up in, the handsome older man seemed so melancholy, so distrusting of us and everything that we represented. Both JP and I had gotten the distinct impression that by meeting with his brother, Terry felt we'd meant to undermine his wishes to honor his parents' memory by keeping the Tudor Revival in its present state.

"Awesome! I know it's what Tommy wants—*wanted*," Terry said, correcting himself.

"Well, we're happy to make it happen," JP promised as he and the dead man's twin firmly shook hands.

Next, I took my turn. Terry's palm against mine felt the same as I remembered his brother's feeling, when we shook inside their family's former home, sealing the deal to save it. They really were identical, Terrence and Thomas Cash, in every aspect, from the features on their handsome faces down to the softness of their skin.

No sooner than we'd made our informal pact, an old-timey telephone ring echoed through the funeral parlor lobby.

Terry quickly removed his beat-up flip phone from his suit jacket pocket. "This damn thing!" he cursed, struggling to silence the gadget. His thick fingers fumbled with the different buttons, until finally, the mobile device stopped making the annoying racket.

Terry placed the cell to his ear. "Hello?" He listened to whoever's voice he heard on the opposite end. Nodding every so often, Terry focused intently on the information he was being fed from the other party. After all of maybe a minute, he hung up and apologized. "Sorry. That was Nick Paczki of the PWPD. There's been a development in my brother's case."

We turned to each other, JP and me, before my partner said to Terry: "That's awesome!"

"The cops've decided Tom's death might not be accidental after all," Terry coolly informed us.

"Really?" I said, pleased that I'd come to that same conclusion and presented it to Detective Paczki myself.

"Yep. They think maybe somebody *killed* my brother," Terry confirmed. "And believe it or not, they've already got a suspect in custody."

"You're kidding," JP said, shocked. "How'd they catch the person so quickly?"

"That phone you guys found at the crime scene . . . they got into it, somehow, and figured out whose it is."

"So, it wasn't Tom's phone?" I asked, my original theory now disproved.

"Nope. My brother's phone wasn't even on him when they found his body."

JP seemed surprised by this new piece of evidence. "Odd for someone to *not* carry their phone on them at all times."

"Any idea what might've happened to Tom's phone?" I asked, thinking the missing mobile device could be crucial to the investigation.

"Not sure," Terry answered. "Nick said he'd let me know if and when it turns up. Knowing Tommy, he probably dropped it in the yard and ran it over with the mower."

JP picked up with our earlier part of the conversation. "Who did Paczki say the phone Pete and I found belongs to?"

"Yeah! Who's the person Nick brought in for questioning?" I asked, excited by this big break in the case. "Is it someone we know, by any chance?"

Terry lowered his voice and looked around the half-empty funeral home. "I probably shouldn't say anything. But since we're going into business together . . ."

We clung to the quiet that hung about us, anxious to learn the identity of the prime suspect.

"You do know the person," Terry divulged, "and you guys know the dude very well, as a matter of fact."

It was at that instance that Terry Cash revealed the identity of his twin brother's would-be killer—a revelation that would set my life, and the life of the man I love, on an entirely new trajectory.

The name that Terry Cash had been given by the Pleasant Woods Police Department belonged to none other than . . .

*Campbell Sellers.*

# Chapter 12

He insisted he didn't do it.

Campbell Sellers swore, on a stack of King James Bibles, that he couldn't harm a fly, let alone *murder* a man.

"Sure, I was angry. I felt totally betrayed," he admitted, in the presence of his criminal justice lawyer, Rana Vakeel.

At just thirty years old, the six-foot tall, brown-skinned beauty could have easily been a model, with her curvaceous figure and legs for days. She looked exceptionally stunning on this particular Tuesday morning, dressed in a traditional Indian sari fabricated from fine snow-white silk. "And what had Tom Cash done to betray you?"

The police detective with the bushy mustache, Nick Paczki, sat poised and ready to tap the real estate agent's response into his cell phone's notes app.

"It's gonna sound silly, but . . ." Cam took a sip from the plastic water bottle that had been provided to him. He felt it best to make known the verbal threats he'd made against Tom Cash, before some witness leaving Chianti wine pub that evening had the chance to report it. "I told Tom he'd rue the day he ever crossed me by not giving me the listing to his parents' house."

Detective Paczki looked up from his phone screen. "You really didn't say *rue,* did you?"

"Of course not. It's called *embellishing* for dramatic effect."

The police officer exhaled with relief. "Good. Because I don't know how to spell it."

The trio laughed at the detective's attempted humor, the tension in the room lifting, if only for a moment.

While most of their neighbors were off paying their respects to Tom Cash at the Scott-Ashley Funeral Home, the three friends had assembled at the Pleasant Woods Police Department, located within Pleasant Woods Town Hall, before heading over together for the formal service.

The colonial-style white brick building housed both the local law enforcement and the governmental meeting rooms. Due to its small size, Pleasant Woods shared its police force with nearby Royal Heights, and the Fernridge branch provided its library services. Each of the three suburbs, however, elected their own mayor and town council commissioners, providing them with political autonomy.

While the potential charge against Campbell Sellers was premeditated murder, as Detective Paczki had summed it up earlier, there hadn't been a cold-blooded killing in the hundred years that people had been living in the city. Hence the name, *Pleasant* Woods.

This was the sole reason the policeman had invited Cam, along with his lawyer, into the station for an informal sit-down meeting. No Miranda rights had been read. The detective had deemed it unnecessary to treat Cam like a common criminal or detain him any longer than needed. His reputation as a successful Realtor made him a model citizen, a pillar of the community.

"Yes, I was mad at Tom," Cam said, conveying his frustration. "I acted like a real brat, accusing him of not trusting me."

Rana Vakeel leaned forward in her chair, the satiny fabric of her choli clinging to her bare midriff. "Not trusting you how?"

"Well," Cam replied, "as a Realtor. And as a friend."

"But you guys were more than friends, right?" Rana said gently, so as not to imply anything lascivious.

Cam nodded. "Yes, we were more than friends. But that was a long time ago." He didn't want to think about that period in his life, when he'd felt truly happy, truly loved. Before Tom had deceived him.

Still, Cam complied and answered the lawyer's question.

"By my calculations," Rana said, consulting the notes she'd already taken, "it's been four years since you broke up with Tom."

"Since he *cheated* on me," Cam quipped, correcting his counsel. "That's the only reason our relationship ended. I didn't want it to. I loved the guy. He loved me. Or so I thought. Guess I was wrong, huh?"

It was now Detective Paczki's turn to speak. He took the opportunity to dive deeper into Campbell Sellers's wounded psyche. "And how did it make you feel when you found out Tom was cheating?"

"Duh! How would you guys feel if you caught your significant others *in flagrante* with someone else?"

The detective looked up from his phone screen again, mid-tap. "Say what?" He rubbed a finger back and forth across his bristly upper lip.

"Just type *in bed*," Cam advised, trying to be helpful. The phrase *all brawn and no brains* came to mind as he smiled at the hunky cop.

"Naveen would never cheat on me," Rana the lawyer reported with confidence to her colleagues. "In Hindu shastras, adultery is considered a serious breach of dharma. Plus, I would take him for everything, if he ever did."

"Neither would Nora," Nick the detective proudly declared. "She's the mother of my child."

Cam couldn't imagine anyone dumb enough to be unfaithful to a woman like Rana Vakeel or a man like Nick Paczki. But he couldn't help feeling that, coming from different cultures and sexualities, they didn't fully comprehend. "Pardon my stating the obvious . . . you're both straight. That's what you wanna believe."

"Are you saying gay guys are different when it comes to fooling around?" the police detective asked, curious to hear Cam's take on the intricacies of intimate relationships.

"I'm saying that Tom cheated on me . . . with a bartender who worked for him. And not only did he cheat, I caught him in the act of doing so. I'll spare you guys the gory details."

Both the policeman and the attorney had no need for further elaboration.

"Well, how did it make you feel when you found out Tom was having an affair?" Rana asked instead.

"In the gay community, we call it *hooking up*," Cam said bitterly. "But to answer your question, it made me mad."

"How mad would you say it made you?" Detective Paczki wondered. "On a scale from one to ten?"

*"Twelve."*

Rana Vakeel laughed softly. "I'd say that's pretty mad."

Cam could sense where the confrontation was now heading, as far as the detective had been concerned. He was trying to sway Cam into a confession: that he'd wanted to kill Tom Cash for fooling around with Danny the bartender from Shout! while they were still a couple.

"Yes, it made me so mad I wanted to murder Tom," Cam said, coming clean. "Four years ago, maybe. Last week? Not at all."

Detective Paczki gave Cam the side-eye. "You sure about that?"

"As Heaven is my witness, I'm over Tom," Cam assured the others who'd been questioning him. "Maybe he didn't trip and fall down that staircase? Maybe somebody did push him? If so," he said, crossing his heart, "that person wasn't me. I'm sorry that Tom's dead. But I didn't kill the guy."

The lawyer leaned across the Mission oak library table. "Campbell . . ." The gold bangles that decorated her delicate wrists lightly jangled as she laced her fingers together. "If you didn't kill Tom Cash, who do you think did?"

"To quote the Bard, better known as the great William Shakespeare," Cam calmly replied, "'that *is* the question.' Too bad I don't have an answer for you."

"Well, it's not a trick," Rana informed her client. "You're not being charged for anything. The detective is just trying to figure out why your brand-new cell phone was found inside a dead man's house."

"Rana, I already told you," Cam reminded his lawyer. "The night before Tom died, I went to a dinner party at Fairway Bob's—"

"For the record," Detective Paczki said, interrupting. "Fairway Bob is—"

"I thought this interview was *off* the record," Cam said, looking to his counsel for assurance.

"It is," the attorney said, jumping into the conversation. "Right, Nick?"

"Right, right," the detective responded. "But I still gotta ask: By Fairway Bob, you mean Bob Kravitz, your neighbor?"

"That is correct," Cam said, answering the officer's rhetorical question. "Bob Kravitz. Lives at Three Fairway Lane."

"He owns the antique shop on the corner of Sylvania and Woodward, correct?" Rana Vakeel asked. "I just love that store!"

"Got it." Detective Paczki entered the information into his phone. "Please, continue . . ."

"What was I saying?" Cam asked himself, having forgotten where he'd left off with his recap of the events leading up to Tom Cash's death.

"You went to dinner at Fairway Bob's," Rana said, providing Cam with a prompt.

"Yes! Then we all went across the street to show PJ and JP—" Cam stopped mid-sentence, deciding he'd better clarify, for the sake of the off-the-record record. "Peter Penwell and his partner, John Paul Broadway." Here, he paused, in case the police detective wanted to jot down the additional details.

He did *not*.

"I'm good," Detective Paczki stated. "So, you went over to Four Fairway . . . ?"

"While we were there, I tripped on a loose stair tread and fell flat on my butt. At which point, my phone must have fallen out of my back pocket. That's why it was found inside the house the next morning, along with poor Tom."

The police detective nodded as he pieced together the details of Cam's account. "Seems strange it took you so long to realize your cell phone was gone. I misplace mine for like five seconds, I go crazy."

"I did go crazy!" Cam cried. "I could barely sleep all night. I need that phone for work. Without it, I'm up the creek without a paddle."

In an attempt to lead Cam like a witness on the stand in court, Rana Vakeel asked: "When did you realize you'd lost your phone?"

"As soon as I got home! But I don't have a landline. I couldn't just call Tom up. And it was too late to drive over to his house. Plus, I'd had a lot of wine to drink," Cam added, to show his respect for the law. "At dinner earlier and after I got home."

"So, you waited till morning," Detective Paczki said, putting together the order of events. "Then you went over to see Tom at his parents' old place, so you could pick up your lost cell phone . . ." The policeman rubbed his stubbled chin, rough like sandpaper. "And while you were there, you got into an argument and you pushed Tom down the staircase and you killed him."

"No!" Cam exclaimed, horrified by the picture the detective had just painted. "That isn't what happened at all." He didn't want to think about such an awful incident taking place.

"Then please tell us what did happen," Rana Vakeel implored her client. "Again, Campbell . . . anything you say is completely off the record. We're just three concerned friends, trying to figure out how our neighbor died."

"I wish I knew . . . but I'm sorry, I don't."

Like Detective Paczki himself had originally surmised, Tom had most likely tripped and fallen down the rickety old staircase. Cam had practically done the exact same thing himself the evening prior. He'd been a witness to the rundown interior of Larry and Linda Cash's former home. It was for the best that TV's *Domestic Partners* were about to honor their son Tom's dying wish by stepping in to save the historic house from further decline.

Out of a need to protect himself, and out of fear for his future, Cam made one more comment: "What time was it that you estimated Tom died?"

Detective Paczki consulted the coroner's report in the case file. "Somewhere between ten-forty-five and eleven-fifteen."

"Then I definitely couldn't have killed Tom," Cam announced. "I was hosting an open house in Royal Heights that morning. It started at eleven o'clock."

The lawyer turned to the police detective, silently checking in. A man's future rested in both their hands, dependent on whether the one could convince the other of the man's lack of culpability in this potential crime.

The policeman looked the suspect up and down, someone he'd known as an upstanding member of the community for the past decade. "Well, in that case . . ."

Both Cam and his counsel took those few words as a positive sign of what would follow.

"You mean you believe me?" Cam exhaled the breath he'd been holding, feeling a sense of relief.

"It's like I told your pal, Peter Penwell, and his partner, the actor," Nick Paczki said casually. "This isn't New York City. This is Pleasant Woods. People don't get killed here."

"Oh, I know!" Cam couldn't agree more. "Peter's always been a negative Nelly. In high school, he wouldn't skip class with me because he was scared we'd get caught."

"As far as I'm concerned," the detective declared, "Tom Cash tripped, fell down a flight of stairs, and broke his neck at the bottom. His brother, Terry, said he believes that's what happened, so why shouldn't we?" The policeman stood and silently exited the room.

The informal meeting was officially over.

The attorney, Rana Vakeel, took hold of her client's hand. "Congratulations, Campbell! You're a free man."

"Thank you! Prison-jumpsuit orange isn't my color," Cam said, grateful to have been spared from a life behind bars.

If only Detective Paczki of the Pleasant Woods Police Department had been accurate in his assessment. The man found dead at 4 Fairway Lane, on that Saturday morning in mid-July, had *not* died an innocent death.

Someone had intentionally entered the historic home once belonging to Larry and Linda Cash . . . then *killed* one of their twin sons.

# Chapter 13

My heart was broken.

A full seven days later, without word—not an email, not a text message, not an old-fashioned phone call—I mustered up the courage to consult the Home FurEver website.

That's when I saw it.

On the page titled *This Week's* Adoptions: our little Clyde, in the loving embrace of another couple.

A sick feeling bubbled in the pit of my belly. I stared at the screen of my cell phone, fixated by the figures of the man and woman cradling our fur baby as they smiled for the camera.

"Oh, no!" I exclaimed, lying in bed on that Saturday morning while JP slept silently by my side.

A tear trickled down my cheek.

I wiped it away before swiping upward on my phone screen. Closing out of the dog-rescue site, I vowed never to return or show support for the nonprofit organization that had just now ruined my life. I couldn't help but feel discriminated against.

This was Michigan, after all, a state that had more recently gone red in its political leanings. No longer were my partner and I part of the so-called east coast elites as residents of New

York, one of the most liberal cities in America, a place where Marriage Equality had been made legal long before it gained acceptance in the more conservative Midwest.

At the sound of my sobs, JP rolled over in bed and opened his sleepy eyes. "Babe, what's wrong?" Whereas any ordinary person would be all puffy, with crease marks from the pillowcase imprinted across their face like train tracks, my would-be husband looked as handsome as ever.

If I didn't love the man so much, I'd totally loathe him for the luck he possessed in the gene pool department.

"They gave Clyde away," I cried, biting my lower lip as it convulsed uncontrollably. Snot oozed from my nostrils and down my upper lip. My reflection in the mirror above my Stickley Mission-style dresser across the room revealed a hideous monster.

I didn't care. Our boy, Clyde, had been stolen away from us by another family, and there wasn't a solitary thing we could do about it.

"What?" This was all JP could say in response to my sudden revelation.

Not *what* as in *What did you say? I can't understand you when you're ugly crying.* More like *what* as in *WTF?!*

In spite of my earlier promise to myself, I pulled up the Home FurEver webpage again and showed JP the awful photo I'd recently discovered. The good-looking man and the pretty woman holding the beautiful puppy made my stomach turn. They were the picture of perfection, with their perfectly whitened smiles and matching wedding bands.

I loathed the sight of them.

"This is discrimination!" my partner declared, upset beyond belief by what I'd just shared with him. "Pure and simple. They didn't let us adopt Clyde because we're a *gay* couple!"

While I, too, had come to a similar conclusion, closer examination of the photos posted to the group's site revealed several same-sex couples—both male and female—as part of the Home FurEver adoption family.

"I don't think that's the reason. Unfortunately." Something told me we'd lose our case had we attempted to take HFE to court on charges of opposition against homosexuals.

"Well, Margot's a stupid fool!" JP declared, frustrated. "She doesn't realize the mistake she's making. We could give her so much exposure. We're on a national TV show, for cripe's sake!"

"Obviously, she doesn't care about celebrity," I speculated, still in shock. "She's like fifty! She's probably never even heard of Insta. She said so herself, she doesn't watch television."

"She's an idiot," JP spat out in disgust. "She should be flattered we wanna adopt a dog from her stupid rescue. She's the one who's losing out by not giving us Clyde."

"She is!" I agreed, showing my full support. "Totally."

Unfortunately, we both knew who the real losers were in this unfortunate incident: *Us.*

We spent the rest of the morning in actual mourning. Usually, we kick off the weekend with JP cooking a fancy breakfast: pancakes from scratch or brioche French toast made with bread from the local bakery, topped with homemade bananas Foster sauce. Or sometimes plain Chiquitas and fresh sliced strawberries. If he's feeling super adventurous, my partner will break down and break out the waffle iron from its dusty cupboard shelf, high above the stovetop. Again, with the utmost culinary expertise, JP will whip up the batter in no time flat from a recipe he's kept hidden away somewhere inside his head.

In a jiff, we'd sit down at the dining room table for the most fabulous Saturday morning brunch—like we're real adults. After eating most meals parked on the living room couch in front of the TV, our plates balanced gingerly in our laps the way we did while living in New York City, the feeling of maturity one felt at age thirty-three came as a well-earned reward after years of sacrifice in pursuit of one's art.

To put it bluntly, our apartment in Brooklyn was teeny-tiny, and up until recently, we couldn't afford to move into a bigger place had we even wanted to.

Instead of enjoying a leisurely meal, followed by several cups of coffee that we'd warm in the microwave until the half-and-half had taken on a sour taste from being reheated one time too many, I poured JP and myself some cold cereal. We crawled back into bed together, where we crunched our cornflakes in silence. Once we'd lapped up the last drops of lukewarm milk, we dumped the empty bowls on our night-stands, pulled the blankets up over our heads, and spooned each other for the rest of the morning. We both tried our best not to think about the sad injustice in the cold, cruel world in which we'd been forced to reside.

But it was all for naught.

In spite of the most valiant of efforts, our thoughts kept returning to the same subject . . . and his name was Clyde.

Well, it *used* to be.

According to the caption posted that morning on home furever.com, the newly adopted beagle-bull we had recognized in the photo as our dear, sweet Clydie Boy had been given a new moniker: Baxter.

*Seriously?!*

He'd already possessed a perfectly fine first name, one that befitted both him and his quirky personality. Why did this stupid straight couple feel the need to go and change it?

#wrongkindofpeople

At 11:30, the alarm I'd set on my phone sounded, startling

me out of the most delightful dream. In my reverie, JP and I played the parts of the proud dog parents of a beagle-bull puppy named Clyde Barker Broadway-Penwell. I watched, overjoyed, while JP tossed an orange rubber ball across our grassy backyard and our happy boy chased after it, his pink tongue wildly hanging out the side of his mouth.

Like a Little League outfielder, Clyde got in front of the object and skillfully caught it between his teeth after a single bounce. Long tail wagging, he confidently brought the ball back to Daddy JP, while Daddy PJ cheered him on, our good little champ. Clearly, he was delighted to be home with us, right where he belonged.

Never had we been this happy in all the years we'd spent together, JP and me. Why did I have to go and wake up from the dream and ruin everything? Alas . . .

*Nothing is forever.*

*All good things must come to an end.*

*Nothing gold can stay.*

JP moaned as I extracted myself from his strong embrace. "Nooo!"

Reaching across the bed for my phone resting on the nightstand, I silenced the noise with a firm tap against the glass. I rolled back over and faced my partner. We lay together, nose to nose, basking in the warmth of each other's morning breath, not caring that we were both in need of a good toothbrushing. JP gazed at me with sad puppy-dog eyes that, of course, reminded me of our lost Clydie Boy. It seemed foolish to think that we both felt such love for a creature we'd only met just once . . .

And yet we did.

We'd had so many hopes for our future: trips to the county dog park, adventurous walks in the Northern Michigan woods, puppy training classes, and all the car rides we'd take in order to get to all these places, each one with Clyde hanging his big head out the backseat car window as the breeze blew across his handsome, furry face.

"Try not to be sad," I told JP, stroking his sandpaper chin. "I'll find us another dog to adopt. I promise."

"But I don't want another dog."

"Neither do I."

Our lips met and lingered in a bittersweet kiss that soon became passionate. Having been so busy for the past twelve months—between the move to Michigan and the taping of season one of our TV show—we'd not had much chance to simply just love each other.

We spent the next sixty minutes or so making up for lost time.

Soon, the clock tower in Town Square struck once. Outside, on Fairway Lane, JP and I strolled across the street and over to the Cash family's former home.

"Are we really doing this?" I asked, stepping up the stairs that led to the wide front porch. It had only been seven days since we'd first set foot inside the home, and already I'd forgotten everything that Tom Cash and his twin brother, Terry, had shown us the night before Tom's sudden passing.

"At this point," JP lamented, "we've got no choice."

He was right.

In less than ten days, we were scheduled to start shooting the sophomore season of HDTV's breakout new reality series, *Domestic Partners*. If anything were to halt production in the slightest, we could both find ourselves suddenly out of employment. Or at least in breach of contract. For sure, we'd end up on our producer's blacklist.

I heaved a heavy sigh. "Have you heard from Ursula?"

"I have. We're all set. The cameras and crew will arrive promptly at nine, nine days from now."

"Well, shoot."

My hope was that JP's best gal pal had found a loophole that would offer us a reprieve from filming. We'd discovered a dead man on the premises of the property we'd agreed to renovate. The personal trauma we'd endured, along with the plethora of outrageous publicity, ought to count for something, one would think.

"Shall we go in and have a look around in the light of day?" JP said, not sounding the least bit enthused by the thought of doing so.

The goal was to assess the situation and come up with a plan of attack. As producers on *Domestic Partners*, in addition to hosting the program, we'd been given free range in mapping out the show's overall season arc. Ursula had pretty much left it entirely up to us to determine the projects we felt we could tackle in the given amount of airtime.

"You got the keys from Terry, didn't you?" I asked, knowing full well that JP had, since I'd been right there with him when the handsome older man had signed his contract and handed them over to us.

Still, I wanted to double-check.

JP held up the brass key ring and gave it a jingle before inserting the silver front door key into the vintage mortise lock set. Most likely we'd want to add a modern deadbolt to the exterior entryway. Personally, I felt it a shame to alter the original. But this was no longer 1929. Most people craved a sense of security when it came to keeping out unwanted intruders, no matter how safe a neighborhood they lived in. Surely the new owners—whoever they may be once the time had come to sell the home—would want a fiberglass front door, if not a solid steel one.

As we stepped through the original storybook archway into the foyer, the reality of what had recently taken place began to overwhelm me. "Jesus, JP," I said, reliving that horrific Saturday morning a mere week ago.

My partner's tone bordered on blasé. "Let's just make the best of an awful situation and get this second season over with."

Casa Cash, as Tom himself had called it, smelled of must and mildew after being shut up for the better part of the past quarter-century. Somehow, I'd not noticed this fact on the night we'd first dropped by for our private moonlight tour. Because of all the alcohol I'd had in my system from Fairway Bob's dinner party, I must have overlooked this hard-to-miss sensory detail.

Holding my breath, I made a mental note to keep an eye out for black mold, a potential toxin due to an overabundance of moisture in an older home. The large living room into which we'd first entered was both stuffy and stifling, with the warmth of the summer season well upon us. Someone needed to turn on the central air, stat.

We moved toward the back of the house, into the tiny kitchen . . .

"Let's put this room on the list for sure," JP decided, tapping against his phone screen as he typed. "I could tell when we first saw it, it's gonna need a major overhaul."

"What is that?" Abruptly, I recoiled, my eyes watering at a rancid odor coming from somewhere deep within the house.

JP stuck his nose out and took a whiff. "You and that sniffer." He was always making fun of my strong sense of smell, a gift I'd inherited from my father.

Without a word of exaggeration, my dad could detect a spoiled jar of mayonnaise in the refrigerator without even opening the door.

Lifting up my shirt, I quickly covered my face with the fabric. "Ew, JP! It's like death! Like something literally died in this place."

As soon as I'd uttered the word, we both stared at each other.

"Some*thing* didn't die here," JP said. "But some*one* did."

I shot daggers in my partner's direction. "Not funny, Mr. Broadway."

"I didn't mean it to be . . . just telling the truth."

I stole a glance over my shoulder to make sure the ghost of Tom Cash wasn't standing behind us. "Do you really think he fell down the stairs and broke his neck?"

"It doesn't matter what *I* think," JP said, his hands falling to his hips. "Your hunky cop friend ruled it an accident."

"He isn't my friend," I insisted, blushing at the memory of Nick Paczki poured into his blue uniform. "He's my sister Pamela's."

"Lucky girl," JP teased, knowing full well of my boyhood crush on the PW police detective. "We should be grateful he did. Otherwise, we'd be standing in the middle of a crime scene right now . . . and we'd have no more TV show to tape."

My future hubby was right. For the sake of *Domestic Partners*, it was best to leave well enough alone.

The last thing we needed was to involve ourselves in a *murder* investigation.

# Chapter 14

The awful stench wafted up from the basement.

JP knelt down and gave a good whiff near the air vent along the baseboard, carefully assessing the situation. "It's coming through the duct work."

"Just look at those register covers!" I leaned in for closer inspection. "Bet they're solid brass."

No expenses had been spared in the construction of this home, from the white oak flooring to the high-end fixtures. I felt it our duty to help restore the house to its original late 1920s state, before some other less-considerate developer could get their grubby hands on it, gut it, and fill it with dry-wall, particle board, and plastic light switch plates.

"They probably *are* solid brass," JP agreed, giving the metal a gentle rub. He held up his soiled finger and made a sour face. "Under all the tarnish."

"Nothing a little Brasso and some elbow grease can't get rid of." Having applied the same method to much success in our own home, I was sure I could clean up those bad boys and make them shine once again.

JP took hold of the little lever at the top of the register cover. "It's probably rusted shut." He gave a firm push, opening the flap that controlled the amount of air flowing into the room.

I almost threw up.

"Ew! You made it worse!" Involuntarily, I gagged on the putrid scent that my partner had just released into the kitchen like the mythical Kraken from Scandinavian folklore.

As quickly as I could, I scooted over to the opposite corner of the room, near the porcelain enameled cast-iron sink. For a moment, I considered sticking my head into the basin, just in case I were to become physically ill.

JP deftly returned the register cover to the closed position. The dreadful smell subsided, if only a little. Still, it seemed clear: Something was indeed rotten at 4 Fairway Lane.

A trip to the basement disclosed no evidence as to what could possibly be giving off such a foul odor.

"Where could it be coming from?" I wondered, glancing around the dark space at the unfamiliar surroundings.

Nothing about it evoked childhood memories of playing spin the bottle, assembled in a circle, with friends from Madison Park Middle School. In our finished basement, there was wood paneling and carpeting aplenty. It wasn't dark and scary and filled with cobwebs and spiders. Not to mention monsters lurking behind the door that led to the wine cellar or inside the fiery furnace. It was more like a family room or what some might call a *den*; it just happened to be located beneath our house.

JP glanced up. "Any idea what's beyond these cinder blocks here?"

"How should I know?" I said, slightly sarcastic. Really, I was just feeling creeped out by being down in a creepy basement/cellar.

"My guess is that's an outside wall. The backyard, I bet, is on the other side."

"Okaaay . . ." While JP sounded pretty sure of himself, I

wasn't quite certain where this guessing game would lead us. But, wanting to be a supportive partner, I gladly played along.

JP led the way up the creaky staircase. "Come on!"

Without risers to mask the backs of the steps, Lord only knew what ankle-biting creature lurked behind, waiting to pull you through the gaps and devour you.

Once more, I followed my partner into the kitchen, where he unlocked a solid wood door with a small skeleton key that had been stuck inside the lock for the past twenty-five years, probably longer.

"Love that!" I beamed, bowled over by all the original character that remained within the Tudor Revival.

JP wasn't nearly as impressed by an old hunk of metal as I had been. At that moment, he was hell-bent on getting to the bottom of what was causing such a stink inside the historic house.

Beyond the solid wood door with the skeleton key lay an old sleeping porch. While the exterior area could become an eventual sanctuary, in its current condition, the space felt un-inviting and just plain sad.

In the actual yard, a cute little chipmunk chirped away in a corner. His entire body convulsed violently with each high-pitched peep, piercing my sensitive eardrums.

"It's a good size," JP said, still holding his nose, as we'd not yet established from where the awful smell emitted.

"Well, those shrubs will have to go . . ." A row of box-woods, in desperate need of trimming, separated the property from the one next door to it. My instinct told me to rip them out and put up a privacy fence. "Look!"

Gray-painted wood steps led down into the large lot. Bits of forest green could be seen beneath the peeling layers. I pointed to a small wood door located directly below the old sleeping porch, held shut by an unfastened padlock.

While the majority of the home rested above the Michigan basement, this section sat above a closed off crawl space. Lord only knew what we'd find once we removed the old lock and took a peek inside.

"I'll go get a flashlight," JP offered, heading inside the house from whence we'd just come.

While I waited for my partner to return, I carefully inspected the area. The sides of the staircase leading down into the yard were masked with white plywood panels. Their purpose, I'd assumed, was to keep any creatures from crawling under and taking up residency. Unfortunately, one of the wood panels had a rather large hole in the lower left-hand corner, either the result of rot or the gnawing of some sort of animal.

"Hey!" a hoarse voice hollered from over in the next yard.

Sure enough, it was Hank Richards, the ornery neighbor we'd run into on the night Terry Cash's twin, Tom, had given us a tour of the Tudor.

"Hello!" I called back, intentionally choosing to remain polite. We'd be spending an ample amount of time on these premises over the next few months. No need to get off on the wrong foot with the old man neighbor.

Mr. Hank made his way through the bushes and into the Cashes' backyard, spying me up and down. "I know you! You're on that TV show. With the other one. Does Tom know you guys are snooping around over here?"

It pained me to have to tell the old man: "Tom Cash died, Mr. Hank."

"I know that!" Hank Richards cried out. "Did I say Tom? Those boys look so much alike, I never could tell them apart."

I began explaining my and JP's business and what, exactly, we'd been doing at 4 Fairway—with Terry Cash's permission—until we'd gotten sidetracked playing Sherlock and Watson.

"Huh?" Mr. Hank pulled the belt on his plaid bathrobe

tightly around his paunchy belly. "Well, I did see something run that way just last week. Our Lola chased after it."

A senior Scottie the color of charcoal, who received a monthly visit from the mobile grooming service to keep her nice and pretty, Lola was Hank and Hennie's dog.

Mr. Hank pursed his lips as he formed his next thought. "Think it might've been a cat. Fine by me! Don't want no stray living in my backyard." His lima bean–shaped nostrils began twitching. "Smell that? I'd bet good money there's a dead animal under that porch."

"You think?" I don't know why I'd bothered asking the old man's opinion. The big question wasn't if something had gone and died. This fact was fairly evident from the foul odor permeating the fresh air. Of more importance was how JP and I were going to suss out the culprit, and better yet, get rid of the carcass.

That poor cat! Surely someone in Pleasant Woods somewhere had been in search of their precious missing kitty. The last thing I wanted to do was find a dead feline under the Cashes' old sleeping porch.

For the first step in our plan of attack—which we'd dubbed *Domestic Partners: Operation Smells Like Death*—we headed home and changed out of our shorts and T-shirts into something more appropriate for entering the bowels of hell in search of Satan's spawn.

"Are you really gonna crawl under there?" JP asked skeptically.

We'd both slipped on our work jeans and threw on old sweatshirts, despite the weather app on our phones declaring that, yes, it was hot outside.

"Well, someone's gotta and it isn't gonna be you . . . is it?"

Whenever a project involved getting the least bit soiled, good old Peter "PJ" Penwell always had to do the dirty work. During season one of *Domestic Partners,* this had actually be-

come a trending meme on social media. Not that my partner was a priss or anything. I just didn't care as much about
my outward appearance, being a writer and not an actor like
he was.

"I'll do it, if you really want me to," JP declared.

"Forget it. You won't fit."

At six-foot-two, my partner towered over me by a good
seven inches. According to dear Ursula and the testing she'd
done with HDTV's target audience, the difference in our
heights only added to our appeal as TV show hosts. Straight
women and gay men alike found JP's stature both sexy and
domineering. My being a shortie made them want to put me
in their pockets and take me home.

Arriving back at 4 Fairway Lane, I'd prayed the offensive
smell would have miraculously dissipated during the time it
had taken us to run home and return.

Alas, it had *not*.

JP moaned behind the N-95 protective mask he'd strapped
on as part of his PPE. "I think it's gotten worse!"

My hands, hidden from view by a pair of gardening gloves,
fell to my hips. "Butch it up, you big baby. If the cameras were
rolling now, you'd lose most of your fan base." Of course, I
was only playing around.

Well, partially.

JP did try his best to project a persona of masculinity
whenever we were filming. I wouldn't say he was *acting* the
part of a manly man, but . . . the person I'd come to know, in
private, had his more sensitive moments.

I loved him all the more because of it.

JP took a tentative step toward the tiny wood door that led
to the depths of the unknown. "What should we do first?"

"You stand here and hold the flashlight," I told him, taking charge of the situation. I wasn't always the passive one in
our relationship, as *Domestic Partners* viewers had witnessed

on more than one episode of our premiere season. I could get particularly defensive when it came to dealing with contractors who tried to overprice their services.

"What are you gonna do?" JP asked, his body posture anxiously closed off.

"Duh! I'm going in."

"Please be careful."

While his concern for me was super sweet, we had an issue on our hands. There was no time for sentimentality.

After removing the rusty padlock, I set it aside and gently pulled opened the small wood door. The hinges creaked like something out of a horror movie. All we needed was an eerie soundtrack to accompany the scene.

In the heat of the summer, I found it hard to breathe with a fabric mask covering my face. Thankfully, it did help in keeping out the heinous smell of whatever was wasting away beneath the sleeping porch.

JP scooted up behind me to steal a glance over my shoulder. "Do you see anything?"

"Not really." Peering into the darkness, I couldn't even make out the far side, where the back wall of the house extended down below porch level. "Shine the light in, would you?"

JP did as he'd been instructed.

As the bright beam cut across the blackness, a menagerie of objects began to reveal themselves. Along with a bunch of old boards, the space under the old porch boasted a collection of rakes, shovels, bricks, wood baskets, metal trash cans, and not one but *two* full-size manual push lawn mowers.

"It's like a clown car," I joked as I reached in to extract the items, one by one, and pass them off to my partner.

JP joked back. "The crap just keeps a-comin'!"

By the time we'd completely emptied out the contents that had been stowed away under the porch, we'd amassed enough loot to have ourselves a yard sale. Not that there was anything worth selling to anyone.

Well, one of the push mowers had a nicely stained solid wood handle that gave it an antique air. I made a mental note to suggest to Terry Cash that he haul it over to Fairway Bob at his vintage shop, and see if he thought it worth anything.

"Guess Larry and Linda were hoarders, huh?" JP said, surveying the items that now cluttered their former property's lawn.

"Maybe they just didn't have room in the garage?"

JP groaned. "I don't even wanna think about what's in there. We'll have the PAs unload it once they get on set next week."

We spent the next hour emptying out the storage space below the old sleeping porch, and yet we still hadn't discovered the cause of the awful stench.

"Can you still smell it?" I asked my partner in crime, afraid that if we removed our masks, we totally would.

"On three?"

"I will if you will."

We took hold of the elastic straps secured tightly around the backs of our heads and prepared to rip them off like Band-Aids.

JP began the countdown. "One . . . two . . ."

Before he reached three, we both took off our face coverings and gave a good whiff.

"Jeez Louise!" I cried out, sounding just like my grandmother, God rest her sweet soul, at the awful odor that still lingered.

"Put 'em on!" JP swiftly ordered, for both our sakes.

Once we were re-masked, we tried coming up with our next move.

"Mr. Hank swore he saw a cat crawl from his yard into this one," I said, remembering. "Now there's the smell of death in the air. Coincidence much? Probably not."

"How would a cat get under the porch? The door was padlocked shut."

"But the lock wasn't *locked*."

My partner regarded me quizzically. "Pete. You really think a cat unlocked a lock, removed it, opened the door, and crawled under the porch? Then somehow replaced the lock— from the inside?"

"No!" I said, feeling foolish. "I didn't say that. Maybe Tom Cash was over here working in the yard and, for some reason, he opened this door? When he wasn't looking, the cat could've crawled in. Then Tom could've closed the door, put the lock back on, and trapped the poor thing inside. If it couldn't get out, it probably starved under there."

JP gave my theory some serious thought. "I suppose so. Or . . ." He stepped around to the far side of the porch steps and pointed at the large hole in the plywood panel that masked the under siding. "Maybe Lola chased the cat into the yard like Mr. Hank said, it got scared, and it crawled in through there? *Then* somehow it got stuck, starved, and died."

"Whatever," I said with a shrug.

It didn't matter how a poor defenseless creature came to be trapped in the crawl space located beneath the old sleeping porch.

It was there.

And, from the smell of things, we needed it to be gone.

# Chapter 15

I screamed out in excruciating pain.

My lower back had just scraped up against the upper part of the storage space located under the old sleeping porch at 4 Fairway Lane.

*"Son of a—!"*

Hunched over like Quasimodo himself, I said a silent prayer of thanks. Fortunately, there weren't any nails sticking down from the floorboards above. Otherwise, they could have easily punctured a hole in my hoodie and pierced right through my sensitive skin.

"Are you okay?" JP called out to me, sight unseen, from the safety of the spot where he stood waiting on the backyard sidewalk.

"Does it sound like I'm okay?" I snapped, in response to my partner's stupid question.

"Sorry, babe."

I'd chosen to crawl inside the crawl space and, armed only with a flashlight and a small shovel, go in search of the dead kitty cat and attempt to retrieve the remains. Once removed, my hope was that the awful stench that had plagued us for the past few hours would eventually subside and drift away

forever into the air. What we would do with the poor unfortunate feline after I'd excavated it from the premises—that
was a whole other matter.

JP kept on talking to keep me company. "Do you see anything?" Or maybe he wanted to hear the sound of my voice to
know that I was still alive? Either way, he just wouldn't shut
up. "Babe?"

"I said I'll be fine!" Shining the flashlight around, I honestly didn't see anything. There was nothing left to see, really,
since I'd already removed all the ancient contents from the
storage space.

However, I could still smell death, mixed with the pungent aroma of dirt. Other than that, it was just an empty area,
approximately twelve feet wide by nine feet deep, by another
three feet high, if even that.

"What about over by the stairs?" JP suggested. "If the cat
crawled in through the side, it could still be under that area
somewhere."

I looked to my left.

A bit of natural light shined in through the hole in the
plywood board that masked the underside of the staircase.
What my partner was advising could have been possible.
To be honest, I was afraid to venture under the porch too
far from the wood door opening, in case I were to run into
anything—an animal that wasn't dead, like a *rat,* maybe?—
or some other type of demon that would, of course, want to
kill me.

"Let me go check it out," I called back, aiming my flashlight in the direction of the wood steps that led down from
the porch into the yard. The stairs were maybe four feet from
where I sat, crouched down with my butt resting between my
thighs.

My body would pay for all this physical activity the next
morning, that was for certain! All I had to do was twist around

to face the other direction; then I could crawl my way over toward the crack of daylight.

Suddenly, the sound of my partner's voice took on a different tone. I couldn't quite hear what he was saying now. But clearly, he was talking to someone outside in the yard with him. Maybe Mr. Hank had returned to check on our progress? It could also have been an on-duty police officer out on a routine Saturday morning Neighborhood Watch drive-by. Another added perk of living in Pleasant Woods.

"Babe! We've got company," JP called out again. "You almost done in there?"

"Just a minute," I said, scooching toward the empty space under the porch steps.

That's when I felt something go *squish*, right beneath my left hand.

Immediately, I stopped moving, lifted my palm close to my face, and took a sniff. The garden glove that I wore reeked.

Sure enough, when I glanced down at the spot in the dirt where my left hand had been resting moments before, what did I see? A fuzzy lump of rotting flesh, grayish in color. Though at one point in time, it could have been closer to white. The thing was in an obvious state of decay. But the long, hairless tail that extended from its posterior told me it could only have been one thing when it was still breathing: a *possum*.

I let out a cry, my second scream that hour, erupting out of pure disgust rather than pain.

"Babe! What's wrong?"

Through the hole in the plywood masking on the side of the porch staircase, I could see JP clearly now. He rushed over to see if he could catch a glimpse of me cowering under the old sleeping porch in pure terror.

"I found it, and it's *not* a cat!" A burst of adrenaline shot through my veins. I grabbed hold of the shovel I'd taken under the porch with me, dug the blade down into the dirt beneath the poor dead possum's body, scooped up the carcass . . . and flung it toward the hole, where my partner, JP Broadway, manly gay man, had just stuck his handsome face.

The remains of the dead marsupial hit him square on his dimpled chin.

JP flinched and cried out, all high-pitched and horrified, just like a little girl. His hands flew up to his face as he swatted at the spot where the dead thing had made contact. Frantically, he wiped away any grossness that his bare skin might have absorbed in that one millisecond of bad timing. *"Get it off me! Get it off me!"*

My partner's hair-trigger reaction totally freaked me out and, as a nervous reflex, I let out a shriek myself. Then he screamed, startled by the sound of my scream. Then I screamed again, startled by the sound of his.

After what had felt like forever, we both finally calmed down. Huffing and puffing and gasping for air, we broke out in a laughing fit that lasted almost as long as the screaming one had.

In that moment, the most devious thought infiltrated my mind: If only the *Domestic Partners* camera crew had been here to get this whole incident on tape. But since they weren't, perhaps we could reenact everything we'd just encountered once we started recording the show the following week? The hijinks would make for an exciting second season premiere episode, for sure!

Once I'd escaped my crawl space nightmare, and JP had succeeded in sealing the dead possum safely inside a plastic bag, he presented our visitor who, of course, had witnessed our entire comic debacle. "Pete, this is Kyle Young."

I smiled at the cute guy, whose name I immediately recognized as that of the late Tom Cash's last-ever boyfriend. "Hey, Kyle."

Catching a glimpse of my reflection in the garage side window, I wished I hadn't looked such a fright. Again, being a writer and not an actor like my partner, I didn't put too much emphasis on my physical appearance. Still, I liked to make a good first impression whenever possible.

Not that I was trying to impress this kid. I was already spoken for. Plus, I never found myself attracted to anyone younger than me. JP always joked that I wanted to be the pretty one. Fortunately, my partner clocked in at seventeen months my senior. Or I'd never have agreed to go out with him, way back when. If memory served, Kyle was still a baby, not even yet thirty.

He extended his hand. He was tall and thin, and it reflected in his fingers. I wondered if he played piano. The short navy shorts he wore, with their five-inch inseam, hugged his hairless thighs, and the tight tank top showed off his well-sculpted shoulders. He had a fit little body, though he was far too waiflike for my personal preference.

"Great to meet you," Kyle told me. "I've read all your books. My boyfriend Tom is—" He stopped himself. "He *was* a huge fan. We both were. I mean, I still am. Tom was when he was . . ." He stopped himself again, unable to continue.

"No worries," I said, sensing his heartache over his recent loss.

As nice as the compliments were, it made me feel awkward to have anyone gush over me or the stories I'd written. Usually, I just said thanks and quickly changed the subject, same as I did right then.

"Sorry about Tom," I added. "We only met him the one time. He seemed like a good guy."

JP interjected awkwardly, not sure of what else he should say: "Totally."

"He *was* a good guy," Kyle confirmed. "Until he started cheating on me."

JP and I silently checked in with each other. On the night before he died, we'd heard Tom Cash mention being in trouble with his boy toy at Fairway Bob's dinner party. He'd mentioned chatting with another young guy on the Lads4Dads hookup app and that Kyle had found out about his indiscretion. But Tom hadn't made it clear if he'd actually been unfaithful.

Kyle continued to ramble on. "Not that I had any proof Tom was messing around. He totally denied it when I called him out. But then, why would he PM that guy Hunter if he wasn't?"

JP and I checked in with each other again. Now things were just getting plain weird. We'd met Kyle Young not more than ten minutes ago, and here he was confessing to us the intimate details of his intimate relationship with a dead man. Some people wore their hearts on their sleeves. We would soon find out that Kyle Young was one of them.

"Are you okay?" This was all I could think to say in response to Kyle's recent revelation.

"Sorry." He wiped his eyes, wet with tears. "It's the reason I didn't come to his funeral. We broke up the morning Tom died. Over brunch!"

Kyle reached into his shorts pocket. He removed a crinkled pack of cigarettes, and with a shaky hand, lifted one to his lips. Then he offered the most crucial of confessions: "Tom made me so mad, I wanted to *kill* him."

JP and I checked in with each other for a third time. Was Kyle Young trying to tell us something?

The bereft boy ran his piano hands through his thick hair, mumbling softly to himself. "I can't believe my daddy is gone."

As I'd suspected, Kyle suffered from a reverse Oedipal complex. Lots of younger gay guys found themselves attracted to older men—me included—be it their rugged good looks, the air of maturity they projected, or for some, the security that came from his having a sizable bank account. Fortunately, I'd already found The One in John Paul Broadway, so I had no need for hookup apps the likes of Lads4Dads.

*Thank goodness!*

"It was a terrible accident," JP told Kyle, doing his best to console the poor kid.

Kyle fumbled with a fancy silver lighter and opened it with a loud *click*. It looked a lot like the Zippo that Tom Cash had used on several occasions, the night we'd first been introduced to him by Fairway Bob. He lit the crumpled cigarette that dangled from his lower lip and drew hard on it. Blowing a plume of blue-gray smoke high over our heads, Kyle stared my partner, JP, straight in the eyes and made his next remark: "It's nice of you to say that. But Tom's death wasn't an accident."

JP chuckled nervously, reading my earlier thoughts regarding Kyle's culpability in Tom Cash's death. "According to Detective Paczki of the Pleasant Woods PD, it was."

Kyle shook his blond head. "I'm telling you guys, it wasn't. Somebody *killed* Tom . . . and I can prove it."

With these few words uttered by the dead man's much-younger former lover, the mystery of what really happened to Tom Cash had taken a sudden turn.

Kyle peeled back the paper cover on a mini coffee creamer and poured it into his half-empty cup. He stared down at the clouds that had formed before stirring them away with a spoon.

"We just love this place!" I marveled, taking in the assortment of old metal signs advertising the likes of Faygo, Vernors, and Stroh's beverages that covered the light blue walls. "You gotta wonder where they got all the cool stuff."

"It's been here since June owned it," Kyle said, unimpressed.

We'd decided to move our impromptu meeting to a spot more conducive to conversation: The Depot Diner, conveniently located right near the railroad tracks. While JP and I regularly enjoyed weekend brunches across the street from our house at Chianti, we occasionally walked the few extra blocks for a more traditional—read: not as fancy and less expensive—breakfast.

The Depot, we'd been told upon our arrival in Pleasant Woods last autumn, was an institution. After the passing of its original proprietress, a cantankerous old woman who cooked and served every meal herself, the owners of The Depot Diner up in Bloomington Hills stepped in to save the greasy spoon from becoming a nail salon. Or so the story goes.

"You probably don't appreciate all this," I said, gesturing to the Detroit-themed décor, "because you've lived here all your life. Did you know you can't get Rock N' Rye in New York City?"

Kyle turned up his nose at my comment. "So what? It's gross."

"No! It's like my favorite soda, ever."

How I wished JP hadn't forced me to give up sugar once we got this TV show hosting job. Or I'd have ordered some of the cream cola instead of boring black coffee. The camera didn't really add ten pounds. Apparently, eating ice cream twice a week totally did.

"You call it soda?" Kyle looked at me like I'd made the biggest faux pas. "This is Michigan. We say *pop*. Aren't you guys from here?"

"I am," I admitted. "But I lived in Brooklyn for a while, so I got used to saying *soda*."

JP shook his head at my pretentiousness. "I'm from Pittsburgh. I say *pop*, too. And for what it's worth," he couldn't resist adding, "Rock N' Rye is disgusting."

"Oh, my God!" I couldn't believe my own partner was

taking the side of a guy we'd only just met. Kyle was more his type—young and cute—which would explain why JP had chosen to gang up on me. "He puts French fries *on* his sandwich," I told Kyle. "Now *that's* disgusting."

Either he didn't agree with me, or Kyle Young had been too preoccupied to care. He sat in the blue vinyl booth across from JP and me, sipping a cup of cold coffee in silence.

"So, do you wanna finish telling us what happened with Tom Cash?" JP said after a long pause.

"You said you think somebody killed him?" I asked, lowering my voice slightly, just in case there were wandering ears in the restaurant.

On our way in, we were stopped by a small group of *Domestic Partners* fans, who asked if poor Kyle wouldn't mind taking a picture of them posing with us, using their camera phone. I wouldn't have been surprised if the pair of giggling young girls at the table across the room, near the windows, was recording our conversation to post on social media and increase their page likes.

"I don't think it," Kyle declared. "I know it." He swallowed his last sip and slammed the ceramic coffee mug down on the laminate tabletop.

"All right," I said, not wanting to seem contrary to a guy whose boyfriend hadn't been dead but a week. "Can you tell us *how* you know?"

Kyle took a deep breath.

The wheels of memory began turning as he traveled back in time . . .

# Chapter 16

*The night before the murder . . .*

Kyle sat at the bar, drowning his sorrows in high-end bourbon. He fumbled with his phone, checking the time on the display: *12:02 a.m.* He beckoned to Danny the bartender like he was Kyle's own personal servant. "I need another drink!"

Danny brusquely walked away to wait on other customers.

Kyle snapped. "Don't ignore me!" He stood and attempted to flag down Danny, who dismissed him, his back to the boy.

The second Kyle lifted his body off the stool, the room spun around him, and he fell backward onto his butt.

"Girl, you messy."

Kyle sensed the tender touch of a soft hand upon his shoulder. He recognized the beautiful blur beside him as everybody's favorite Queeraoke host, Ms. Harmony House.

"How come you haven't sung tonight?" she asked Kyle, squeezing in between the barflies to lean against the counter. "Oh, wait. Cuz you're too wasted to read the lyrics on the monitor, maybe? If you could even make it down to the mic."

At a loss for words, Kyle crunched hard on the ice in his

rocks glass. The drag queen had hit the nail squarely on the head. He was indeed a disaster, more so than usual.

When he didn't reply with his normal snarky response, Harmony placed her hand on Kyle's back and gave it a gentle rub. "Tell Momma what's wrong?"

It felt nice to hear a friendly word, considering the awful night he'd had. After confronting Hunter27 earlier, Kyle had come to the conclusion that the younger boy had been telling the truth: He may have private messaged with Kyle's boyfriend on the Lads4Dads app, but Hunter27 hadn't actually had an affair with CashMan. Though, if this were the case, why did Kyle fear the worst with regards to his current relationship status?

With the toe of his tennis shoe, he kicked at the metal footrest attached to the bottom of the bar, bleary eyes cast down. "My birthday is next month."

"Happy birthday next month, Baby Face!" Ms. Harmony beamed, showing off a sparkly set of perfect pearly whites. "Remind me on the night of. I'll serenade you."

Kyle hung his head, dreading the idea of everyone at Shout! knowing he was one step closer to hitting a major milestone. "I won't be celebrating."

"Of course you will! Remind Momma how old you're gonna be?"

Kyle frowned, cursing his swiftly fading youth. "Old."

"How old?" Harmony House stared down her broad nose at the boy.

"Twenty-nine." He knew that he sounded ridiculous. But with the upcoming turning of the calendar, Kyle realized he'd be on the verge of losing the love of his life, come next year. Tom Cash would never remain in a relationship with him once he'd turned thirty.

The drag queen let out a husky laugh. "When you're *forty*,

see me. We can talk about what old is." She slapped Kyle lightly on the cheek and signaled to Danny at the far end of the bar. "Be a doll and get Baby Face some H-two-oh," Harmony House said sweetly. "Then call him a car and get him the hell outta here!"

"I got this."

At the sound of the deep baritone, Kyle's heart sank in his chest. He didn't need to see the man who'd stepped up behind him to know the identity of his savior.

It was none other than Daddy Tom, there to rescue Kyle from his own self-destruction.

"Danny!" Tom shouted over the roar of the crowd, capturing the bartender's divided attention. "These drinks are all comped," he ordered, sliding the glasses Kyle had emptied along the bar toward the opposite end.

"For sure," Danny said, smiling, having no other choice than to comply with his boss's command.

Moments later, Kyle slouched in the passenger seat of Tom's SUV, parked out behind Shout! in a space marked RESERVED, his head slumped against the side door. He could barely keep his eyes open, the lids growing heavy from all the alcohol he'd consumed.

"What are you doing?" Tom asked the younger guy, like an actual father confronting his troubled son. "How much did you drink tonight?"

Kyle turned to his handsome lover just as Tom lit up a cigarette. "What do you care?" he asked, his words tumbling out all slurred together.

"I'm a respected member of this community . . ." Tom rolled down his window to allow some fresh air inside the vehicle. "Everybody knows me."

The warm breeze felt nice as it wafted across Kyle's flushed face. He leaned his head back and shut his eyes tightly as Tom carried on with his lecture.

"My boyfriend can't be flat-out drunk, making a scene in the middle of my bar."

Kyle knew that he was caught.

He didn't bother questioning the comment or denying his own earlier drunken outburst. Clearly, Tom had found out about Kyle's confrontation with Hunter27 in the dark corner, and he wasn't happy. Would this public display of poor judgment on Kyle's part give the handsome older man reason to put a premature end to their relationship?

Tom raised his voice in exasperation. "Are you even listening to me?"

Kyle opened his eyes with a start and sat forward, only half-hearing the question his boyfriend had just posed to him. "I am!"

Kyle focused his attention on the familiar surroundings, his brain conjuring up a fuzzy image: being led out the back door of the bar, barely able to walk, across the paved patio and over to Tom Cash's car, where he'd been gingerly placed inside by Tom Cash himself.

"I'm only telling you this because I care." The bar owner's harsh tone softened. With his large hand, Tom stroked the young man's hair, the blond locks damp with perspiration.

"You do?" Kyle asked, too ashamed to look directly at the other man.

"Of course, Kiddo!" Tom promised, calling the boy by the nickname he'd given him on their very first date night. "You're my guy. I love you."

Kyle wanted to believe the words. He wanted to believe that Tom's feelings for him were both genuine and true. He wanted to believe that Tom found him different—more *special*—than any of the other younger men he'd ever been with before.

Most of all, Kyle wanted to believe that Tom Cash would stay.

"I love you, too," he whispered, before finally passing out in the passenger seat of the SUV.

Kyle woke up alone.

For close to eighteen months, he'd slept most nights in the arms of the man he loved, safe and secure in the big house on Borman Avenue.

The stunning late-1930s Art Deco–influenced home boasted over three thousand square feet, with an equal number of bedrooms and bathrooms, totaling four apiece. The first-floor master suite had been added on by its previous owners, longtime residents of the community who, due to advanced age, could no longer easily access their second-story sleeping quarters. Such respectful attention had been paid to historic detail, even the most seasoned architect would vouch for the room's original authenticity.

Pulling back the satin sheet, Kyle exposed his bare torso to the cool air that blew in through the open casement windows. The morning sunlight caused the colored stained glass to sparkle, reminding the young man of a kaleidoscope from his not-so-happy childhood.

He rolled over, reaching for his cell phone resting on the black lacquered night table, and checked the time on the screen: *8:13 a.m.*

Kyle couldn't recall the exact moment that he'd gone to bed the night before. He couldn't recall much activity, for that matter, from the previous evening. The throbbing in his brain served as a painful reminder of the cause of his lost memory.

The opposite side of the bed lay abandoned.

No matter how much rest he may have gotten, Tom awoke each morning along with the sunrise. He referred to that magical time as *Michigan's Finest Hour.* The expression, Kyle had learned, had been coined by Tom's late father, Larry, back when Tom and his twin were both still boys. Long before the elder Mr. Cash and his lovely wife, Linda, fell victim to the tragic fate that had claimed both their young lives.

Kyle decided to dress comfortably, in his favorite navy shorts and cotton collared shirt. As a rule, he preferred to wear shades of blue, as the color went best with his eyes. His hope was that Tom would notice how nice he looked that morning and forget the unfortunate incident of last night.

"Good morning!" Kyle cheerfully greeted his lover as he strolled through the double doors of the four-season room located at the back of the house.

"Good morning, Kiddo!" Freshly showered after his 6:00 a.m. workout, Tom Cash sat with one meaty thigh crossed over the other on the crescent-shaped, coral-colored vintage velvet couch.

A cup of hot coffee rested on the chrome-accented oval coffee table, beside a Baccarat crystal ashtray overflowing with cigarette butts. The smell of stale tobacco hit Kyle in the face like a sucker punch, making him sick to his stomach.

Despite participating in his fair share of destructive behavior less than twenty-four hours prior, Kyle couldn't bear the thought of smoking before the sun had actually gone down. He squinted at the bright light glaring off the floor-to-ceiling windows behind his boyfriend. Outside, the landscaped gardens along the perimeter of the property flourished with the summer season.

"How's my little sleepyhead?" Tom could sense Kyle's queasiness. He kissed the boy tenderly and eased him down on the sofa.

"Sleepy," Kyle replied, forcing a yawn for dramatic effect as he ignored a wave of nausea.

"You look handsome this morning."

"So do you."

Nicely tanned from their recent Key West trip, Tom

sported a tight T-shirt under a zip-up hoodie and track pants that accentuated his muscular lower limbs. Even after all the time they'd been dating, Kyle found it hard to believe the over twenty-year age difference between them. For a man of fifty, Tom Cash possessed a better physique than most guys who frequented the bar he owned, where Kyle spent most of his free time.

"Hey, is my brother awake?"

"Not sure." Kyle leaned back against the tufted sofa cushion. "His door was shut when I passed by on my way down."

"I gotta talk to him about something," Tom said, almost to himself, as he rose from the couch and threw on his favorite blue and gold U of M ball cap.

Kyle watched Tom walk into the formal dining room and over to the marble staircase alongside the far wall. Firmly, he gripped the custom wrought iron railing and urgently shouted in the direction of his twin's bedroom, at the top of the steps: "Yo, Ter! You up?"

After a moment of radio silence, Tom looked to his lover, waiting by his side. "Guess I'll let him sleep. Hopefully, he won't miss his brunch date with Fairway Bob."

"What time is that happening?" Kyle wondered, not that he really cared about Terry Cash and his weekend plans. He was purely making polite conversation, happy that last night's indiscretion seemed to have been forgiven.

Tom consulted the gold wristwatch that he wore, a present to himself for his golden birthday. "Pretty sure they agreed on eleven o'clock. If I heard them right."

"You can always text Terry from the diner and make sure he's awake," Kyle suggested. "He probably won't text you back, but . . . that guy really needs a new phone."

"I offered to buy him one," Tom said, shrugging his broad shoulders. "Not my problem if he won't upgrade."

Kyle patted his empty belly, his six-pack abs even flatter than usual. "You hungry?"

Tom took hold of Kyle's hand. "Starved. That protein shake I drank after the gym didn't do squat."

They waltzed through the cozy eat-in kitchen, complete with professionally restored metal cabinetry, and out the side door into the heat of the summer.

The couple had taken to having breakfast on Saturday mornings at The Depot Diner. As per tradition, they would arrive around the same time, sit at the same table with a view of the train tracks, and order the same items off the menu.

"Gentlemen, good morning!" Within moments of Kyle and Tom's arrival, Olivia, the young waitress, bounded over with a pair of steaming coffee cups.

"Somebody's happy," Tom teased, taking note of the girl's giddy glow.

The soon-to-be senior at Fernridge High could hardly contain her excitement. "Well . . ."

"Did you have a date last night with that hunky dude? Tell Uncle Tommy all about it."

"Hashtag-me-too!" Kyle interjected excitedly, acting like a lovestruck teenager himself.

The young woman blushed. "I did have a date with Wes. We went to see a movie at the art house up in Royal Heights. Then after, he took me to that fondue place around the block."

Tom raised a dark eyebrow. "A football player into foreign films? Athletic *and* intellectual. Sounds like a keeper."

"Any luck, we'll be going to homecoming together in the fall," the girl gushed, crossing her fingers for good luck.

"How did you like *La Fondue*?" Kyle lifted the ceramic mug to his lips and blew gently before taking a sip. "That's where we went on our first date," he recalled, beaming at the remembrance.

"Really?" Olivia the young waitress asked, amazed at the coincidence.

"A long time ago," Kyle told her, once again feeling his advancing age.

"It wasn't *that* long ago," Tom declared, in good humor. "Not even two years."

"Two years?" the teen girl gasped. "I can barely remember being a sophomore."

"Not me," Tom said, his voice filled with nostalgia. "Fifteen feels just like yesterday. Got my first girlfriend that year, so it was a pretty big deal." He smiled to himself, mentally conjuring up an image from his youth. "She had this crazy red hair and a crazy personality, to boot. Liked dogs better than she did people."

The waitress gave Tom Cash a look. "No disrespect, but . . . you had a girlfriend?"

Tom chuckled as Kyle choked on his coffee, suppressing a laugh at his boyfriend's expense. "It was a totally different time. What can I say? You couldn't be gay in high school, the way you kids today can."

"I was gay in high school," Kyle confided to the young waitress, Olivia.

"And how long ago was that?" Tom joked.

"No comment."

"Well, it's awesome you guys are still together," Olivia said, granting full approval to Tom and Kyle's relationship. "Maybe you should think about getting married?" She tossed her mousy hair and winked mischievously at the couple. "I'll be right back with your breakfast."

As the waitress disappeared through the swinging door into the kitchen, Tom folded his muscular arms across his muscular chest and locked his gaze on his lover. "That Olivia is a smart girl."

Regardless of the fun and frivolity they'd had that morning thus far, Kyle felt an ominous sense of foreboding.

Something bad was about to happen; an event so sinister, it would result in the end of Kyle's relationship with Tom Cash . . .

Forever.

# Chapter 17

*One week after the murder . . .*

The giggling teen girls whispered to each other. Judging by the precocious way in which the pair looked over at us, they clearly had recognized my partner and me from our cable TV show.

From our booth against the wall, Kyle Young pointed in the direction of the two-top table, near the windows, with a view of the train tracks. "We were right over there . . ."

JP swallowed the last drop of cold coffee in his cup. "You and Tom?"

"No, him and the Queen," I said, frustrated by how long it had taken us to get to this point in our conversation. We'd finally gotten around to binge-watching that streaming show, *The Monarch*, and this was the first clever retort that I could come up with.

After spending nearly an hour at The Depot Diner, all we'd done was fuel up on caffeine and make small talk with Kyle. Literally, the clock was ticking. If someone had murdered Tom Cash, and his ex-boyfriend knew the killer's identity, we needed him to tell us who it was, so that we could go to Detective Paczki and have him reopen the case. At which point, he could go and arrest the assailant and immediately close it again.

"Yes, me and Tom," Kyle confirmed. "We came here every Saturday morning. When we first started dating, we used to go to the wine pub, over by you guys."

"Chianti?" JP asked.

"No, Cabernet," I said sarcastically. "Of course, Chianti! There's only one wine pub in all of Pleasant Woods! Now would you please stop interrupting and let the guy finish his story?"

The sound of my raised voice drew attention from some of the other customers. The giggling young girls at the table across the room got out their phones and started filming us, just as I'd predicted they would.

To show that I'd gotten used to being on display, I waved and smiled for their cameras. Then I went right back to listening to Kyle's tale.

"We started coming here after Tom got into it with Andrew, the owner. Super-hot older guy. Korean, I think."

JP leaned his elbows on the table, grinning at the thought of the sexy restaurateur. "We know Andrew."

"Well, not *from* Korea," Kyle continued. "But he's Asian American. He's got like a fourth-degree black belt in karate."

"Pretty sure it's Taekwondo," I said, remembering the threat that Andrew's wife, Brianna, had made the last time we stopped by Chianti for brunch.

Something told me we'd be at The Depot a while longer, so I signaled for the young waitress, Olivia, to bring over more coffee.

"Why did Tom and Andrew get into it?" I asked Kyle, thinking it a legitimate question, unlike the ones my partner had been bombarding him with.

"He kept bugging Tom to sell him the Tudor."

"So they could build a parking lot for Chianti," I said, recalling the other detail that Brianna had recently divulged.

"Something like that," Kyle said, indifferent. "Tom got tired of them bringing it up every time we ran into them. So, we started coming here for breakfast on Saturdays instead."

Now that we'd established *why* Kyle was with Tom at The Depot Diner on the morning that he died, we needed to know something more important: How could Kyle Young prove that someone had actually murdered Tom Cash?

"Can we backtrack to what you told us over at Four Fairway?" JP asked, cutting into the conversation once again. "You said you and Tom broke up on the morning he died."

Kyle picked at a cold fried potato on his plate and popped it into his mouth. "That's the part I'm getting to."

"Let the guy tell his story!" I playfully chided my partner.

JP sat silent as Kyle leaned forward, placing his elbows on the table. "I decided I needed to drop Tom . . . before Tom could drop me."

My jaw fell open. In the writing world, we referred to this type of plot point as a *twist*.

"You broke up with Tom?" JP said to Kyle, equally dazed by his revelation.

Olivia the young waitress returned, wielding a fresh pot of coffee. "Can I get you guys a warmup?"

The nutty aroma of chicory and chocolate notes tickled my nostrils as she poured another round of hot dark liquid into my mug. I couldn't wait to down another cupful. Or maybe five?

"Thanks, Liv. We'll take the check whenever you get a chance."

"No problem! It's a beautiful day. Better get out there and enjoy it."

"We sure hope to!" JP told the young woman with a smile.

Olivia blushed. She'd had the biggest crush on JP Broadway, handsome home rehab TV show host, ever since we'd first set foot inside The Depot Diner. Unlike the pair of giggling girls at the table across the room—who, thankfully, had finally left—the waitress remained professional in her weekend interactions with us.

Before returning to the cash register at the counter, Olivia paid her respects to Kyle. "Again, I'm sorry about Mr. Cash."

Kyle nodded. "You know he'd hate you calling him that. Mr. Cash was his dad. He was Uncle Tommy."

Olivia bowed her head and somberly walked away.

"Why did you break up with Tom Cash?" I cried, diving back into the conversation right where we'd left off.

"You're BFFs with Campbell Sellers, aren't you? Then you're well aware of Tom's track record when it comes to dating younger guys."

"He's got you there, Pete," JP laughed. "Why'd you even ask?"

"Just because Tom broke up with Cam when he turned thirty," I informed my smart aleck partner, "doesn't mean he'd do the same thing to poor Kyle."

"You don't think so?" JP said, his tone dripping with sarcasm. "He dropped that bartender, Danny, when he got too old for him, didn't he?"

"How would you know? We weren't even living here then."

"But I heard the story enough times from Campbell, after he got his heart broken for the exact same reason."

Out of the corner of my eye, I noticed Kyle sitting quietly as my partner and I carried on like bickering old biddies. "Sorry, we're being totally rude," I apologized on behalf of Team *Domestic Partners*.

"You are. But you're buying me breakfast, so I won't complain. Now where was I?" Kyle thought for a second. "Oh, yes. I broke up with Tom. Right over there in that very spot . . ." As he gestured to the two-top across the room with a view of the train tracks, the horror of that fatal Saturday morning, a mere week ago, haunted Kyle Young's memory.

"How did he take the news?" JP inquired. "What did Tom say when you told him it was over?"

"He told me to shut up," Kyle confessed. "He told me I was being stupid. He said he wouldn't let me break up with him. He said I was stuck with him, *till death do us part.*"

Kyle's choice of words struck me as significant. The specific way in which he had phrased the comment could only mean one thing . . .

"Tom Cash asked you to marry him?" The pitch of my voice escalated to a screech as I proclaimed: *"Get out!"*

Kyle looked at me, crestfallen. "Actually, he didn't ask. He was gonna, I'm pretty sure of it. But he never got the chance."

"Well, why not?" JP demanded, sounding like his partner— me—a hopeful romantic who loved a good happy ending.

"He got a phone call."

"You're kidding," I said, in total astonishment. "Nobody calls anybody anymore. That is so twentieth century!"

"I know, right? And . . . he left his volume on inside the restaurant, which is totally annoying. But not nearly as bad as that stupid xylophone ringtone Tom always used."

Something told me that Kyle wasn't familiar with the word *marimba.* At that moment, I didn't bother schooling him on the proper names of wooden percussion instruments. I felt it would have been rude.

"Better yet," JP said, drawing a conclusion to the bizarre situation. "Why did Tom take the call? If he was about to propose marriage . . ."

"Good point!" I said, giving my partner his due props.
"Who could've called that was so important, Tom interrupted
a major moment in his life?"

Suddenly, I recalled a crucial piece of information that
we'd learned earlier in the week: *The pink mafia!*

Elaborating, I explained to Kyle why I'd just gotten so
excited that I practically jumped out of my skin. "At Tom's
memorial, one of our neighbors mentioned a rumor that's going around . . ."

While I wasn't one to give power to gossip, I proceeded to
tell Kyle what Stephen Savage-Singer had told us with regards
to where Tom had gotten the cash to remodel Shout!

"Well, you can't believe everything you hear," Kyle said.
"Because I actually asked Tom that same question when he
first brought up redoing the bar. He swore to me he got the
money from a totally legit source: his brother."

JP drummed his fingers against Formica. "Interesting . . ."

"How so?" I said, failing to follow my partner's train of
thought.

"Remember what Fairway Bob said at the funeral? There
wasn't much love lost between the Cash brothers. Why would
Terry give Tom a bunch of money to renovate his bar, if he
couldn't stand the guy?"

"Another good point!" I cried, proud of my partner's skills
of deduction. "You sure you only played a cop on TV?"

Kyle sighed, ready to get this show on the road. "I'm just
telling you what Tom told me."

"Well, if it wasn't the pink mafia calling to shake Tom
down," I said, trying my hand at some police detective lingo,
"who was it?"

"No idea. I didn't stick around long enough to find out. I
told Tom we were finished . . . and I left."

"Nooo!" JP and I shouted in unison, slamming our fists
on the table like something out of a courthouse drama.

Kyle shrugged. "I was upset! Here I am, breaking up with the man I love, and he pulls out a velvet ring box. Then his phone goes off, and he actually stops to answer it?"

"What if the person on the other end of the line was the actual murderer?" I said, desperate to learn the mysterious caller's identity. "I mean, presuming that somebody killed Tom—besides the pink mafia—and his death wasn't an accident after all."

"That's exactly what I'm thinking," Kyle said. "I got up from the table and stormed off. But before I could get out the door, I heard Tom say something to the caller . . ."

JP gasped, drawn into the mystery unfolding before us. "What did he say?"

"He said: 'You don't like what I'm doing? *Kill* me!'"

Staring at Kyle Young, I shook my head incredulously at the evidence he'd laid out. Could it really point us toward the person who'd possibly murdered Tom Cash?

"So, what happened after you walked out of here?" JP asked Kyle. He reached into his wallet for his credit card. "Did you ever hear from Tom again?"

Kyle picked up his phone from where it rested on the table, next to the napkin holder, and stared at it reverently as he spoke. "He left me three voice mail messages—between like nine-thirty and ten-thirty—begging me to take him back. He said he was heading over to the Tudor. He'd be there like an hour or so, doing some yard work. Then he'd give me another call, and we could chat."

Kyle scrolled through his photo stream until he came to a picture of Tom Cash, looking handsome as ever, posing on the back patio at Shout! "He told me he loved me . . ." Kyle gazed longingly at his dead lover's image. "And that's the last thing he said."

"Speaking of Tom's phone . . ." I'd been wondering if

anyone had ever located the missing mobile device. "Did it ever turn up?"

"Terry found it," Kyle confirmed, "in the middle of the lawn at Four Fairway, chopped up into a dozen pieces. Tom must've dropped it when he was cutting the grass and ran it over with the mower. Terry gave what he could salvage to Detective Paczki. But it's pretty much a moot point."

Funny how Terry had precisely predicted the fate of Tom's missing cell phone when we were talking about it with him at the funeral. If only he'd had a similar hunch as to what had happened to Tom, himself.

After settling our bill with the young waitress, Olivia, we departed The Depot Diner and headed toward home. Outside, as JP, Kyle, and I began the walk back to Fairway Lane, I wondered what course of action we might take next . . .

"I think we need to go to the police," JP decided. "Let Detective Paczki solve the mystery of *Who Killed Tom Cash?* He can get a subpoena and have the CDRs pulled for Tom's phone."

Kyle and I gaped at JP as he spouted his cop lingo. Neither one of us knew what a CDR was or why we'd want it pulled by the police.

"Certificate of digital receipts?" I guessed, taking a stab at deciphering the abbreviation.

"Call detail records," JP clarified. "We did an episode on *Brooklyn Beat* with a similar plot. A woman files for divorce on the grounds her husband is having an illicit affair. The police pull the CDRs for his phone and check if he's been calling his mistress."

"I remember that one! The guy got busted and his wife got everything."

"I'm telling you . . ." Kyle reached into his pocket for his cigarettes. "Paczki isn't gonna do a thing to find Tom's killer."

"What makes you think that? Nick dated my sister," I said. "I've known him a long time. He's a good guy."

"I'm not saying he's *not*." Kyle exhaled a puffy white cloud into the blue summer sky. "But this is Pleasant Woods. People don't get killed here."

"He did tell us that," JP reminded me. "When we first found Tom's body at the bottom of the staircase, those were pretty much Paczki's exact words."

"Well, what if we tell Terry about the phone call Tom got?" I suggested, grasping for a long straw.

"I did tell Terry," Kyle said. "He informed me the police ruled Tom's death an accident and told me to drop it. He said I wasn't married to his brother, so I have no legal say with regards to anything concerning Tom."

"That seems rather nasty," I said, reconsidering our business agreement with Terry Cash. "Why would he be so mean?"

"Because he hates me," Kyle complained. "Terry insists I only got involved with Tom because he had money. Like I couldn't possibly be in love with a man over twenty years older than me. Personally, I think he's jealous. Terry just wishes he had a cute young boyfriend, the way his brother always did."

I could see where that might be the case. But if Kyle truly felt somebody had killed Tom, we needed to make his brother believe it, too. "Did you tell Terry we have proof that someone threatened Tom's life?"

JP played devil's advocate. "But we don't have proof."

"Weren't you listening back at the diner?" I asked my partner, more frustrated than ever. "Kyle said he heard Tom being threatened by whoever called him that morning."

"No. He said he heard Tom say the caller could kill him, if they didn't like what he was doing."

JP had a point. But it was simple semantics. *Po-TAY-to, po-TAH-to.*

"Well, what do we think Tom was doing that the caller might not like?"

We'd crossed the train tracks and found ourselves on the far side of town, near Gainsford Park. The newly installed playground equipment, paid for by our Pleasant Woods tax dollars, was getting a real work out. All the little kiddies took turns swinging on the swings and sliding down the curly slide as their helicopter parents looked on, clutching their iced coffee cups.

"I've thought about it," Kyle admitted, in response to my last statement. "Maybe it had something to do with Shout!?"

"That could be it," JP said, giving Kyle's assessment some thought. "But the bar's an even bigger success now. Why would anyone *not* like that fact?"

"Well, is there anything else?" I asked, coming up short with an answer myself.

Kyle plopped down on a nearby park bench and hung his head. "Tons of things! Tom made lots of people mad."

"Like what? Like who?" My hope was to come up with a list of reasons why this crime could have been committed . . . and by whom.

"Like . . ." Kyle considered a moment. "Like Brianna and Andrew Kim. They were peeved at Tom for not selling them the Tudor."

JP placed a hand on his hip and gave Kyle his full attention. "Go on . . ."

"Danny, the bartender at Shout!" Kyle continued, the list of suspects starting to grow longer. "He never forgave Tom for breaking up with him, just cuz he turned thirty."

"If that's the case," JP said, "what about Campbell? Tom did the same thing to him."

"The cops already questioned Cam," I reminded JP and Kyle both, "after they figured out the phone we found inside the house was his. They concluded that Cam couldn't have killed Tom. The coroner determined he died between nine-forty-five and eleven-fifteen. Cam was at his open house up in Royal Heights during that time frame."

JP folded his arms over his chest in defiance. "But how do we know Cam was telling the truth when he talked to the cops?"

"Yeah," Kyle said. "Why should we take Cam's word for it?"

I'd heard enough.

"I can't believe what you guys are insinuating! I realize you don't care for my best friend, JP. But I will tell you both this: I've known Campbell Sellers for over half of my life. He could never *kill* anyone."

The three of us stood in the middle of the park, eyes focused everywhere but on each other.

After a moment of awkward silence, Kyle Young broke the tension with a pleading request: "Could you guys please help me? I need to find out what really happened to Tom. No matter what anyone thinks, no matter what anyone says, I loved the guy. If he ended up asking me to marry him that morning, I would've for sure said yes. And if somebody killed him and they get away with murder . . . I couldn't live with myself."

I felt terrible. Putting myself in Kyle's place, I tried to imagine what he must've been dealing with since Tom died. If something similar ever happened to JP—my partner in life, my one true love—I'd stop at nothing to make sure his assailant was caught and justice was served.

"What can *we* do?" JP asked, sounding hopeless. "I'm an actor, Pete's a writer . . ."

"But you played a detective on TV . . ." Kyle grinned in remembrance. "And PJ, you write mystery novels. There's always a killer in the story who gets caught in the end."

Biting my lower lip, I considered Kyle's logic. "True."

Maybe, using the skills that both my partner and I had acquired in our real-life line of work, we could parlay those talents into yet another profession?

*JP Broadway & PJ Penwell: Domestic Partners in Crime.*

# Chapter 18

We formulated a plan.

Arriving back at 1 Fairway Lane after breakfast, we ascended the limestone steps and made ourselves at home on the screened-in front porch.

JP plopped down in one of the white recycled plastic rockers we'd gotten last fall and patted his full belly. "That was some good French toast."

Kyle perched himself along the edge, between the pair of pillars that held up the overhang. He glanced up at the slatted beadboard that we'd painstakingly refinished that past spring. "The ceiling looks nice."

"It turned out pretty good," I said, trying to be modest. "Took us weeks to scrape off all the old primer and caulk between the cracks."

JP gently rocked back and forth in his chair. "Pete did most of the work."

"You painted! He used this roller attached to a long pole," I told Kyle. "Finished it in like fifteen minutes."

"Well, you guys did a great job fixing up this old house," Kyle said sincerely. "I can't imagine the responsibility that comes with home ownership. Now that I moved out of Tom's house, I'll probably live in my crappy apartment forever. I still can't believe he's gone."

With the subject of death and destitution on the table, a lull fell between the three of us.

"So . . . ?" JP said.

"So . . . ?" Kyle said.

It was time to get down to business and plot out our plan to catch Tom Cash's killer.

"So . . ." I said, preparing to advise my fellow compatriots. "I think we should head up to Shout! Kyle can introduce us to Danny the bartender. We can find out his alibi for the morning Tom died. And . . . we can finally get Stephen off our back about never coming to Drag Queen Queeraoke."

"Are you talking about Harmony House?" Kyle asked, taken aback by my cavalier comment.

"He's our neighbor, two doors down," JP said, answering for me.

"You call her *Stephen*?"

"Well, sure," I said. "Should we give him special treatment or something?"

"Ms. Harmony is a Detroit legend," Kyle answered in awe, "in case you guys aren't aware."

"If you say so," JP said. "Guess we'll find out for ourselves soon enough."

Having performed on stage with the likes of A-list New York actors, in addition to the Hollywood types that were flown in for *Brooklyn Beat*, JP was never one to appear starstruck around celebrities. For someone who had achieved his own success, my partner took pride in deeming himself a regular Joe. Or in his case, a regular John Paul.

The next point, I'd made sure to give additional thought.

"If anyone asks why, all of a sudden, we've showed up for Queeraoke when we haven't been one time since moving here . . ." I paused a moment to get the specifics of our story straight. "We'll just say we've been too afraid of going out in public."

JP gasped, horrified. "We can't say that! We want all those gays to watch our TV show. If they think we think we're better than them, they'll totally turn on us and never tune in."

"I'm not saying we think we're better than anyone," I said, trying to untwist the words my partner had just put in my mouth. "What I meant is: We can tell anyone who asks that I'm an agoraphobic. I don't do well in social settings."

I wasn't overexaggerating. What I'd said was totally true. In fact, in recent months I'd come to the conclusion that I might be a bit on the spectrum. Lots of writers were known eccentrics. So, why not me?

The more I'd thought about it, the more evidence led me to believe I wasn't like most everyone else. As a child, I had a terrible time making friends. Sure, I was friendly enough. From an early age, my mother instilled in me her cardinal rule: *If you can't say something nice, don't say anything at all.* But it was my sense of humor that others just didn't get. Whenever I'd meet a new person, I'd make a joke to put them at ease. More often than not, they'd stare at me like I'd uttered the most peculiar thing.

The summer before high school started, when all my classmates were off playing baseball or riding bikes across Madison Park, I spent the afternoons sequestered away in my bedroom writing my very first novel, *The Butler Didn't Do It.* Well, I pretty much ripped off the plot to Agatha Christie's *Ten Little Indians* and changed the location from England to Michigan. At the time, I never told a living soul about my literary masterpiece, mostly because I didn't deem it a real book. Plus, I knew the other kids would think me weird if they'd gotten wind that I wasted my vacation. But the older I got, the less I cared about impressing other people. In fact, apart from my partner JP and Campbell Sellers, I didn't have any friends.

And honestly, I didn't mind.

I'd never been one for forced frivolity or making small talk with strangers. A global pandemic could disrupt the planet, causing widespread quarantine among the human population . . . it wouldn't faze me in the slightest.

"How about we say we've been super busy with the move to Detroit and taping the show?" JP suggested. "We haven't had any time for going out and having any fun. Until now."

"Well, what changed?" I wondered, stopping to consider the plausibility of our backstory like a good little author.

It was at that moment that Kyle Young stepped in to intervene, yet again.

"Why don't we just tell people I invited you guys to come to Queeraoke, since you still haven't been to Shout! since the remodel? Not that anyone's going to care either way," he added. "They'll probably just ask you to take a selfie and be done with it."

"Won't people wanna know how you know us?" I asked Kyle, still in writer mode.

Part of plotting a good story involved getting inside the characters' heads and figuring out their motivation. If Kyle Young randomly showed up at Shout! on a Saturday night, with a pair of semi-famous HDTV show hosts, weren't all his karaoke comrades going to want to know how he'd made our acquaintance?

"We can say we met online," Kyle offered as a possible riposte. "That's where I meet most of the guys I know. Either on social media or some hookup app."

"Well, we can't let people think that!" I didn't mean to sound like a prude. I just wouldn't want people thinking that JP and I were up to no good. If the media got hold of that story, they'd have a field day. We'd made such a name for ourselves as the poster boys for gay monogamy over the past almost five years, I didn't want to give anyone any reason to suspect otherwise.

"People meet online all the time," JP said, suddenly an expert on human behavior, "and not just for hooking up."

"Please!" I scowled at my partner's naïveté. "We're three attractive gay men . . . nobody will believe we're not involved in a throuple."

"Fine. We can just tell everyone we met Kyle in the back-yard of his dead lover's dead parents' old house," JP stated flatly. "He asked us if we could help find his ex-boyfriend's killer, since both the ex-boyfriend's twin brother and the PW police believe the ex-boyfriend's death was an accident. But Kyle feels otherwise, based on a phone call he overheard at breakfast on the morning his ex-BF died. So, here we are now at Shout!, trying to find a murderer . . . does anyone have any ideas as to who it might be?"

Shaking my head at my partner's detailed recap of our current predicament, I made up my mind and made a deci-sion: "Let's not worry about what we'll tell people at the bar. Nobody's gonna ask, anyway. If they do, we'll just say we met Kyle through his ex-boyfriend—our neighbor—Tom Cash, before he passed away."

"But how did we meet?" JP asked, just to annoy me.

If he wasn't so gosh darn gorgeous, I would have hauled off and hit him. Throwing my arms up in defeat, I declared: "I don't know! Maybe we double-dated?"

"And where did we go on this double date?"

"You just love to push my buttons, Broadway," I told my partner, trying hard not to laugh at his antics.

JP chuckled. "You know I do, Penwell!"

With that, he took me in his arms and kissed me.

★ ★ ★

I hadn't been out to a bar in forever.

Like JP had said, we'd been so busy with the move from Brooklyn to Detroit, coupled with a rigorous shooting schedule and all the actual renovation work that took place off camera, we hadn't time for much of a social life.

We'd attended the local community festivities: the Pleasant Woods Historical Society's annual Historic Home Tour, the Pleasant Woods Foundation's Gala and Auction, the Christmas tree lighting ceremony in December, the Ice Cream Social in June. We'd spent our first Halloween gathering in Fairway Bob's driveway with the other residents of Fairway Lane, giving out candy to all the trick-or-treaters, all the while sitting around on camp chairs eating pizza and drinking red wine. But other than those few occasions, we'd passed the majority of our free weekends at home, in front of the TV, binge-watching some streaming series or original movie based on some other YA author's book.

"Do I look okay?" I asked JP as he parked our car in the lot behind Shout! "Don't forget to feed the meter."

For my big gay night out, I chose to wear a pair of new shorts that I'd bought on a recent shopping trip with our fashionista neighbor, Stephen Savage-Singer, paired with a tight-fitting graphic T-shirt that some might consider too young-looking for a person my age. According to the fortysomething Stephen, just because I'd soon find myself in my early mid-thirties didn't mean I had to dress like an old person.

"You look awesome," JP assured me, "and I won't." He pulled up the local parking app on his phone screen. "Oh, look! After ten o'clock . . . free, free, free."

"Seriously? This town is losing out on a fortune. Wasn't it like a dollar for like fifteen minutes back in New York?"

"Yes, Michigan!" my partner cheered, quoting an old slo-
gan from my childhood that I'd told him about at some point
during our courtship.

JP, who had a firm policy against wearing shorts out to
a bar—not even during summer or in South Beach—looked
sexy, as per usual, in lightweight dark jeans that clung to his
backside and a short-sleeved button-down shirt that showed
off his guns, along with a bit of chest hair.

"Where did Kyle say we should meet him?" JP took my
hand and led me across the street toward the rear entrance
of Shout!, off the already packed patio filled with the finest
queer folk in Metro Detroit.

"Inside, near the bar," I said. "Why can't we enter through
the back door?"

It was right there in front of us, albeit barricaded by a
bunch of would be Queeraoke-ers, waiting for the show inside to officially get underway.

"Let's cut through this alley. It'll be quicker," JP concluded.

Dance music wafted up into the warm air. Many of the
establishments located on that particular stretch of downtown
boasted outdoor gathering areas, all of them bustling on a
summer Saturday night. Fernridge really was a great little
town! Out of all the suburbs, it felt the most like NYC, with
lots of tasty restaurants, bars, and shops that one couldn't find
other places in the area. A vintage record store sat directly
across the street. Next door, the cutest little café served the
best coffee from Red Hook, Brooklyn. Down the long block,
drunk twentysomethings could throw actual axes at a tiny
target, after signing a waiver, of course.

Past a mammoth mural of a Motown cityscape, painted on
the side of an old brick building, the open-air corridor gave
way to the front, where the entrance could be found to Shout!

"There's Terry Cash, working the door," JP said, pointing
out a familiar face on the highly trafficked strip of street.

The burly man sporting the dark hoodie, track pants, and MSU ball cap physically resembled our new business partner. Except in that particular moment, puffing away on a cigarette, he more closely mirrored his deceased twin.

"Dudes!" Terry greeted us, all the while scrolling through the screen of what looked like a new smartphone.

"How goes it?" JP asked casually as we approached the bar.

Either it was early or we were late. But thankfully, as we arrived, there wasn't much of a line for us to get stuck waiting in.

"What brings you guys down here?" Terry asked, surprised to see us finally showing our faces at his place of business.

"We're meeting Kyle Young for Queeraoke," I answered, acting as nonchalant as possible given the awkwardness of the situation.

"Better late than never, I always say," my partner said, stealing a page from my playbook.

I took the opportunity to apologize to Terry for our negligence as good neighbors. "Sorry it took us so long. We're dying to see the renovations."

"Welcome! I'm looking forward to your critique," Terry told us. "You dudes are the rehab experts. Why I wanted you to redo the Tudor."

Rarely did I like putting someone on the spot. I could have easily reminded our new business partner that it was his brother's dying wish for us to tackle the renovations at 4 Fairway Lane—*not* his. Terry had made the confession to us, himself, at Tom's funeral.

Even had I wanted to rib him, I wouldn't have gotten the chance, as the doorman-turned-bar owner next hit us with the million-dollar question I'd been hoping all day to avoid: "I didn't know you guys knew Kyle."

JP grinned at me. I'd concocted many cover stories earlier, and now he waited to see which one I'd go with as my answer. Unfortunately, I'd expected this question to come from a total stranger. Or maybe Stephen Savage-Singer, aka Harmony House, when he, aka *she*, had seen us chatting over drinks with a dead man's ex-boyfriend.

I couldn't rely on the double-date scenario since I presumed that Terry, being his brother's twin, knew most everything about Tom Cash's past. He was aware of the fact that we'd only met Tom for the first time on the night before he died. That left hardly any chance for Tom and Kyle and me and JP to take in a foreign film at the art house cinema up in Royal Heights. Or head downtown to a Tigers game, before we'd discovered Tom's lifeless body lying at the bottom of a rickety old staircase.

So, instead, I told a little white lie: "We met online."

"But *not* on a hookup app," JP promised, intentionally trying to make me lose my cool.

"Of course not," Terry said, a naughty twinkle in his eye. "Tommy didn't meet Kyle on a hookup app, either." He dropped his cigarette to the ground and crushed out the embers with his massive sneaker. "Filthy habit, huh? Quit when I turned fifty. But it's been a tough week, with my brother dying and all."

"Sure, sure," I said, embarrassed at being caught silently judging Terry's bad behavior, when it was none of my business what he did with regards to his own health.

Terry flashed the latest model iPhone, as proud as his twin had been to show off his own, on the night of Fairway Bob's recent dinner party. "Like my new gadget?"

JP took notice of the shiny piece of technology. "What happened to the flip? That thing was a classic. Made me want one again."

"You can have it," Terry teased. "Talk about a piece of crap! Only reason I kept it so long was I got it from Tommy."

The subject of his dead sibling put a damper on his otherwise playful banter. Terry Cash grimaced and softly bowed his head.

"Have you seen Kyle?" JP asked, eager to venture inside from what I could read of his body language. He shifted anxiously on the balls of his feet, hands shoved deep in his pockets, the corded muscles in his forearms tense and tight.

"He got here a while ago," Terry answered. "Head on inside. You'll find him bellied up to the bar, I'm sure." Then, after a slight pause, he added a request: "Do me a favor, would you?"

"If we can," JP said, never one to make a promise before knowing the full extent of what the commitment entailed.

"Keep an eye on Kyle tonight, okay? Last week, he had way too much to drink. My brother practically had to carry him out to the car."

"We can do that, no problem," I pledged, touched by Terry's concern.

"Now that Tommy's gone, the kid's got nobody to take care of him. Bad enough he broke up with my brother on the day he died. Probably feels terrible and full of guilt."

This show of kindness made me stop to consider: When, exactly, did Terry Cash learn of his brother and Kyle Young's separation?

According to Fairway Bob at the funeral service, Terry had told him that Tom and his boyfriend had recently broken up. But how could Tom Cash have had the opportunity to share this news, when shortly after the actual breakup, he tragically lost his life?

According to the story that JP and I overheard Terry telling Detective Paczki on the day his brother died, Terry hadn't seen Tom that morning. If this were indeed the case, how would Terry have known that Tom and Kyle had broken up earlier over breakfast?

Unless Terry Cash had blatantly *lied* when questioned in our presence by the Pleasant Woods police detective?

"Thanks, dudes." Terry smiled his gap-toothed grin and graciously held open the door for us to pass through.

There'd been a time when the booming bass in a bar would make my heart skip a beat. With each lap around the perimeter, scoping out the territory, the thrill of possibility in finding a potential boyfriend outweighed the overwhelming fear of spending life alone.

Thankfully, those days were long gone.

JP and I, for all intents and purposes, were now a married couple, paperwork pending. We'd not paid this late-night visit to the local, somewhat gay watering hole on the hunt for Mr. Right Now, as we might have in our younger—and single—days.

We'd come to Shout! for one solitary purpose: *to catch a killer.*

# Chapter 19

Kyle leaned against the bar.

Bourbon before him, exactly as Terry Cash had predicted, we had no trouble finding the guy.

Weaving our way through the densely packed crowd, I couldn't help but notice how much younger—and more attractive—the patrons appeared to be than the ones we'd encountered a half dozen years before, on our last visit to Shout!

The interior of the establishment, from a design point, looked spectacular. Entire walls had been knocked down and rebuilt elsewhere. Hardwood flooring replaced the bland beige carpet that once lay beneath our feet. The bar itself, formerly located on the left side of the main room, now found itself positioned against the right. Flat-screen TVs hung mounted on the walls, all on mute, showing an assortment of premium channels as high-energy dance music blared all around us.

"Hey, boys!" Kyle called, breathing whiskey in our faces as we squeezed in beside him.

A pair of empty rocks glasses remained, just off to the side of where Kyle stood. I couldn't be certain he was already on drink number three, at just barely ten o'clock, but . . . the odds were in my favor, based on what Terry Cash had told us on our way inside.

"Well, what's the plan?" JP asked, leaning in for a huddle so he could be better heard.

"To get you boys some alcoholic beverages," Kyle said, "so you can catch up!" He beckoned to the bartender at the far end: a good-looking, dark-haired guy in his early thirties, pouring cocktails from a silver shaker.

I recognized him from the Shout! website as Danny Murphy, Tom Cash's most recent boyfriend before Kyle Young had entered the picture . . . and our prime suspect in Tom's alleged killing.

"All right, all right!"

Startled, JP and I both recoiled as a giantess of a drag queen sashayed her way toward us. We'd never seen our neighbor, Stephen Savage-Singer, in full costume, except in photos posted online to his social media pages for his 5K followers to feast on.

"Hey . . ." I paused, unsure of how to politely address a drag performer. Did I call him *Stephen*, as I'd done on a daily basis? Probably not the best protocol.

I hadn't officially made the acquaintance of his alternate persona, Harmony House, so I didn't want to appear too familiar. Also, if I chose to follow the more formal route, did I go with *Ms. House* or *Ms. Harmony*?

Stephen enveloped us in sleeveless slender arms. "So excited you boys finally made it down for my show!" His look was very 1990s hip-hop girl group: shimmery satin puffy pants and Lycra sports bra/bustier with cross-your-heart straps, all in basic black.

"We're excited to be here," I said, without going into detail as to why we'd finally shown our faces for the big gay event.

"You can't be *too* excited . . ." Stephen scrutinized us standing there empty-handed. "You're still sober."

"I tried getting Danny's attention," Kyle said, directing his comment toward the far end of the bar, irritated. "He's ignoring me. Just like he did last time!"

Unfortunately, with the din of chatter bouncing off the tin ceiling and the distance between them, the bartender couldn't hear a word of Kyle's complaint.

Losing all patience, he threw up his arms. "I'm sick of this! That old queen thinks he can treat me like dirt just cuz Tom's dead."

"Easy, boy," Stephen warned, taking offense at Kyle's choice of epithet. "If Danny Boy's an old queen at almost *thirty-two*, what's that make me?"

Kyle steamrolled ahead with his barrage of disdain. "He forced me to pay for my first two cocktails! Now he won't bring me another one."

The drag queen wagged a finger at Kyle. "Baby Face . . . if I recall correctly, when I saw you here last Friday night, you'd already done had enough to drink. That is the only reason Danny Boy refused to serve you."

Stephen turned his attention to me and my partner and further elaborated. "You boys should've seen this poor child. Momma practically had to pick him up off the floor, he was falling down drunk so bad."

"I wasn't that drunk," Kyle muttered.

"Lucky for Baby Face," Stephen said, "Old Tom Cat showed up to save the day. Carried the boy outta here—literally—like the fairy princess he fancies himself."

The drag queen's painted lips morphed from a pert pucker to a mournful pout. "Was the last time I seen the old guy alive, now that I come to think of it. God rest his miserable soul."

Kyle started pushing his way through the three-deep row of revelers. "Stay here, I'll be back." He stormed off toward the other bar at the opposite end of the room, in search of better service.

With Kyle out of earshot, it was time to make our move on Stephen, aka Harmony House . . .

"So, Danny doesn't like Kyle?" I said, careful to pose the loaded question in such a way that it sounded more like small talk.

"The feeling is mutual, I presume," Stephen answered as Harmony, pitching his voice half an octave higher. "You guys know all about their sordid past, don't you?"

"We know Tom Cash broke up with Danny once he turned thirty," JP replied, taking on the authoritative tone of his police detective character from TV's *Brooklyn Beat*, "and he started dating Kyle, shortly after."

"Well, ever since, from what I could tell . . ." Harmony batted her false lashes toward the bartender with the flippy bangs. "Danny had a personal vendetta against Tom Cat and Baby Face both."

"What kind of vendetta?" I asked, genuinely interested in learning the answer.

Whatever Harmony, aka Stephen, was about to reveal, JP and I had the feeling it could be the break in the case that we'd been hoping for.

"Right after Tom Cat took Baby Face home last Friday," Stephen clarified, dropping his voice down to his natural, lower register, "Danny got this wild look in his eye."

"What kind of wild look?" JP wondered as I tried to envision the picture that our neighbor was drawing for us.

"You didn't hear this from me . . ." Stephen said slyly. "But you wanna know what Danny said as soon as Tom and Kyle were outta here?"

*Of course we wanted to know!*

"Sure," I casually replied, acting as if I couldn't care one way or another, when really I was dying inside.

"Danny said . . ." Stephen came closer to us, his voice a husky whisper. "He'd get even with Tom for leaving him, if it's the last thing he ever did." Without skipping a beat, the drag queen turned on a dime. "Let's do some shots!"

Silently, JP and I checked in with each other. The last thing we needed was a drunken night of debauchery. We had come to the bar with a single agenda. Getting wasted wasn't part of it. But, before we could protest, the Drag Queen Queeraoke host began plying us with tequila.

"Thank you, Danny Boy!" Ms. Harmony graciously commended the bartender as he filled the tiny glasses full of gold liquid. "Did you meet my friends? They're famous TV stars."

"Well, we're on TV," I said, blushing. "I wouldn't say we're *stars*."

Danny replied, with a wink: "I have not."

He was certainly cute enough, with his perfect smile punctuated by a pair of deep dimples. I could certainly understand why Tom Cash, at one point in time, had taken an interest in the guy.

"I'm JP Broadway, and this is my partner, Pete Penwell."

"You can call me PJ," I said politely, gazing into the dark eyes of a potential killer.

"JP and PJ?" Danny raised his brow. "Cute." He nodded his flippy-haired head flirtatiously. "Both of you. Now bottoms up."

Having no other choice, JP and I each took hold of a shot and held it aloft, taking care not to spill the precious contents. Stephen gently clinked his glass against ours, then he abruptly banged it on the bar top. Placing the brim to his full lips, he opened his throat and swallowed down the sweet nectar in one fell swoop.

As Ms. Harmony, Stephen gave me an order: "Peter, start

warming up your vocals. By which I mean, get yourself a beer and loosen up! Now if you boys will excuse me, I've got a show to host."

With Stephen Savage-Singer up on stage—and our new friend Kyle nowhere to be seen with the beverages he'd promised to bring us—we took it upon ourselves to order a round directly from Danny.

"Can we get a couple Manhattans?" JP leaned one elbow against the bar and immediately captured the bartender's attention.

"You got it, Daddy."

As Danny walked away to prepare our drinks, JP turned to me, insulted. "*Daddy? That guy's only a few years younger than me!*"

If what our neighbor Stephen had told us were true, the bartender had all but admitted his desire to see Tom Cash dead. We just needed to ask a few simple questions to determine whether or not Danny Murphy had a credible alibi for the morning that his former lover had possibly been murdered.

With Queeraoke in full swing, the crowd in the bar area had begun to grow thin. As we slowly drank our cocktails, JP and I carried on the conversation we'd struck up with the good-looking mixologist.

"Seriously! You guys think somebody killed my ex?" Danny topped off our beverages. "Don't forget your sidecar," he said, referring to the bit of leftover liquid that remained in the shaker after the initial pour.

We'd moved on from Manhattans to simple bourbon and Cokes, figuring the high-fructose corn syrup would counteract the effects of the high-proof alcohol.

"Wait! You don't think I killed him?" Danny said, aghast, putting two and two together after all the casual questions we'd been confronting him with.

"Well, did you?" I asked, my confidence increasing along with my blood alcohol level.

"No!" Danny swore. "Sure, I hated Tom after he dumped me for that kid, Kyle. But not enough that I'd wanna see him dead."

"That's not what we'd heard," JP revealed, without divulging Stephen Savage-Singer as our source. "We heard that you vowed to get even with Tom, on the night before he died. If it was the last thing you ever did."

"Look . . ." Danny leaned across the bar top, taking on a much more serious tone than he'd employed all evening. "I might have said that—and on multiple occasions. But the bottom line is . . . what time do the cops estimate Tom died?"

"Between ten-forty-five and eleven-fifteen," I answered, providing the info that I'd been made privy to by Tom's twin brother, Terry.

Danny coolly wiped down the counter in front of us with a damp dishrag. "Then I couldn't have killed Tom because, at that time, I was home in bed. And I wasn't alone, if you get my meaning."

JP sipped his drink through the plastic stir straw. "So, you had a little sleepover?"

"You could say that." Danny grinned devilishly, the cat that ate the canary.

This steamy plot point reminded me of my *Murder High* series, book 4: *Killer Quarterback*, in which Madison Park High's star football player, after spending the night with the cheerleading captain, is framed for a murder he didn't commit.

"Do you recall what time you and your . . . guest woke up on Saturday?" I said, trying to steer the line of questioning to something more serious. "If you don't mind my asking."

"Let's see . . ." Danny thought back to the morning of the incident, a little more than a week ago. "A few of us hung out here late, the night before. We're not supposed to . . . but

Tom wasn't around, so we figured why not? Think me and my friend were at my apartment by four."

Suddenly, I felt nostalgic as the whiskey warmed my insides. "I remember those nights, living in New York City!"

During my mid-twenties, my friends and I would close down the bars, most weekends, along with some weekday nights. How I missed those carefree times, before I'd amounted to some sort of success and lacked real responsibility.

"Not to pry into your personal life, Danny . . ." JP began, about to do just that.

"I'm an open book," the bartender assured us. "Ask me anything you want. You wanna know if I killed Tom Cash? I did not. You wanna know if the guy I brought home on the night before Tom died can vouch for me? Go ahead and ask him . . . he's right outside."

Danny gestured toward the far end of the room. Through the glass windows that lined the front wall, we could see a dark male figure standing outside on the street, checking the IDs of incoming customers and collecting their cover charges.

"Terry Cash!" JP just about choked on his drink. "He's the guy you slept with on the night before Tom died?"

Seriously, I couldn't make this up if I were writing a new novel. That being said, I stopped to think that maybe I could borrow this particular plot point and rework it for a Young Adult book-reading audience.

"What can I say?" Danny said humbly. "Things got a little flirty between us at after-hours. One thing led to another . . . next thing I know, Terry's following me back to my apartment." Danny shrugged. "I'm surprised we didn't do it a whole lot sooner. He looks so much like his brother."

"That's because they're twins," I said, stating the obvious. "Well, they *were* twins."

JP knocked back his bourbon. "So, that morning . . . ?" He set the empty glass down and, laser-focused, looked

Danny the bartender directly in the eye. "Got any idea what time you woke up?"

"I do, actually," Danny admitted. "I rolled over in bed. Terry wasn't there. I thought maybe he bailed on me, so I checked the time on my phone. It was almost nine-thirty."

"Why would you think Terry took off?" I asked, curious as to the cause of Danny's paranoia.

"I don't know," he said, sheepish. "He's not the drunken hookup type of guy, I guess. Unlike his brother."

"I thought Terry doesn't drink," JP recalled. "He made a comment at Fairway Bob's dinner party the night we met him."

"He doesn't," Danny confirmed. "But I do. And I had a lot of alcohol at after-hours that night. You know how some people get? They do something wild, the next morning they feel guilty."

"What would Terry have to feel guilty about?" I wondered. Danny was a rather attractive guy. It wasn't as if he was someone to be ashamed of going home with on a Friday night. "Other than the fact that you guys work here together."

"And I dated his brother."

"Well, there is that," JP stated stoically.

"But everything ended up being just fine," Danny said. "A few minutes later, Terry came back to bed. Guess he went to the bathroom or something. Another cocktail?"

JP declined as I chewed on the ice from the bottom of my glass. "So, then what happened?"

"Well, I won't go into details," Danny decided, giving us the PG version of his confession. "A little before eleven, Terry said he needed to go meet a friend for breakfast up in Pleasant Woods. So, he got up. And he left. Excuse me a minute, guys?"

Danny stepped away to wait on another customer, leaving me and my partner to reflect on the earlier conversation between Terry Cash and Detective Paczki: the one that we'd witnessed as we stood together outside the Tudor Revival on the morning Tom died.

"Why would Terry say he'd come over from his own house," JP pondered aloud, "if really he woke up that morning at Danny's apartment?"

"Good question. Either Terry deliberately lied to Nick . . . or maybe Terry was telling the truth? He could've left Danny's place, went home to take a shower, *then* went to meet Bob for brunch."

"Guess there's one way we can find out for sure," my partner speculated.

We stepped outside to speak with Terry.

When we asked him his whereabouts on the morning his brother died, before he'd met our neighbor Bob for brunch, he flat-out proclaimed: "I already told you . . ." He completely stuck to his story about waking up at home—alone—until we revealed what Danny Murphy had just revealed to us.

At first, Terry seemed confused, as if he'd actually forgotten that he'd spent that Friday night at someone else's place. Then he offered an apology of sorts. "I only told Nick Paczki what I told him, cuz I didn't want him knowing what I did with my brother's ex."

Remembering what Danny had said about Terry's potential embarrassment at his sexual indiscretion being uncovered, I assured him that we passed no judgment. In fact, this new piece of information had provided Terry with an ironclad alibi. As long as he could back up Danny's claim, both the bartender and the doorman could no longer be implicated in the death of their employer.

"Danny told you guys I was at his place until almost eleven?" Terry asked skeptically.

"He did," JP affirmed. "Then he said you left to go meet Fairway Bob at Chianti for brunch."

Terry sighed, as if a weight had been lifted off his broad shoulders. "Well, that's good to know."

"It is!" I agreed, grinning. "This means you didn't kill your brother."

As serious as my comment was meant to be, Terry didn't care for the cavalier tone I used in making it. "Is that what you guys think?"

"Terry, no," JP said sincerely. "We're just not so sure Tom accidentally fell down that staircase."

"You think somebody pushed him?"

"It's possible. Kyle Young told us your brother had a lot of enemies. Can you think of anyone who wanted to see him dead?"

The burly doorman stifled a laugh. "I can think of lots of people."

After asking him to narrow down the list of potential suspects, Terry Cash provided us with a single pair of names: *Andrew and Brianna Kim.*

Could the nice married couple, co-owners of Chianti and our neighbors across the street, be actual cold-blooded killers?

We would find out soon enough.

#  Chapter 20

Another Sunday morning saw the popular wine pub packed with Pleasant Woods's hungriest. JP and I had made sure to arrive around nine o'clock, when Chianti first opened, so that we could secure time to chat with the Kims before they got too busy serving other customers.

We ordered our usual.

"Potato latkes with eggs over medium and the *migas*, plus black beans and avocado," Brianna repeated back to us. "I'll go grab you guys some java. Sit tight!"

As soon as she disappeared, I dropped my cheerful façade and hissed at my partner: "Why didn't you say something?"

JP stared blankly at me, as if he were still half asleep. "I will. Once I get some coffee and can actually form a sentence."

Our whole plan hinged on confronting Brianna and Andrew with the accusations that Terry Cash had leveled against them.

According to the doorman, on the night before his brother's death, the married couple had attended Drag Queen Queeraoke. Shortly after midnight, Tom arrived to retrieve his intoxicated boyfriend, Kyle Young, only to be confronted by the restaurateurs. The grievance, as Danny the bartender and several other bar patrons had overheard, stemmed from the recent real estate development, in which Tom Cash had solicited our services to renovate his former family home on reality TV.

Clearly, the Kims weren't happy to have their parking lot dreams dashed to dust. But were they angry enough to murder the man whom they felt had wronged them?

JP winced in pain. "My head is pounding."

"Shouldn't've ordered that last round last night. I told you three was plenty."

"I didn't order the round! Danny bought it for us, remember?"

My memory was a little fuzzy around the edges. I could vaguely recall our bartender bringing over yet another pair of cocktails near the end of the evening, all the while flirting with my fiancé.

Two tables over from where JP and I waited patiently for our coffee, a silver-haired couple in their sixties—straight out of the Summer of Love—sat sipping Bloody Marys. The woman called out to us with a wild wave: "Yoo hoo! Domestic Partners!" For her sake, the overt gesture drew attention away from the floral print caftan she wore over a modest one-piece bathing suit.

"Good morning!" Given the lack of sleep we'd gotten after our late-night, not-so-undercover adventure, the chipper sound of my own voice came as a surprise to even me.

In briefly thinking back to the bar, I suffered a momentary flash of PTSD. Had I really been coerced by a fortysomething drag queen to get up onstage with her and belt out a schmaltzy duet from a cheesy '80s romantic comedy about a department store mannequin brought to life by a guy with a penchant for bowling shoes?

The silver-haired woman stood. Her brightly colored

coverup billowed behind her as she strolled the few steps over to us. "Quinn and I were just talking about you guys," she told us. "We heard you're remodeling that old Tudor Revival next door for your TV show."

"Fairway Bob strikes again," JP muttered in reply.

I saw no point in beating around the bush with the silver-haired woman, Vicky Marshall. Her husband, the esteemed mayor of Pleasant Woods and the gentleman with whom she'd been brunching, appeared well-tanned from days of leisure spent at the community pool. Despite the difference in our ages, we considered the couple as friends.

"You've heard correctly!" I confirmed, exerting the enthusiasm that my partner had lacked in his response to Mrs. Marshall's query.

"How terrific! We can't thank you both enough! That place has been such an eyesore for the past I-don't-know-how-many years. Ever since Quinn and I moved here, and that was like . . ." Silently, Vicky calculated the math. "Well, it was a long time ago!"

JP and I joined the mayor's wife in her nervous laughter, so as not to make her feel awkward cackling away in the middle of an upscale wine pub during brunch.

"Quinn and I won't even walk our dogs past that creepy old house," she continued, stealing a furtive glance around and lowering her voice, "for fear of the *rats* that could be living inside."

Normally, I would have taken the time to defend the property. Yes, there'd been discussions about the abandoned home harboring vermin. Especially with its close proximity to Chianti. But we'd been inside on enough occasions to deem it fairly clean. However, I simply couldn't be bothered to argue until I'd gotten my—

"Coffee?" Our host, Brianna Kim, returned with a couple hot cups.

JP lunged for his mug and gulped down the black gold, scalding his mouth.

Consciously, I took a more careful approach and blew on mine first before daring to take a sip. "Thank you!" The warm goodness gave me new life.

"No problem. Your food will be up in a jiff."

Before she could walk away a second time, I made a point to catch Brianna's attention. "When you get a minute, could we talk to you and Andrew about something?"

Brianna regarded me sideways. "Is everything all right?"

I turned to my partner for backup. "We're not sure . . ."

"Everything should be fine," JP promised Brianna, "once we speak to you both."

"I'll go get Drew." Brianna anxiously walked away in search of her husband.

"So, how are the dogs?" JP asked Mrs. Marshall, who had continued to remain by our table, trying *not* to eavesdrop on our chat with the wine pub co-owner.

"The dogs are great!" Vicky gushed. "I gotta show you guys the picture I took yesterday." She reached into her deep pocket, removed her cell phone, and pulled up the photos app.

A trio of dashing dachshunds posed for the camera, each one displaying his own quirky personality. There was Moto, cuddled up beside his brother Phippie Gene Castlebury, affectionately known as Phipp. The pair of pups were mostly black in color, whereas the newest addition to their family, Rex, sported a shiny dark coat, with tan around his face and on his lower legs, and a furry patch of white covering his chest.

*"Awww!"* I couldn't help but coo. "They're adorable! Where did you take this shot?"

"Over at the dog park," the mayor's wife replied. "It's right around the corner from our house, so it's super convenient."

Hearing this tidbit, JP inquired: "How do the dogs like it? We're hoping to rescue one ourselves soon. Maybe two."

Even though we'd been sorely disappointed with things not working out in our favor with Clyde Barker, we continued to peruse the online pet listings in search of the perfect puppy.

"Our boys love it!" Vicky beamed. "When you guys do adopt, be sure to stop by Town Hall and pick up a dog park pass. It's the best service you can spend your money on."

"Good to know! We will," I pledged, already envisioning the three of us joining Vicky and her three fur babies for a day of fun in the sun.

"We'll let you get back to the mayor," JP said, with just enough edge that Mrs. Marshall would hopefully take the hint and leave us alone. But just in case she wasn't biting, he threw in: "Quinn's starting to look a little lonely all by himself."

Vicky glanced over at her husband, the mayor, his sunburned nose buried in his own phone screen. "He may have officially retired," she teased, "but he can't stop reading his advertising blogs. I keep telling him he should go back to work at the agency, if he's not happy. But he's almost seventy, so . . ."

"Please tell Quinn we said hello," I begged, anticipating Brianna's return with Andrew at any moment.

"I will!" Vicky clasped her hands together and firmly stood her ground. "Before I forget . . ." She pulled out a seat from under our table and sandwiched herself between my partner and me. "I told you guys how I used to teach drama at Fernridge High, didn't I?"

JP and I nodded and smiled, out of respect for our elder.

"Since I took an early retirement myself, I've been bored staying home and not satisfying my artistic side. You guys must know what I'm saying," she commented, seeking out the sympathy of her fellow creative types.

"We do!" I said, feeling the older woman's pain. "I haven't

written anything in forever. JP hasn't performed in years. Not since we started working on this home rehab TV stuff."

"Well, that's why I'm bringing this up . . ." Vicky's gray eyes sparkled in the sunlight that filtered through the stained glass windows. She took a dramatic pause, allowing the suspense to build as she stared through us.

We had no idea what she was about to suggest. Nor did we wish to disappoint the woman when JP and I had to turn down whatever it might have been.

"Have you guys heard of the Royal Heights Players?" Mrs. Marshall folded her hands in front of her like a schoolteacher at her desk. "We're a community theatre troupe. I'm directing a show this upcoming season. I would love for you both to be involved with the production."

"That's awfully kind of you to think of us . . . but I'm not an actor."

"But you're a writer, Peter, aren't you? You've written some stage plays."

"A couple," I said, ashamed to ever consider myself a *playwright*. "Most have never been produced."

"Even better! We've been looking to do a world premiere," Vicky explained, her enthusiasm escalating with each detail that I divulged. "If you've got something we can take a look at, I'll place it on top of the pile."

Giving it some quick thought, I came up with a response to the mayor's wife's request. "I do have this one play I'm rather proud of. It's a four-hander. Two couples—one gay, one straight—living in New York City. Their lives intersect after the woman meets one of the men on the Brooklyn Promenade, totally by chance."

I'd finished writing the piece right before I published my first novel, with the hopes of seeing it produced as an off-off-Broadway showcase or maybe as part of the Fringe festival.

Once the positive pre-pub reviews for my book started to arrive on my publicist's desk, my editor, Sabrina, realized she needed to push forward the release date of the follow-up. The play script got locked away in a file on my laptop somewhere, never to see the light of the stage.

"Is it a mystery?" Vicky asked, her voice filled with suspense. "Like your novels? Which my grandchildren love, by the way. As do I!"

"It's not a mystery," I revealed, worried my candor could be a deal breaker. "I wrote it before I switched genres."

"Well, I'm sure it's brilliant. What's the play called? Not that it matters, I'm just curious."

"*Blue Tuesday.*"

The mayor's wife sighed. "Oh! Sounds sad."

"It's only sad in certain parts," JP said, having read several different drafts of the script, several times.

"I consider it more of a romantic *dramedy,*" I said, "so it's not a complete downer."

"Perfect!" Vicky exclaimed. "Email it to me, I'll read it *tout suite.*" Her eyes lit up, as if she'd just gotten the most brilliant idea. "And you, John Paul . . . you can perform in Peter's play! I'm sure he's written a role for you." A road map of wrinkles appeared on the older woman's high forehead as she raised her silver brows, hopeful.

"Unfortunately, I can't legally perform in anything non-professional," JP said sadly. "I'm in the actors' union."

"I had a feeling you might say that," the mayor's wife mused. "So, I looked into the rules, and guess what? There's something called a Guest Artist Contract that we can offer you. The pay won't be great. But everything will be above board. To be honest," she said, lowering her voice to a hushed whisper, "our little company isn't doing so hot. Your celebrity could help bring us some attention. A play by PJ Penwell, starring JP Broadway . . ." If this were a cartoon, we'd have seen dollar signs reflected in Vicky Marshall's eyes as she proclaimed: "It's a guaranteed sellout!"

I had to hand it to her. The woman really knew how to work the room. Flattery, as they say, could really get her far.

Caught between the old rock and a hard place, JP and I were both at a loss for words. Until—much like the fantastical plot in my aforementioned stage play—providence intervened.

"You guys wanted to talk to us?"

Glancing up, we discovered Brianna Kim and her handsome husband, Andrew, ready for our little chat. Talk about perfect timing!

"We'll definitely think over your proposal and get back to you," JP promised Vicky.

"I do appreciate your consideration," she acquiesced. "Peter, you'll send me the play?"

"Soon as I'm back at my laptop, and I can find it."

"Wonderful!"

With that, Vicky Marshall, the mayor's wife, rose from our table and returned from whence she had come.

"Bri tells me there's something wrong," Andrew said, sounding alarmed. His hands fell to his hips, revealing hairless, muscular forearms under the rolled-up sleeves of his chef's coat.

As the restaurant had quickly filled up, I felt it best not to cause a public spectacle in our confrontation with the Kims. "Can we take this conversation somewhere a little more private?"

Inside the storage room, among industrial-sized cans of fruits and vegetables, fifty-pound bags of flour, sugar, and various other sundries, I quickly recounted for the couple what we'd earlier discussed with Kyle: how Tom Cash hadn't fallen down a rickety old staircase to his death—he'd been intentionally *pushed*—and why, exactly, Kyle believed that someone had murdered his former lover.

After JP rehashed what Terry had told us at Shout!, regarding the witnessed altercation between the Kims and Tom Cash, Mrs. Kim cried out: "This is completely crazy! We didn't kill anybody!"

"You're right," I said, in full agreement with Mr. Kim's wife. "It *is* crazy! We're just trying to figure out what really happened."

"You said so yourself," JP reminded Brianna, "you guys were angry with Tom after you'd found out about our deal to renovate the Tudor on our TV show."

"You said you wanted to buy the vacant house, tear it down, and put in a parking lot for the restaurant," I added, in case Brianna had conveniently forgotten what she'd stated on the very morning that Tom Cash had died.

"Yes, we did," Andrew admitted. "But . . . we couldn't have murdered Tom even if we'd wanted to. Bri was here on the morning Tom died. I was up in Royal Heights, looking for a new space to move the restaurant."

"That's right!" I said excitedly, thankful for this saving grace. As much as I'd wanted to prove Tom Cash's death wasn't accidental, I also didn't want to go around unjustly accusing our neighbors of a crime. "The open house that Cam hosted . . ." I said, remembering. "I almost forgot about it."

"Well, Cam forgot about it for sure," Andrew said, exasperated. "He never showed up. I arrived right at eleven. He wasn't there. I texted him, I called him. No reply and no answer."

I recalled sending Cam a message myself that morning, to show off the picture of Clyde that I'd taken at the pet store. He didn't text me back all day. When I finally heard from him, he gave me the excuse that something had gone wrong with his phone. But he didn't—or wouldn't—say what the problem had been.

Eventually, we'd learned that Cam had lost his mobile device on our drunken excursion over to the Tudor, on the night of Fairway Bob's dinner party. Hence the cause for his ghosting all who'd reached out to him before he picked up a replacement.

"I stuck around for as long as I could," Andrew Kim continued, returning me to reality in the restaurant storage room. "But I promised Bri I'd get back here A-sap, so I left the open house around eleven-thirty. Still no Campbell Sellers in sight."

If what Andrew Kim had just revealed to us was true . . .

Well, it could only mean one thing: My best friend had totally lied to the authorities about his whereabouts that Saturday morning.

The question was: *Why?*

# Chapter 21

A scream rang out from the second floor of 1 Fairway Lane.

I'd been standing in front of the bathroom mirror, performing my nightly ablutions, when I heard a cry: *"Babe! Come quick!"*

I could only imagine the worst of scenarios, like JP had gotten a text from my sister, after I'd failed to respond right away, informing him that one of my parents had been rushed to the hospital. They were both getting on in age, well into their sixties, although in good health. Still, I couldn't resist going to the dark place. I dashed across the hall and popped my head into the open doorway. "Hon, what's wrong?"

"Look!" My partner lay in our queen-size Mission-style bed, shirtless, beneath the gentle breeze of the overhead ceiling fan. His bare back propped against a pair of fluffy pillows, he held up his cell phone and flashed it at me, along with a ginormous grin.

The image on the screen showed the cutest white puppy, with brown brindle markings on the right side of his face, and a half-moon patch over his left almond-shaped eye.

"Oh!" I cooed, suddenly filled with mixed emotions. "He

reminds me of . . ." I couldn't bring myself to finish the sentence.

JP scooted over and gently patted the empty space beside him on the bed, inviting me to sit. "Come closer."

I didn't want to. While I'd consented to our continued search for a dog to adopt, deep in my heart I didn't *want* to find another dog, because I'd already found the dog that I wanted.

"Read the post . . ." JP offered me his phone. "See what you think."

> *ABOUT ME*
> *Breed: Beagle Mix*
> *Color: White w/ tan*
> *Age: 7 months*
> *Size: Small (25 lbs or less)*
> *Sex: Male*
> *My story: Part of a litter of four surrendered by a*
> *neglectful owner, along with mother, Freckles, a 15 lb*
> *beagle. Clyde is shy at first, but he loves to be held and will*
> *cuddle up for a puppy power lap nap. He is energetic and*
> *loves to play, but not rough like his big sisters.*

My jaw dropped. Had I read the post correctly? The adoptable part beagle puppy's name was *Clyde.*

"Is it—?"

*He had to be our long-lost boy!*

"Just look at that face! How could you not recognize him?"

Ecstatic, I stole another peek at the photo in the post, to be certain our eyes weren't deceiving us. "But Clyde's already been adopted."

JP smiled softly. "Guess the other couple gave him back. Why they'd wanna . . . ?"

I couldn't imagine an acceptable reason to return a poor creature after giving it a home. How heartbreaking it must have been for poor Clydie to be taken to live with his Forever Family, only to be sent back to his foster mom, once again an orphan.

*Were those people insane?*

They'd been given the most precious gift—an adorable animal to love—and they didn't want it?

*Shame on them!*

JP and I vowed, right then and there on that Sunday evening, that we'd see to it that Clyde come to live with us on Fairway Lane in Pleasant Woods, no matter what it took to get him there.

"What're we gonna do?" I mumbled to myself, after agreeing to take on such a daunting task.

"I say we reach out to that woman . . . the one who runs the dog rescue."

"Margot," I said, not one to forget a name. "I'll send her a message right now!"

JP took note of the time on his cell phone. "Babe, it's late. You can just call her in the morning."

It wasn't even midnight.

"It'll just take me a minute." Now that I'd made up my mind, there was no stopping the force that was Peter "PJ" Penwell.

Hopping off the bed, I scurried around to my own side, taking care not to scrape myself on the sharp corner of the frame's footboard. I snatched up my mobile phone from the nightstand, sitting back down, and opened the internet browser.

JP cozied up next to me and glanced over my shoulder. "Do you have Margot's email?"

My thumbs tap-danced across the on-screen keyboard. "I'll contact her via the Home FurEver website."

After locating the proper page, I began putting down the most important words I'd written in a long time . . .

*Dear Margot,*

*I hope you'll remember me. My name is PJ Penwell. My partner, JP Broadway, and I host a rehab show on HDTV called Domestic Partners.*

*A few weeks back we had the pleasure of meeting you at an adoption event in Madison Park, my hometown. You may recall that we recently moved to Michigan after living in New York City for almost 10 years, which is where JP and I met.*

*At the adoption event, we spoke to you about a little beagle-bull puppy named Clyde, and we even put in an application to adopt him. Sadly, we later discovered on your website that you had posted photos of Clyde with a happy looking couple and their children, which led us to believe he had been adopted by another family.*

*But tonight, we came across a new posting with Clyde's picture, so we're wondering if he is once again available for adoption?*

*JP and I live in Pleasant Woods, between Royal Heights and Fernridge. We'd be happy to meet with you at your convenience, if Clyde is indeed still looking for a new home.*

*Could you please just let me know? Thank you!*

I hit send, without bothering to proofread or to ask for JP's approval. We couldn't afford to waste a single precious moment.

I couldn't sleep.

Reaching for my cell phone resting atop the nightstand,

I powered it on and checked the time of the early morning hour: *6:23 a.m.* JP lay next to me, facing the opposite direction. Outside, the sun had already begun to light up the bedroom, through the crack in the blackout curtains. Still, I lowered the brightness level on my screen, so as not to rouse my partner with the blue-white glow.

Since I always woke up earlier than he did, I'd use the extra time in bed to scroll through the daily news, starting with my horoscope . . .

> SCORPIO (October 20–November 21)
> Today's Sun-Mercury aspect in your sign favors big life
> changes. You could soon see the expansion of your household
> with a new addition to the family. Be wary of close friends,
> or relatives, harboring a secret. All is not what it seems.

Miss Zelda, the online astrologer that I followed, could be spot-on when it came to her readings. Other times, she got it totally wrong. More than ever, I wanted to believe what she'd predicted for me on this particular Monday. Surely, the family expansion meant a new fur baby! The person harboring a secret, I feared, could only be one friend: Campbell Sellers.

Since our meeting with Andrew and Brianna Kim the morning before, I'd been contemplating what we'd learned from the couple, regarding Cam's missing his open house on the day that Tom Cash died.

Where might Cam have been at that moment . . . and what could he have been doing . . . and did I really want to learn the answers to either of these questions?

I needed to get my mind off the negative thoughts and focus on the positive meaning of Miss Zelda's zodiacal message!

With a tap on the tiny envelope icon on my phone screen, my email popped open. A quick scan of the spam that flooded my in-box caused my stomach to drop. Three lines down from the top—directly below an almost realistic warning that my online credit card account password had been compromised—I discovered exactly what I'd been hoping to find: a message from Margot at Home FurEver, with the subject line: *Clyde*.

*Hi PJ & JP,*

*So good to hear from you! Yes, Clyde was adopted, but the family decided that an adult dog would be better suited for their home, so he is available once again.*

*When we met last time, I don't think I realized that you guys lived in Pleasant Woods. I grew up on Roycroft Road, near the library and cultural center. I will be dropping by there later this afternoon to visit my parents.*

*If you are free, I could stop by your house when I'm in the neighborhood to conduct a home visit. If everything goes well, I'd be happy to grant your adoption of Clyde.*

*Please give me a call to arrange a time that works well for you both.*

*Best, Margot*
*248-555-0842*

My heart had begun to beat faster with each word of the email that I'd read. Everything was coming together, according to the master plan we'd laid out for our future. We'd found ourselves an historic house to renovate, and move into, just like we'd wanted. Now we were being given a second chance at adopting the dog of our dreams, after thinking all hope had been lost.

As my mother always said: *Everything happens for a reason.*

We may not have gotten our Clydie Boy the first time around, but . . . *It doesn't matter how you get there. The point is you arrive.*

As much as I wanted to, it was far too early to call Margot on the phone. The email she'd sent had come in late last evening, so I presumed her to be a night owl and probably still asleep, like JP. A freight train passing through our bedroom couldn't wake the guy once he was dead to the world. Me, I suffered from chronic insomnia. Anxiety only made the condition worsen. No way could I fall back to sleep with my veins full of adrenaline. So, I did the next best thing: I emailed Margot back.

> *Hello again!*
> *Thanks for your prompt reply to my totally random message. I appreciate your getting back to me with the news about Clyde being available for adoption again.*
> *JP and I will definitely take you up on your kind offer to stop by this afternoon for a home visit. We will be here all day, so just let us know what time you will be in your old neighborhood.*
> *Take care,*
> *PJ*
> *347.555.5927*

My partner rolled over and caught me staring at my phone. "What time is it?"

"Early," I whispered. "But since you're awake . . . guess what?" Bursting at the seams, I gave JP the good news, in full voice: "Margot emailed me back!"

After reading over the message, we were both too excited to remain in bed, so we got up and headed downstairs. I began the morning's task of brewing a half pot of coffee and unloading the dishwasher, while JP commenced cooking our breakfast.

As we ate, listening to *Detroit Today* on our local NPR station, WDET, we prepped for our meeting with Margot . . .

"We need to totally puppy-proof this place!" JP anxiously announced, blowing on a bite of steamy scrambled egg.

"I know!" Suddenly, I felt super nervous. "But what, exactly, does that entail?"

"No idea."

"Me neither."

"When we were kids," JP said, "we got our dog from a breeder. There wasn't any quote-unquote adoption process, let alone a home visit."

"Well, we got Lucky from the neighbor on the corner. They asked did we want a puppy? We said yes. They said pick one out. We did."

"*Pete!*" JP cried, bordering on hysterical. "We can't blow this meeting. Margot will never let us adopt Clyde if she thinks we're unfit."

"We aren't *unfit* . . . are we?"

JP's fear of our not making a good impression had started to wear off on me. I began doubting my own ability to love and care for a small animal. Finally, I could comprehend how parents felt, being handed a newborn infant at the hospital and told to take it home and see what happens. The possibilities for disaster were endless!

"We can do this," JP decided, after careful consideration . . . and several cups of coffee. "We need to come up with a master plan. Like we did with proving Tom Cash was really murdered."

"But we still haven't proven a thing." I didn't mean to be a downer, just simply state a fact.

"But we *will*."

I took hold of my partner's hand as it rested on the recently waxed antique tabletop. "I admire your confidence, Mr. Broadway."

"First we adopt a dog," JP determined. "Then we catch a killer."

Famous last words, I hoped these weren't, as I cleared away the remains of our morning meal.

We cleaned the entire house from top to bottom; vacuumed the rugs, mopped the floors, dusted every exposed surface. Down in the dusty basement, we discovered an old screen tucked in the cubby under the stairs and positioned it in front of the living room fireplace. We'd yet to have it serviced, so it wasn't something we were using. But we had every intention of having a new gas line installed, since we'd been told before we bought the house that the current model was more than likely original. A *flamethrower* is how the home inspector had described it.

We wanted to make sure that Margot realized that *we* realized that having a wide-open hole in the wall, full of soot, wasn't a safe place for a puppy to play.

Outside, our backyard gave us additional cause for alarm . . .

JP peered around for potential hazards to address before Margot's eminent arrival. "What about the fence?"

"What about it? We don't have one."

Well, we had a divider on part of our property line, separating our yard from Fairway Bob's: a white cedar shadow box that he'd installed when he first got Willie. The man who'd lived in our home prior to us, Mr. Voisin, must have preferred a more natural—read: overgrown—look to his yard. His idea of a border had been to plant a wall of unruly shrubs along the perimeter and then never trim them. Those we tore out on *Domestic Partners* season one, episode one.

"I know we don't have a fence!" JP whined. "That's why I'm worried! Did your backyard have one, when you were a kid and you got a dog?"

"It did. A short, ugly, steel gray cyclone. Just like all the other houses in Madison Park."

"So did mine! Well, ours was wood," JP said, in not so

many words reminding me that he'd grown up in a more well-off neighborhood. "We can't have a puppy, Pete, without a fenced-in backyard!"

As much as I wanted to tell my partner that now was not the time to take this factor into account, I could sense his anxiety and didn't want to stoke the flames. "We're having a fence built. We've already discussed it. We just need to get the number of the guy who did Bob's next door, so our fence can match his."

JP shook his head spastically, starting to panic. "Do you think Margot will believe us?"

"Um, yes . . ." Placing my hand on his shoulder, I eased my partner down onto the wood steps of our sun porch. We sat together in silence a few moments, feeling the warmth of the summer sun on our faces.

As I gazed out over the quiet, I tried imagining what the yard would look like come next spring. Once we'd finished up with shooting season two of our TV show, we could take some time to focus on fixing things up the way we'd wanted. Our goal was to put in a patio, along with some outdoor furniture covered by an umbrella, string up some lights between the oak trees, and set up a grilling area for holiday barbecues.

All my dreams were finally coming to fruition.

Never had I imagined, five years ago, that I'd be back in Michigan, living in my very own home with the man I loved and our very own doggie . . .

And yet, I still harbored a feeling of dread.

# Chapter 22

Margot arrived promptly at one o'clock.

With open arms, we welcomed the dog-rescue woman into our home for our official home visit. We had no other choice. No sooner had she stepped through the French door of our front foyer, and across our living room threshold, did Margot reach out her milky-white arms and envelop both me and my partner in the warmest of embraces.

"So good seeing you both again!" Her attitude toward us had done a complete one-eighty, and it all had started the moment I'd mentioned that JP and I resided in Pleasant Woods.

"Thanks for coming by on such short notice," I said, intentionally trying to show Margot my gratitude. I almost hadn't recognized her, save for the shock of scarlet hair.

She wasn't wearing her purple HOME FUREVER T-shirt as she had been when we'd first met in person and in every photo of her posted on the website. Instead, she'd dressed more conservatively, in pale summer slacks and a muted cotton blouse. Was the change in appearance meant to impress us, I wondered, or perhaps her parents?

"You have a beautiful home!" Margot glanced around at

the olive vine-painted plaster walls, the Pewabic tile fireplace, complete with newly added safety screen covering the opening, and the Stickley spindle sofa, cube chair, and coffee table, all in matching Fayetteville finish #035.

"Thank you," PJ humbly replied. "Won't you please come in and have a seat?"

Margot positioned herself on the Stickley ottoman. It wasn't meant to be an actual sitting spot. But I didn't want to insult the woman by asking her to move elsewhere.

"We were very lucky when we found this place," I said. "As you know from growing up here, buying in Pleasant Woods is no easy feat."

"Definitely not! Someone pretty much has to drop dead for a house to hit the market," Margot joked. Her statement, while no laughing matter, held a weight of truth.

"That's literally what happened," I revealed. "The man who lived here before us *did* die. Poor guy."

Margot nodded with recognition. "Whit Voisin? Yes, I heard he passed," she said mournfully. "He was only in his mid-sixties, can you believe it?"

JP and I stared at each other, startled by Margot's remark. "He was?" we both said, practically at the exact same time.

This bit of information came as a surprise.

"Everyone we talk to keeps referring to Mr. Voisin as an *old* man," I explained to Margot. "We assumed he was more like ninety."

The dog-rescue woman tossed her red head back and chuckled at the overexaggeration. "No! Whit went to high school with my brother, Mike. He's sixty-four."

"So, you actually knew Mr. Voisin?" JP asked. He relished the prospect of discussing our home's former owner whenever he'd gotten the chance. "What was he like?"

"Well, he was older than me, so I didn't know him all that good," Margot said. "He never married, so he lived here with his folks till they died. I assume he inherited this house, being an only child."

"See? That all makes sense," I said. "We were told by the historical commission that we're only the second owners. Explains why so much of the house is still original."

"That's the thing I love about Pleasant Woods," Margot said. "People here take care of their historic homes. Lots of places, the yuppies come in and buy up the old houses. They either tear 'em down and build brand-new or they gut the insides and make 'em all modern. Breaks my heart."

"Us too," I said, chiming in as a fellow kindred spirit.

"That's pretty much the whole premise of our TV show. We renovate and restore. Rarely do we remodel," JP told Margot.

She rose to her feet and peered through the archway into the dining room. "And that's what you guys did with this place? I can tell! It was in pretty bad shape by the time Whit's parents retired. I can only imagine it got worse once they were gone."

"Fixing it up was a project, that's for sure," JP admitted. "But we're glad we took it on."

"So glad," I gushed. "We love living here."

Margot nodded, agreeing with our enthusiasm. "That's cuz it's a great house! It was always one of my favorites. A guy I dated in high school grew up across the street. I used to ride my bike over to see him . . . always passed by here on my way down the alley."

"Really?" I said, my mind racing to unravel the mystery of who Margot's old beau might have been. "Your boyfriend lived here on Fairway Lane?"

Margot reflected within, thinking back to her childhood, some thirty-odd years ago. A soft smile indicated that the memories of her past were nothing but pleasant. "He did!

You know the vacant Tudor at number four? It belonged to his family."

"Did you say number four?" Clearly, she had. But I wanted to carry on this conversation with the dog-rescue woman a bit longer, for purely personal reasons. "The Cashes lived in that house, didn't they?" Obviously, they had. We knew that for a fact. But, again, I hoped to keep the dog-rescue woman talking, to show that JP and I were interested in her for more than just what she could give to us.

"They did! Terry and Tommy. The three of us went to school together . . . kindergarten up through graduation."

In Pleasant Woods, a small town without its own educational system, the majority of children who lived in the suburb attended Fernridge Public Schools. Especially the ones from the east side.

"Do you guys know the twins?" Margot asked us, sounding thrilled by the prospect of her worlds colliding. "Or I should say . . ." The words caught in her throat. She silenced herself, before she could fully acknowledge that one of her classmates was no longer of this world.

"We do know Tom and Terry!" JP answered. "Well, we met Tom once, right before . . ." He, too, couldn't bring himself to finish his sentence, out of respect for the dead man's childhood friend.

"A terrible tragedy, wasn't it?" Margot's voice softened, full of great sadness. "Tommy was so young! I mean, I know we're a lot older than you guys . . ."

"Not by much," I said. "Like fifteen years, maybe?"

Margot balked, bewildered. "You're only thirty-five? Such babies!"

"I'm thirty-five," JP revealed, ready to rat me out. "Pete's only thirty-*three*."

At any other given moment, I'd want to make someone

fully aware of just how young I was, compared to my partner. But with Margot, I felt the need for her to see me as a responsible adult, capable of caring for a special puppy like Clyde. "I'll be thirty-four on November twenty-first," I stated, dreading my upcoming natal day.

We needed for Margot to tell us more about her past relationships with the Cash twins, in case any detail—sordid or innocent—might point us toward a suspect in the deceased brother's murder.

"So, you dated Terry Cash in high school, you said?"

Margot stared at me blankly. "Did I say that? Because I didn't. Say it, or date Terry."

"Oh. My bad. I thought you said you dated a guy in high school who lived across the street."

"I did. But he wasn't Terry Cash. I used to go out with *Tommy*. He even took me to prom, senior year."

Why had I assumed that, out of a pair of gay twin brothers, Terry Cash would have been the one in his youth to date a girl? They were both masculine men, in their own right. Either could have passed for straight had they wanted to. But with Tom having gotten around with so many guys—my best friend Cam, Danny the bartender, Kyle Young—I figured his sexuality would have long ago been fixed.

It seemed odd, though, as identical twins, that Tom received all the attention when the men looked exactly alike, down to the slight gap between their two front teeth. Why weren't any men—or women, for that matter—attracted to brother Terry now? He was plenty good-looking enough, and as prime a physical specimen as his sibling, maybe even more so.

Perhaps something deep within his heart had, all these years, prevented Terrence Cash from finding true love?

"We're actually working with Terry on a project," JP

informed Margot, "for the upcoming season of our TV show."

"Is that a fact?" The dog-rescue woman's Michigan accent pierced the air with her nasally vowel placement. "How is old Ter doing? I haven't seen him since his parents' funeral, like twenty-five years ago. I looked for him on social media, could never find him."

"Terry's good. Seems like he's a bit . . . ?" Searching for the right word to describe his disposition, I hesitated.

Margot offered a suggestion: "Shy?"

"Well, he was for sure when we first met him," JP said. "But he's starting to warm up the more we get to know him."

"That's true, come to think of it," I concurred. "Ever since Tom passed, Terry's been a lot more . . . ?"

Margot supplied yet another descriptor for her former boyfriend's twin brother: "Friendly?"

"Friendly, open, eager," JP decided. "It was actually Terry's idea for us to renovate his parents' old house."

Margot gaped at JP in disbelief. "The project you're working on with Terry Cash is at Four Fairway?"

"It's not *at* Four Fairway," I answered. "It *is* Four Fairway. We're renovating the entire home."

Margot scratched her chin lightly as she contemplated this tidbit. "No kidding?"

"Once we finish, we're pretty sure Terry plans on selling," JP presumed.

Had Margot been an animated character, her eyes would have bugged out of her head, and her tongue would have unraveled like a paper noisemaker on New Year's Eve, accompanied by the honk of an antique car horn or maybe a kazoo.

"You're pulling my leg," she said, laughing. "Last time I seen Terry Cash, he was dead set on keeping his folks' old house exactly the way it was when they died."

Neither of us knew what to say in response to the dog-rescue woman, other than what our signed contract with Terry Cash had stated.

"He was pretty against the project at first," JP recalled. "But after Tom passed, Terry asked us to tackle the rehab in honor of his brother."

"Right," I said, adding my two cents. "Terry said it was Tom's dying wish to have us renovate the house, so he wanted to make sure it happened. We start work on the project a week from today."

Margot broke down in hysterics.

Once she could finally catch her breath, she divulged an incredible piece of information: "There's no way on God's green earth that Terry Cash would touch his dead parents' house. Especially in honor of his dead brother. Terry resented Tommy with every fiber of his being."

Margot's statement checked out with what Fairway Bob had told us at Tom Cash's funeral, with regards to no love being lost between the brothers . . .

But *why* did Terry despise his twin, Tom?

"All through school, Terry was nothing but mean to poor Tommy," Margot elaborated. "He made fun of him cuz he got good grades and people liked him. Just about broke my heart, since Tommy showed nothing but love for his brother. That's the reason he took Terry in, after their folks died, and gave him a place to stay in that big house on Borman Avenue."

"So, they didn't always live together?" JP inquired, trying to piece together the puzzle that Margot had been presenting. "You hear about twins being inseparable . . ."

"Not those guys! Terry had his own apartment down in Fernridge. But he got kicked out cuz he couldn't pay the rent, on account of he couldn't hold down a job. That's why

Tommy hired him to work the door at that bar of his when he opened it." Margot lowered her voice, as if the ghost of Mr. Voisin were eavesdropping through the plaster walls. "No disrespect. But Terry was always a bit of a screwup. Even his own dad preferred Tommy as a son . . . and Terry could tell. To be honest, I was worried sick for Tommy's safety."

"May I ask why?" I said, growing fearful with each additional detail of Margot's story.

"Between us, Terry was so jealous of Tommy . . . heck, I wouldn't be surprised if Terry up and *killed* Tommy and made it look like an accident."

A hush fell over our home as JP and I reflected on Margot's last statement. Had Terry Cash been our prime suspect in his brother's death all along, and we'd failed to consider it, all because he'd simply proclaimed his innocence?

Margot let out a huff. "Well, enough depressing talk about the Cash twins. I'm here for a happy puppy home visit."

JP and I both sat up straight and tall, as if having good posture would help to impress the dog-rescue woman. "What do you need from us?" I asked, crossing my fingers for good luck.

"Nothing. I've seen enough," Margot said with a smile. "You guys are great. I know you'll take good care of Clyde." She started toward the front door, pausing a moment to turn back for one final bon mot: "Feel free to mention Home FurEver on your TV show sometime."

*That was it?*

Everything had all come together so easily. Now we just needed to pick up our new fur baby at the upcoming adoption event on Sunday and bring him home.

The next six days would be murder—hopefully not in the literal sense.

As soon as Margot had gone, I called my best friend. We'd gotten out of the habit of actually talking on the phone, unlike in high school where our conversations could go on for hours. But this news was big. I wanted to share it with Cam himself. Not via a text or some other automated message.

"Is everything okay?" he asked, picking up on the very first ring. "Are you in trouble? Where's JP?"

"Yes. No. He's right here," I answered playfully. "We just had our home visit with Margot from Home FurEver."

*"And . . . ?"*

After sharing the details of the past half hour—including Margot's scandalous high school love affair with our late neighbor, Tom Cash—I felt the need to confront Campbell with what my partner and I had recently learned while brunching at Chianti.

"You told Nick Paczki that you couldn't have killed Tom Cash because you were at an open house up in Royal Heights at the time Tom died."

The sound of silence filled my earbuds.

"Didn't you?"

"I did."

"Okay. Well, the PWPD determined that Tom Cash died between ten-forty-five and eleven-fifteen . . ."

"Uh-huh."

"And Andrew Kim said he showed up to your open house right at eleven, and he stayed until around eleven-thirty."

"Uh-huh."

"Well, according to Andrew, the entire time he was at your open house . . . he didn't see you."

"So, what are you trying to say?" Cam said, from the comfort of his home down the block.

Inhaling deeply, I mentally prepared myself to pose the question I'd been formulating all day, but I'd been too afraid to utter aloud: "What, exactly, did you do on the morning Tom Cash died?"

Through the speaker on my cell phone, I could hear Cam's breath quicken.

He was definitely hiding something.

# Chapter 23

*The morning of the murder . . .*

The Realtor Extraordinaire woke up late that Saturday, having gotten home close to eleven o'clock the night before. Instead of heading right to bed, as he knew he should have, Campbell Sellers had settled down on the couch for some cuddle time with his American Staffordshire terrier, Snoop, after pouring himself another glass of wine.

It was his *fifth* of the evening.

There'd been the four chardonnays, courtesy of Fairway Bob, at dinner, followed by a flinty Sancerre with a ripe gooseberry aroma that he'd opened upon his return. The chilled French vintage sure did hit the spot, particularly after the falling out he'd had in the middle of Fairway Lane with his ex-lover, Thomas Cash.

Cam knew that his behavior had bordered on the hysterical. Blame it on the alcohol, but he'd felt a serious betrayal when Tom flat-out refused to grant him the future listing to his parents' former home. Once the updates were completed, and the house ready to hit the market, Cam felt that he could fetch four—if not five—hundred thousand dollars for the sale of the newly renovated property, seizing a sizable commission for his efforts.

To learn that the agent Tom had chosen over him was a novice in the real estate biz . . . this revelation made Cam feel both jilted and humiliated. Not to mention the national exposure he'd miss out on, as a result of appearing on his good pals' hit HDTV home rehab program.

Cam didn't necessarily *need* the attention. Already he counted himself among the top-performing Realtors in the state of Michigan. Still, the accolades and monetary rewards weren't quite enough. Deep within, Campbell Sellers felt a longing. Never would he admit to being jealous of his best friend Peter "PJ" Penwell's success, first as a published author and more recently a television personality.

Yet he was.

More so, Cam envied the longtime, committed relationship of the TV show cohosts.

At thirty-four years old, he'd grown tired of the local gay scene. He'd run into the same old queens, weekend after drunken weekend, since moving back to Metro Detroit in his mid-twenties, after graduating from Central Michigan University. A full decade Cam had spent looking for love at places like Shout! Truth be told, he just couldn't seem to find the right guy.

Nor did he think he ever would.

*My phone!*

Cam shot bolt upright in his king-size bed, where he'd slept close beside his beloved Snoop on yet another Friday. After he'd polished off the bottle of vino the night before, he'd realized his brand-new mobile device had mysteriously gone missing. He'd been in such a manic state the rest of the evening that he could barely fall asleep, thinking how all his contacts—the lifeblood of his business—were contained in that single piece of technology. Plus, Cam had nothing to do before drifting off, without access to a news feed, social network, or one of the real estate apps he habitually perused, checking out the competition.

He had contemplated hopping into his car, driving across town to Tom Cash's house on Borman Avenue, and forcing the man to return to the Tudor Revival, so that he could retrieve his missing cell phone. But Cam passed out from all the alcohol he'd consumed, which in retrospect, had probably been for the best.

Thinking back through the foggy haze, he came to the conclusion that he must have lost the mobile somewhere between leaving Bob's house and heading back home, after making the drunken trip across the street to 4 Fairway, along with TV's favorite domestic partners, PJ and JP.

*I need to find that phone, ASAP!*

Cam could feel Snoop's sleek, fawn-colored fur, snuggled up close against his lower lumbar. He rolled over, trying not to rouse the snoring canine, when a sharp pain set the side of his hip aflame. Immediately, a flash of lightning lit up the darkness of his mind's eye . . .

He remembered his right hand grasping frantically for the carved wood banister affixed to the rickety old staircase. In his memory, Cam could clearly see the heel of his left foot slipping on the loose stair board, his center of gravity being thrown off balance. He recalled the moment he'd regained his composure and fell backward on his bottom. Perhaps this was the source of the dull soreness he was now feeling along his left flank?

Cam flipped off the covers and pulled down the waistband of his plaid boxer shorts. Sure enough, a bluish-colored bruise graced the side of his upper thigh. He breathed a sigh of relief, thankful that he'd only suffered a minor injury. He could easily have fallen face-first down the old steps, landed on his head, and broken his neck.

*What an awful way to leave this world!*

Cam shuddered to himself before crawling out of the big bed, closely followed by his furry shadow. "Easy, boy," he told the pit bull in a china shop, staring into the pup's light brown eyes. Poor Snoop! He always looked so anxious. "Wanna go outside?"

Cam didn't have to ask the dog twice.

On his way downstairs, he lamented the fact that he couldn't drag himself out of bed any sooner. He'd reached over, once too often, to hit the snooze on the old-timey alarm clock that he hadn't used in more years than he could recall. It pained him that he'd already lost his brand-new phone.

Sure, he'd purchased an insurance policy. He could easily pick up another and have all his content transferred over from the original. But Cam had an open house scheduled for eleven o'clock that very morning. He knew there could be potential clients trying to reach him; one in particular who'd been eyeing this specific piece of property, the oh-so-attractive co-owner of the wine pub at the end of the block, Andrew Kim.

Cam let Snoop out the back door into the yard, hoping his barking wouldn't wake the neighbors if he should happen upon a chipmunk or squirrel. Or perhaps a bunny rabbit, trying to invade the pooch's turf?

By the time Cam's bare feet hit the heated floor of the bathroom, it was already close to nine. This left him with less than ninety minutes to shower, shave, dress, eat breakfast, take Snoop for his morning walk, and drive up to Royal Heights, still arriving plenty early to set up for the event.

As the steamy water cascaded across his weary body, Campbell Sellers kept telling himself there was something else he needed to take care of, in addition to retrieving his lost cell phone. Before he could truly get on with his day, he needed to make amends with a certain someone.

Dressed in a cool linen summer suit, Cam walked briskly into his open concept kitchen. The heels of his Italian leather loafers clacked lightly against the ceramic tile. He quickly flashed his wrist, checking the time on the gray-blue face of his Shinola Guardian watch: *10:18 a.m.*

As he filled an insulated travel mug with piping-hot coffee, Cam snuck a peek out the side window, just above the deep stainless-steel sink that he'd had installed upon moving into 11 Fairway Lane ten years ago.

Kitty-corner across the street, Tom Cash continued his task of tidying up his parents' former property, in order to appease the old man who resided next door. He yanked the starter cord on a gas-powered lawn mower, causing the motor to spring to life after a single pull.

Campbell Sellers had approximately ten minutes to run over, apologize for his immature behavior—and see if he could find his missing phone—before jumping into his Jeep and heading to Royal Heights for the upcoming open house.

While he was groveling, Cam thought he could try convincing Tom Cash, one more time, to give him the future listing for his childhood home. He figured it was worth a shot; why not? The worst that his former lover could do was remain steadfast in his decision to bestow Cheri Maison, lesbian chic Realtor—and Cam's newest rival—with the honor.

"Be a good boy," Cam cooed. "Daddy will be back soon." He gave Snoop a firm pat on his big melon head and a scratch behind the ears, then headed through the front door.

Outside, at the Tudor Revival, Cam kept his distance on the sidewalk, so as not to startle the handsome older man pushing the potentially hazardous piece of machinery. "Hey, Tom!" he shouted over the roar of the mowing machine. "Can I talk to you?"

Tom came to the far end of the yard, leaving a trail of lawn clippings in his wake. He turned the mower around in the opposite direction and diligently began pushing again. After a few feet, he looked up.

Cam wiggled his fingers in a friendly wave.

Tom released the safety shut-off lever he'd been holding onto tightly, and the engine sputtered to a stop. He wiped the perspiration from his brow with the back of his large paw. "You here to murder me?" Tom put up his two hands, just to playfully prove that he wasn't armed or dangerous. *"Stop! Please! Don't!"*

"Funny," Cam replied, blushing slightly.

Before he could continue explaining why he'd showed up unannounced that morning, Cam found himself interrupted by a hoarse cry coming from next door.

"Keep up the good work!" Hank Richards called from his Cape Cod's cinder block front porch.

"The yard is starting to look lovely!" Hank's wife of over fifty years, Hennie, complimented. "Hi, Campbell! How are you, sweetie?" She blew her favorite neighbor a big kiss, then headed inside the house with her husband.

"They must have Tigers tickets," Cam remarked.

The Richards were most likely on their way to a baseball game at Comerica Park later that afternoon, judging by the way the older couple was dressed in matching navy and orange gear.

"Sorry, you were saying?" Tom said to Cam, picking up where they'd left off.

The Realtor thought a moment. "I was saying . . . ? Right! I think I left my brand-new phone at your house. It's got all my work contacts in it, so I really need to get it back."

"When were you at my house?" Tom asked, intentionally playing dumb. "Been a few years since we . . ." He made a lewd gesture.

"Your parents' house," Cam clarified, growing tired of Tom's little game, charming as it may have been. He nodded toward the Tudor Revival. "*This* house."

Tom took a step closer to Cam. "Well, what'd you do that for?"

"I didn't mean to," Cam huffed. "I tripped coming down your crappy old staircase. Almost killed myself. My phone must've fallen out of my pocket when I landed flat on my butt."

Tom snapped the spearmint gum he'd been chewing, working his square jaw. "Your *cute* butt."

"Easy, mister! You lost your right to compliment me four years ago . . . when you broke up with me. Besides . . ." Cam folded his arms in defiance. "I don't think your new *boyfriend* would appreciate you noticing my backside. So quit it."

"I didn't notice it," Tom admitted. "Got a good memory, is all."

Cam rolled his eyes, refusing to be played. "Whatever."

"You want your phone? You need to start being nice to me."

"I *am* nice to you!"

"You weren't nice to me last night."

"That's because you betrayed me."

"Stop being so dramatic!" Tom Cash ordered his ex. "It's not gonna kill you to lose out on one listing. You think you really need it more than Cheri does?"

"This isn't about whether I need it. It's about the fact that you were my boyfriend for almost three whole years. Now you're not, you act like I'm nothing to you."

"Soup . . ." Tom called his former lover by his pet name, which he'd coined after the food giant, famous for their condensed tomato in a can that shared Cam's full first name. He reached out to touch the younger man tenderly on the shoulder.

"Please don't." Cam jerked away, feeling the sting of salty tears. "You broke my heart when you cheated on me with Danny. And you broke Danny's heart, I'm sure, when you cheated on him with . . . what's his name? The new kid."

"His name is Kyle," Tom said. "And he's not a kid, he's almost twenty-nine."

"Oh! And we know what that means," Cam quipped. "Somebody'd better warn poor Kyle, pretty soon he's gonna be too old for Daddy Tom to play with anymore."

Tom Cash looked his former lover in the eyes. "You want the phone or not? Let's go and get it."

"Can we please make it quick?" Cam said, snappish. "I'm running late for work."

"Then stop talking and start walking," Tom told him, giving the attitude right back, before he turned and led the way.

Cam followed the handsome older man through the storybook entrance into the rundown Tudor Revival. Before he could search for his missing mobile phone, they were interrupted by marimba music playing at full volume.

Tom didn't answer the call right away. Instead, he glanced at the screen, a sour expression on his handsome face. "Give me one sec." He firmly tapped the glass on his phone screen, before forcefully placing the device to his ear. *"What?"*

Cam intentionally gazed away, out the front windows onto Fairway Lane. "Yes, I'm busy!" he could hear Tom bark from behind him.

Across the street, Cam could see Fairway Bob returning home from his morning walk with Willie. He looked particularly summery, sporting a floral print shirt, khaki shorts, and woven sandals. Willie's shiny dark coat glistened in the morning sun.

Starting to grow impatient, Cam checked his wristwatch as he waited for Tom to finish his phone call: *10:33 a.m.* Up in Royal Heights, potential home buyers would start arriving for the open house soon enough. Cam's anxiety level shot through the roof as he realized he needed to move along on his merry way.

"If you listened when I talk," Tom calmly told the person he'd been arguing with, "I wouldn't have to tell you twice."

Cam turned around in order to try and get Tom's attention. All he got was a view of the other man's broad back.

"I'm *not* changing my mind about the house!" Tom shouted, his booming voice reverberating off the plaster walls.

During the course of their relationship, Campbell Sellers and Tom Cash had had their fair share of disagreements. The berating tone, in that moment, made Cam grateful that he wasn't on the receiving end of his ex-boyfriend's anger. "I gotta go," he whispered, waving goodbye.

The missing new cell phone would have to wait.

Cam darted down the steps of the Tudor Revival's wide front porch, completely unaware. He'd just said farewell to his greatest love for the final time . . .

Ever.

# Chapter 24

*Ten days after the murder . . .*

The detective met us on the sidewalk outside Town Hall. Under the pretense of casually catching up, I'd scheduled an appointment to chat with my sister Pamela's high school boyfriend, Nick Paczki. In all actuality, JP and I had made the short walk across Woodward, from our home on Fairway Lane, to ask for the hunky officer's help in catching Tom Cash's killer.

After what Cam had confessed forty-eight hours ago, we *Domestic Partners in Crime* had decided it was time to bring the police on board with our private, possible murder investigation. Since Nick had been a close family friend for a number of years, I felt that he could be completely trusted.

"Another beautiful day, huh?" The detective led the way, past the community gardens, just south of the old-timey police booth that served as Pleasant Woods's modern-day Historical Museum.

"I can't get over this weather," I marveled, the afternoon sun warming our faces as we strolled along.

During that final week of July, the mercury had barely climbed past the seventy-five degree mark, while the relative humidity remained rather low, making for a pretty good hair day.

"We promise we won't keep you long," JP assured the policeman. "We're just waiting for Campbell Sellers to join us."

Nick looked at us, warily. "Oh?"

"He's showing a house over on Roycroft Road," I explained. "He'll be here in like ten minutes, as soon as he's finished."

"Okaaay . . ." The handsome cop flicked the tip of his tongue against his bristly upper lip. "Why do I feel like this is an ambush?"

We settled on a spot near the Grecian fountain situated in the center of Town Square. The cool spray felt refreshing as I leaned against the marble base, listening to the dialogue between Detective Nick Paczki and my best friend, Campbell Sellers, Realtor Extraordinaire.

"Let me get this straight," the police officer said, piecing together the details that Cam had just presented. "You lied to me and your lawyer when we brought you in for questioning?"

"I didn't *lie*," Cam said. "I just didn't completely tell the truth. Besides, you and Rana kept insisting our chat was completely off the record. We were just three friends talking about our poor dead neighbor, and you wondered if maybe I knew anything about his unfortunate death?"

Nick consulted his notes. "Well, I thought we already cleared that up. It says here . . ." He scrolled to the next page on his phone. "You said: 'I definitely couldn't have killed Tom. I was hosting an open house in Royal Heights that morning. It started at eleven o'clock.' Now you tell me you didn't arrive at the open house till after eleven-thirty. So, where were you between the time you left Fairway Lane and the time you got to Royal Heights?"

"Believe it or not," Cam said, clearly embarrassed by what he was about to reveal, "I was stuck in traffic. I thought I could get up to Royal Heights quicker if I hopped on the freeway. So I did. But I totally forgot about the stupid construction, all thanks to our fair governor's obsession with fixing the damn roads. Don't get me wrong, I love the woman. I gave money to her campaign. I even canvassed on her behalf. But every weekend there's another detour? I mean, seriously! It took me like forty-five minutes to drive two miles. And . . ." Cam's pitch escalated, along with his blood pressure. "I couldn't call anyone to let them know I was running late, since I lost my phone the night before."

"Which is why you went over to Four Fairway on the morning Tom died," Detective Paczki recalled, "so you could get your phone back?"

"Correct."

"Then why did you lie to Rana and me?" Nick asked next, questioning Cam's less-than-honest actions.

He cried out like a wounded animal, caught in a trap. *"I didn't lie!"*

Without raising his voice, the police detective continued berating the real estate agent. "You told us you were at the open house in Royal Heights when Tom Cash died . . . now you say you were stuck on the freeway."

"Well, what's it matter?" Cam said, clearly confused. "So long as I was nowhere near the Tudor at the time of Tom's death . . . which I wasn't."

It pained me to watch two people I'd known for as long as I could remember having words over an issue that I'd had a hand in bringing about. It had been my idea for my best friend to tell my sister's ex-BF the truth about where he was on the morning Tom Cash died, in order to save his reputation—and save himself from serving time for a crime that he didn't commit. Once word had gotten out, via Andrew Kim, that Cam wasn't where he said he'd been at the exact time he said he'd been there, he was going to look guilty for sure.

The least I could do was step in and say something to Nick Paczki to try and help clear the air.

"What I think Cam is trying to say," I said. "I think he was worried you and Rana, his lawyer, would think he had something to do with Tom Cash's death, being Tom's spurned ex-boyfriend and all. He knew that if he gave you guys a credible alibi, you'd believe he was innocent."

Cam regarded me with a sense of relief. "That's exactly it! Thank you, Peter."

"Cam," the police detective said, sounding slightly betrayed. "How long have we known each other? I may be a cop. But I'm your friend first. You could've just told me the truth."

Cam stood up from where he'd been sitting beside me at the base of the fountain and stepped closer to the detective. "I'm sorry, I panicked. When I told you about the fight Tom and I got into the night before he died, you accused me of coming back the next day to get my phone . . . and pushing him down the stairs to his death in the process."

Nick placed a firm hand on Cam's shoulder. "For that, I apologize," he said sincerely. "But you gotta understand. I'm just doing my job, turning over every stone I can to uncover the truth. I don't really think you killed a man. You're a decent human being. That much I know."

Cam blushed a beautiful shade of crimson. "Apology accepted."

Detective Paczki began pacing back and forth, between the babbling water feature and the giant Douglas fir that served as Pleasant Woods's official annual holiday tree. "Speaking of your phone . . . I been giving it some more thought, ever since we first discussed this. You said you went to see Tom Cash on the morning he died to get your lost cell phone back, right?"

Cam remained silent as he allowed the detective to continue with his spiel.

"But then you *didn't* get your phone back, because these guys . . ." Nick gestured to me and JP, standing idly by, pretty much twiddling our thumbs. "They found your phone when they came across Tom's body at the bottom of the staircase." He halted, hands on his hips as he stared directly at my best friend. "If you specifically went to get your phone back from Tom . . . why didn't you get your phone back?"

Cam looked at me uneasily, hoping for some sort of lifeline, maybe? Then he turned to the police detective again, in order to address the point of the man in dark blue polyester. "Well . . . that's the other thing we wanna discuss with you."

"Okaaay . . ." The handsome cop flicked the tip of his tongue against his hairy upper lip once again. "Why do I feel like there's something else you forgot to tell me?"

*Another ten minutes later . . .*

We'd decided to carry on with our stroll, due to an abundance of Pleasant Woodsians out enjoying the summer afternoon along with their four-legged furry friends. Detective Paczki had felt it best that we didn't conduct our private, personal business in the all-too-public Town Square.

So, at the northernmost end of Paisley Park, in the shadow of the zoo tower, we continued our clandestine conversation.

"Let me get this straight," the police detective said, once we'd finally come to a rest. "You were standing with Tom Cash inside his parents' old house . . . ?"

Cam nodded, giving Nick his full attention. "Correct."

"You were there looking for your lost cell phone," the officer said, "when Tom got a call. And the person who called . . . tell me again, what did Tom say to him?"

"He said," Cam said, recalling the would-be killer's exact words, "'I'm *not* changing my mind about the house!' I assume Tom meant, he's not changing his mind about the deal he worked out with Peter and JP to renovate his parents' old place as part of their TV show."

Nick Paczki proceeded to slowly spell things out, more for his own benefit than ours. "And the three of you think . . . whoever called Tom was so upset by this deal . . . he later showed up at Four Fairway . . . and he *killed* Tom . . . by pushing him down a flight of stairs?"

Once the detective had uttered it out loud, I could see how ludicrous our theory might have sounded to anyone outside of our circle.

"No disrespect," JP said cordially. "We know you've already determined Tom Cash's death was an accident. But we just find it odd . . . his own brother—his *twin*, no less—has been so quick to agree, when there's far more evidence that points to foul play."

My sister's hunky ex-boyfriend folded his muscular arms across his even beefier chest. "And what evidence would that be?"

"Come on, Nick!" I cried, growing frustrated by his refusal to see our point of view. "On the morning Tom Cash died, he received two phone calls. One, around nine-thirty while he was having breakfast with Kyle Young over at The Depot . . ."

From our vantage point across Woodward Avenue, we could see the maroon-colored awning with white stenciled letters that spelled out the diner's name, situated right near the railroad tracks.

"The other call came about an hour later . . ." Bound and determined to make the man whom I'd known since before I'd turned ten come around to my way of thinking, I continued with my train of thought. ". . . when Cam stopped by Four Fairway to look for his lost cell phone."

Detective Paczki raised his callused hands in resignation.

"Did you guys try talking to Tom's brother about all this evidence?"

JP picked up where I'd left off, as our spokesperson. "We did! Terry told us to mind our own business, same as he told Kyle Young."

"We tried telling Terry we thought maybe the pink mafia killed Tom," I said, picking up the proverbial ball from my partner.

The police detective let out a laugh. "The pink mafia?"

"If they gave Tom the money to renovate his bar," I elaborated, "and he couldn't pay it back . . . then maybe they came after him and killed him?"

Nick Paczki rocked back on his heels. If I didn't know better, I'd have thought he was enjoying himself listening to us spew out our amateur sleuthing theories. "Guys, I keep telling you: This isn't New York City. People don't get murdered in Pleasant Woods, Michigan. Especially by something silly like the pink mafia."

"Are you sure?" I asked, sounding like a small boy who'd just learned the Tooth Fairy was a total fraud.

"Yes, I'm sure. I'm a cop, I should know." Nick turned to Cam, who'd been lost in a trance, counting the copper coins that lay lost on the bottom of the fountain. "Now let me ask you this: Why didn't you tell me and Rana about this phone call you overheard, back when we first brought you in?"

Startled by having the attention thrust back on him, Cam breathed deeply. "I didn't mean to *not* tell you. I guess I forgot. Things were so crazy that morning. Tom just died. I was on my way to his funeral. You found my phone near his dead body. You said so yourself, you thought maybe *I* killed him."

"That's understandable," Nick said easily. "But it's been over a week now since you gave your statement. Why didn't you come to me earlier about the phone call Tom got, while you were inside the Tudor with the guy?"

"I only just remembered it the other day," Cam said. "I swear! I must have blocked it out or something. It wasn't until I learned about the similar call Kyle overheard at the diner that I even thought of it."

The police detective glanced up at the clock tower in the square, his patience wearing thin, along with the passing time. "So, you overheard Tom on this phone call, arguing with somebody who eventually might have killed him . . . then what happened?"

"Unfortunately, nothing," Cam answered. "I didn't wanna damage my professional reputation by being late for my open house. Tom kept yammering away on his phone, so I figured I'd just leave and come back later to look for mine. Hopefully, I wouldn't miss any important calls or messages before I could find it."

"Then you left Four Fairway and you drove up to Royal Heights," I said, leading Cam along by the hand in his story-telling, as a professional storyteller.

"I did. I waved to Tom and walked out the front door," Cam said softly. "Thinking back, I wish I would've waited till he finished his call. I wish I would've stayed long enough to find my missing phone and thank him for helping me find it. I wish . . ." At the thought of seeing his former lover's face for the last time, Cam felt the sting of tears in his eyes. "I wish I would've given him a hug goodbye."

The police detective seized the moment of silence that followed to change his interrogation tactic. "Did anyone see you at Four Fairway with Tom?"

Cam thought hard.

Suddenly, he recalled the exterior exchange he'd had on the morning of Tom's alleged murder. "Hank and Hennie Richards! They were on their way to a baseball game. Well, they were dressed for one, at least."

"Oh, yeah," the police officer remarked. "Mr. Hank got

them season tickets for their sixtieth wedding anniversary. Hennie's crazy about the Tigers! So, did either of them see you leaving the Tudor?"

"Unfortunately not," Cam admitted in defeat. "They were already inside their house by the time Tom and I had our . . . little chat."

"So, nobody saw you leave Four Fairway. But, on a stack of Bibles, you swear that Tom Cash was still alive when you left him?"

"I do, Nick! As my friend of almost ten years, you've gotta believe me."

Detective Paczki sighed. "I am your friend, Cam. And I do believe you. But if you want me to also believe Tom Cash's death wasn't accidental, then you guys gotta give me something to go on."

"What about the phone calls?" I suggested. "Based on what Kyle and Cam overheard, whoever called Tom Cash on the morning he died most likely murdered him."

"But we don't know who that someone is, now, do we?"

"We don't," JP answered. "But if we can find out who called Tom . . . ?"

A bright light appeared in Nick Paczki's blue eyes. The police detective understood exactly what my partner was suggesting.

Now that he did . . . he felt all the more obliged to act.

# Chapter 25

I begged Cam to go with me.

He resisted at first, stating his resentment.

Ultimately, I wore him down.

"I really hate this place," he complained, taking a seat at the bar.

Squeezing myself in beside him, I sympathized. "I know you do."

Friday night at Shout! seemed pretty much the same as it had the previous Saturday, only slightly less busy. Funny how, in the almost year I'd been living back in Michigan, I hadn't once been to the place. Now I was there for the second time in less than a week.

"So, how long is JP out of town for?" my best friend inquired, still acting as if I'd put him out by inviting him to have drinks with me in my partner's absence.

"He left two days ago," I told him. "He's supposed to be back tomorrow, early evening."

"Lucky guy! I wanna go up to Traverse City."

"Well, outside of Traverse City," I said. "And it's not like he's on vacation, having fun without me."

I, personally, had never been to the Up North resort

town, known for its annual cherry festival and local wineries, located at the base of the Leelanau Peninsula, which is basically the top of the pinky finger on the Michigan hand map. Hailing from lower-middle-class Madison Park, families like mine spent their summers in more accessible—read: cheaper—towns like Gaylord and Lewiston.

Cam craned his neck, in search of Danny the bartender. "What's the movie?"

"It's actually a limited streaming series," I explained. "He's playing a small-town sheriff's deputy."

"Isn't he always a cop? Nothing like being typecast." Cam stood up and waved obnoxiously, nearly knocking over the martini belonging to the guy sitting next to us. "Hello!"

As much as I didn't approve, I chose to ignore my pal's antics, focusing instead on my partner's recent good fortune. JP really needed this job. Not because of the money, which amounted to scale, which was still a fairly decent chunk of change. But he'd been feeling down, not doing anything dramatic for a while. A part of me felt guilty for suggesting that we pack up our New York City lives and move to my native Detroit, despite our newfound success as TV show hosts. The last thing I'd wanted was to stand in the way of JP accepting the role. Especially when he'd received the offer without having to audition.

"The part's pretty minor. But it's three days of work, plus travel."

"Well, that's cool," Cam said casually. Then he let out a loud groan. "Who's a guy gotta do to get a drink around here? Seriously!"

"JP was pretty excited when he got the call from his agent," I said, trying to reel in Cam with my story. "She remembered we're living here, so it worked out perfectly. Hopefully, he'll get more opportunities now that our show is airing. You never know who might see it."

This had been the grand scheme all along, regarding the reality series: for us both to gain some exposure, leading JP to more acting and me to more book sales. Maybe I'd even sell that screenplay I'd shelved—about the transgender teen girl, based on the classic high school rom-com—but secretly hoped would finally make its way into production.

"Hey, guys!" Danny stepped over to take our drink order. "Sorry to keep you."

I couldn't help but notice how quickly Cam's attitude toward the bartender went from hostile to lackluster. He barely looked at the guy as I asked for a couple pints of craft beer.

While we waited for Danny to return with the adult beverages, I took the opportunity to fill in my best friend on the latest development pertaining to *Murder at the Tudor.* "So, I heard back from Nick Paczki . . ."

Cam fanned himself with a cocktail napkin like a Southern belle on an Alabama plantation in the middle of August. "OMG! He is so. Cute."

"OMG! He is so. Straight," I said. "And married. With a kid."

Cam crumpled the paper cloth in his hand and tossed it at me. "A gay can still lust." He deflated, sinking down into himself. "So, what did Detective Hottie McGee have to say?"

"He was able to pull Tom Cash's cell phone records," I reported. "And, just as we'd suspected, he received *two* phone calls on the morning he died. The first one came in at nine-twenty-six, the second at ten-thirty-two."

"But we already knew that." Cam pivoted on his stool and searched for Danny at the far end of the bar. "We need our beers, please!" He turned back to me and scowled. "This is why I stopped coming here. The service is terrible."

That wasn't the real reason why Campbell Sellers avoided

setting foot inside of Shout! I'd almost forgotten Cam's ha-
tred for the bartender on duty, after he'd been left four years
earlier by his then-boyfriend, Tom Cash, in favor of the
younger Danny. I decided against offering my own personal
opinion, not wanting to wound my best friend's pride any
further.

Glancing in Danny's direction, I noticed he seemed to be
moving rather slowly for someone who relied on tips as a big
chunk of his income. A pained expression filled his handsome face. His dark eyebrows knit together anxiously. He
seemed preoccupied, lost in thought over something trouble-
some.

"Yes, we knew Tom had gotten two phone calls that
morning . . ." I focused my attention on Cam and the previous topic: Tom Cash's cell phone records. "One, while he was
having breakfast at The Depot with Kyle. The other, while
you were with him inside his parents' old house."

"Right, right. But did Nick tell you who called Tom?"
Cam wondered, just as Danny appeared, his fists full of golden
amber deliciousness.

"Here we go," he said, placing a pair of pint glasses on the
bar top before us. "Two Hearted Ales, all around."

"My new favorite," I said, happily accepting the award-
winning, Michigan-made, American-style IPA. I handed
Danny my credit card. "Can we keep it open?"

The bartender stared at me blankly.

With the background music at full volume, I thought
maybe he hadn't heard me. "Danny?"

He blinked, shaking off his stupor. "Sorry! Keep it open?"

"Please."

Danny took my Visa and walked it over to the cash register.

"What's her problem?" Cam said spitefully as we watched
the dark-haired man drop off my card with a stack of others.

Bar tabs were all the rage in Metro Detroit. In New York, we always paid cash, due to most establishments not wanting to deal with credit card fees.

"He definitely seems distracted," I decided. "Hope he's okay."

"I hope his boyfriend dumped him for a younger guy," Cam said, taking a sip of his beer. He cringed. "OMG! This is so. Bitter."

"OMG! Like you?" I teased.

Cam ignored my comment. "Tastes like a Christmas tree."

It totally did. But I loved the piney-ness, coupled with hints of grapefruit, that came from the incorporation of one hundred percent Centennial hops from the Pacific Northwest. The seven percent ABV was an added bonus, in terms of the buzz factor.

We clinked glasses, toasting our long-lasting friendship. "Cheers, dah-ling!"

I hadn't been out for drinks with my bestie—just the two of us—in more months than I could recall. I missed the company of a platonic relationship. Especially with someone who'd known me for as long as Campbell Sellers had. We'd been through so much together, from puberty through the coming out process.

*Almost twenty whole years!*

How did we ever get to be so old?

Pondering Danny and Cam's mutual predicament when it came to men, I thanked my lucky stars for the special person in my life and said a silent prayer for JP to get home safely . . . and soon.

"His boyfriend did dump him for a younger guy," I reminded Cam, referring to Tom Cash's leaving Danny the bartender for Kyle the twink, shortly before Danny turned thirty.

Cam drained half the liquid from his glass. "Serves him right after what he did to me."

This statement caught me off guard. "I'm surprised you don't get along better with Danny, based on what Tom did to you both."

Cam tilted his head in the bartender's direction. "He's not a bad guy. I just feel like a loser every time I see him." He gulped down the rest of his beverage and grimaced. "Next round I'm ordering a *real* drink. I don't even like beer!" He set down the empty pint on the bar and pushed it away. "So, what were we saying?"

I adjusted in my seat, making myself comfortable before sharing my exciting news: "Nick pulled Tom's cell phone records—"

Cam cut me off. "Broken record much?"

"You asked me what we were saying!"

"I know. Just razzing you, Penwell. Continue, please."

"Tom received two calls on the morning he died. And . . . guess who they came from?"

Cam bit his lower lip. "If I had a clue, Peter, I wouldn't be sitting here in this godawful bar with you right now. Please just tell me, so we can do whatever we came here to do and get the hell out."

"Fine!" I said, fed up with my best friend's perpetual pessimism. "The calls came from Tom's brother."

Cam let out a surprised shriek. "Just like in *The Drum Major Did It,* my favorite novel of yours!"

He was referring to *Murder High,* book number 3. Matt and Marty Music are rivals for leader of Madison Park High's marching band. After Matt receives a series of threatening phone messages, his girlfriend, Marissa, stumbles upon his lifeless body, stuffed inside the bell of a sousaphone. Later, it comes out that the calls had come from none other than

Matt's brother, and Marty is taken into police custody. Now it's up to our teen sleuth, TJ Inkster, to step in and prove the boy's innocence, before he can lead the Band Geeks down Main Street, in the annual Homecoming parade.

Cam and I shifted our gaze toward the front door of Shout! Something about Terry Cash seemed different from the first night I'd met him. He looked more fashionable, having exchanged the casual athletic wear and hoodie for a pair of snug-fitting dark jeans and a sleeveless denim shirt that showed off his sculpted shoulders and muscular upper arms.

"Well, Tom was Terry's brother," Cam quipped. "Makes sense Terry would call him."

"Sure," I said, in full agreement. "But the thing is . . . JP and I were there when Nick questioned Terry, after we found Tom's body. Nick asked if Terry had seen Tom on the morning he died. Terry insisted he did *not*."

"Okaaay . . ."

"But if he talked to Tom on the phone, why didn't Terry mention it?"

"A bit odd," Cam said. "But Terry's always been a bit of an odd bird."

"Well, you know him better than I do. Have you noticed anything unusual about Terry since Tom died?"

Cam gave my query some consideration. "I actually think Terry seems less odd now."

"How so?"

"Less awkward, more confident, maybe? I know he and Tom didn't get along great. Maybe with Tom gone, Terry's finally relaxing a little?"

The time had come for the next phase of our plan . . .

We stepped out into the warm summer evening. A small crowd of smokers stood off to the side, beneath the overhang of the haberdasher next door. The suburban hipsters puffed away on their nicotine sticks without a care in the world. I wondered if they realized that a potential murderer lurked among them?

Cam and I sidled up to the doorman. "Can we talk to you?"

Terry Cash lifted his eyes from the screen of his fancy new cell phone and slipped the device into his back pocket. "Sure thing! What's up?"

I shared with Terry what Nick Paczki had shared with me and JP: how the call detail records for Tom's cell phone had confirmed Terry as the person who'd *twice* spoken to him on the morning he died.

"Okay, I talked to my brother a couple times," Terry said coolly. "So what? He was my brother. I talked to him a lot on the phone. That piece of crap flip I got rid of . . . took forever to type out a text on." He gave us a thumbs-up to show off the enormous digit on his rather large hand.

"Then why didn't you tell Detective Paczki you talked to your brother on the morning he died?" I said easily.

"Nick didn't ask me if I talked to my brother . . . he asked me if I *saw* my brother."

Again, semantics. *Po-TAY-to, po-TAH-to.*

The fact that Terry Cash had openly admitted to intentionally withholding information from the police led me to suspect him in his brother's murder, even more than I'd already begun to.

"Look, you guys," Terry continued. "I might've talked to my brother before he died. But I didn't kill him."

"You threatened him," I stated, deliberately daring the doorman to deny the accusation. "Why should we believe that's all you did?"

Terry retaliated, playing right into my trap. "I did no such thing. As God is my witness, I'm telling you guys straight: I did not threaten my brother on the morning he died."

He was definitely a good actor, Terrence Cash. But Campbell Sellers and I both knew differently.

"There are two witnesses who say otherwise," I informed him, much to Terry's surprise.

"What two witnesses?"

"Kyle Young and myself," Cam said, finally opening his mouth to speak. "Kyle heard Tom talking to you at The Depot. I heard him when we were together inside your parents' old house."

Terry clenched his jaw. "And what did I say to my brother, Cam? Tell me how I threatened him."

Cam fell silent, at a loss for an answer. Both he and Kyle had only witnessed the one side of the conversation. What Terry had said on the other end of the cell phone line could only be inferred, based on Tom's replies. In either instance, it sounded as if Terry had informed his brother that he didn't approve of the deal he'd made with the hosts of *Domestic Partners* to renovate the Tudor Revival.

"It's my house now," Terry told me, mincing no words. "If I didn't want you and your partner redoing it, I wouldn't've signed off. My brother's gone. He has no more say in anything I do, okay?"

Terry glanced up at the streetlight. Tears pooled in his eyes as he spoke of his dead sibling. Clearly, the memory of the man had upset him. So out of respect, I said nothing in response to his rant.

"We weren't just brothers," Terry continued, after taking a moment to compose himself. "We were twins. We got a bond not even death can break. And making a threat," he said defiantly, "it ain't the same as actually killing somebody. Plus, we already went over this with your partner. You guys know exactly where I was on the morning my brother died."

Keeping calm, I carried on with my questioning. "Please forgive my saying so . . . but you lied before." I could feel my heart begin to race as I called out the doorman. "You told Nick Paczki that you came from home, before you met Fairway Bob for brunch. Then you admitted to me and JP later, you spent the night with Danny and you went straight to Chianti from his apartment."

Cam gawked at Terry in total disbelief. "You had a hookup? Good for you!" He punched me on the arm, hard. "Peter! I can't believe you didn't tell me about this scandal!"

Terry, the strong man, placed his hands upon his hips, temper rising as he accosted me. "Since you seem to know so much . . ."

Out of nowhere, Terry lunged. He grabbed me and gave me a forceful shake. A few hipster heads might have turned. But for the most part, it didn't seem as if anyone had noticed the physical violence, other than my best friend.

"Hey, now!" Cam warned the doorman. "I've got Nick Paczki on speed dial. He's a personal friend, you know?"

Terry Cash slowly loosened his grip on my shoulders. "My bad for losing my temper."

The hard look on Terry's usually handsome face said that he no longer appreciated my accusations. He was definitely more massive than Cam and me both and could easily take us down. So long as we remained outside in public view, I knew we'd be safe from harm.

But what might happen to us later?

With JP still away until tomorrow, I began to fear for my well-being. At the rate things were progressing, I planned on asking Cam if I could spend the night at his house, knowing Snoop would be there to protect us.

"I certainly don't mean to offend you," I told Terry sincerely. "But . . ."

"Unlike a lot of dudes that can't keep their mouths shut . . ." Terry towered over me, his dark eyes cast down indignantly. "I only lied to Nick cuz I didn't want him—

and you and your nosey partner—knowing about my hookup outta respect for Danny. But if you think, for one second, I killed my brother . . . well, you dudes better think again."

Having made his threat against me, Terry Cash spun on his heels and headed back inside the bar.

# Chapter 26

My phone rang at midnight.

But, instead of my partner's handsome headshot appearing on the screen, the caller ID displayed: *Unknown Number.*

I'd been expecting a call from JP from his film shoot Up North, so with a reluctant tap against the glass, I answered. "Hello?"

"Hey!" my partner greeted me from two hundred–plus miles away. "What's up?"

"Sitting on the sun porch in the moonlight." I rested my feet on the outdoor coffee table, even though I knew full well that I wasn't supposed to. "Hon, why are you calling me from someone else's phone?"

JP groaned in my ear. "Like an idiot, I lost mine."

"Oh, no!"

"Oh, yes! We were shooting a chase scene through some woods, and I must've dropped it. Totally my fault. I wasn't supposed to keep it on me. But I was worried about you being there alone, with everything going on."

I leaned my head back against a red-and-white–striped throw pillow. "Well, that's awfully sweet of you. Guess we'll have to ask Ursula for those new iPhones after all."

The paper lantern we'd hung from the ceiling beam gave off a warm glow, lighting up the outdoor space. In just two days, a little doggie named Clyde would be there to keep me company on the couch, the next time JP went out of town for work. I couldn't wait till we made his adoption official.

Suddenly, I remembered something that I'd almost forgotten to ask about: "How did the shoot go?"

"Okay," JP answered casually. "Until all this lost phone business. They gave me another one to use temporarily. But still . . . I feel sort of stupid."

"Well, did they wrap you?" I asked, in an attempt to subvert my partner's self-deprecation.

"Not yet. We've got like six pages left to film tomorrow."

This news came as a disappointment. But JP hadn't done any acting in such a long time, I didn't want to spoil his fun, so I didn't complain.

"Did you and Cam end up going out for drinks tonight?" he asked me, changing the subject.

JP had put the idea into my head that I should drag my best friend along to Shout!, in order to question Terry Cash, regarding the results we'd received from Nick Paczki, re: Tom's cell phone records.

I reiterated the events of the past two hours, including the confrontation that Cam and I had with the burly doorman, in which he'd blatantly denied any wrongdoing in his twin brother's death. Conveniently, I left out the part about Terry's manhandling me and his indirect threat, not wanting to worry my partner while he was still away.

"You're kidding," JP said, exasperated. "He lied to Nick about spending the night at Danny's. Now he wants us to believe he's telling the truth?"

"That's what I told him."

"And what did Terry say to that?"

"He said he didn't want Nick—or me and my nosey

partner—knowing about his hookup, out of respect for Danny."

Through the phone's speaker, I could hear JP audibly gasp in offense. "Terry called us nosey?"

"Well, he called *you* nosey," I teased.

"How dare he!" JP bellowed. "If Terry doesn't like us, he can find someone else to renovate his parents' old house on a top-rated TV show."

"Unfortunately," I said, acting as the voice of reason, "we start taping in three days. Where are we gonna find another house to renovate before Monday morning?"

Realizing we were pretty much stuck with the hand we'd been dealt, JP's attitude shifted. "Well, the good news is: The second A.D. promised I'd be on my way back to Pleasant Woods tomorrow, no later than three. Five o'clock at the latest."

If I'd learned anything spending the past year co-starring on a television program, it was that when it came to film production, everything took longer than initially anticipated . . . and to always expect delays.

"Please hurry," I pleaded.

My hope was to have my partner home as soon as possible. With the first taping day of season two fast approaching, we had some additional details to get ready—namely giving 4 Fairway a final once-over. I didn't like the idea of being alone in an empty house. Especially one where a man had recently died.

Or worse yet, where he'd possibly been *murdered* by his own brother.

Tom Cash had been dead for a total of two weeks.

In just two days, JP and I were set to resume taping *Domestic Partners*.

While I impatiently waited for my cohost to return from

Up North—minus his mobile phone—I decided to head over and work on camera-readying the Tudor Revival.

The first order of business was to clear out the clutter from the second-floor master bedroom. Stepping across the threshold, I felt myself transported back in time. Everything appeared exactly as it had on the day that Larry and Linda Cash perished in the tragic snowmobiling accident twenty-five years before.

The room itself was of ample size. Without taking out my tape measurer, I estimated twelve by fifteen feet. While considered cramped by today's standards, the area was large enough to fit a queen-size bed with end tables on either side, a man's chest of drawers, a woman's bureau with mirror, and a Mission oak Morris chair in the corner. There was even a closet, big enough for a small person to dub a *walk-in.*

How could I resist turning the cut glass doorknob, opening the solid wood door, and taking a peek inside?

The interior hanging system entailed a few wood pieces placed around the perimeter, on which a series of brass coat hooks had been hung, for the purpose of holding garments. There weren't any rods or shelves, amenities found in modern-day closet design. Forget about drawers or pull-out trays! When the Cash brothers had stated that their parents' former home remained in its original condition, they hadn't been exaggerating.

On the oak floor, toward the back of the closet, I found a water-stained cardboard box labeled in black Magic Marker: TWINS.

How could I resist pulling open the flaps that had been pushed inward, the corners securely folded one over the other, and taking a peek inside?

As indicated by the handwritten label, the box contained keepsakes belonging to Tom and Terry Cash, collected over the decades. From the looks of it, the items dated back to the time of the brothers' birth through the next eighteen or so years.

Among the articles enclosed within the time capsule: a pair of baby books that chronicled the small miracles and milestones—such as *Tom's first tooth!* and *Terry's first steps!*—with photographic evidence, along with every school report card, progress report, and English paper written by each boy.

There was far too much history for me to sift through, though tempted I'd been to peruse it all. I always enjoyed a good trip down memory lane—especially if it weren't my own—and I relished the idea of stealing a glimpse into someone else's private past.

The photos themselves I found to be of the most interest: the twins' first birthday, each toddler held tightly on one of his parents' laps, before a single lit candle stuck into a child-sized chocolate cake; the twins' first day of kindergarten, as they posed on the wide front porch of the Tudor Revival; the twins' senior prom picture, with both handsome young men standing beside his respective date, each brother a carbon copy of the other, down to his dress tux.

Based on the wild red hair belonging to one of the young girls, I guessed her to be the dog-rescue woman, Margot, and her twin of choice, Tom Cash. Upon closer inspection of the image, the boy on the left smiled a noticeably gap-toothed grin. The other pressed his lips together tightly, betraying not the slightest bit of glee. I remembered, on the night I'd met him, taking note of the slight space between Tom's two front teeth, as I'd found it strangely sexy. More recently, I'd observed that Terry also possessed the same imperfection, piquing my curiosity. Exactly how much alike could identical twins be?

In my snooping, I happened upon two sets of legal documents worth note: 1) the birth certificates of both Terrence and Thomas Cash, born on the twenty-first day of June, a half-century before; and 2) the deed to the piece of property in which I'd presently found myself.

What made these particular papers so intriguing was the way in which they had been filled out.

As my mother always said: *The devil is in the details.*

Apart from the birth certificates being printed on black paper with white type, it was the time of birth recorded on each that threw me for a loop.

According to the Certificate of Live Birth for the Cash baby christened Thomas Alton, the boy had entered this world at precisely 7:15 in the morning, whereas the baby known as Terrence Lawrence arrived twelve minutes earlier, promptly at 7:03.

While this evidence might not seem substantial, personally it shook me. I'd been under the impression that Tom had been the elder of the brothers, based exclusively on the way in which he'd wielded authority over his twin in their interactions.

Regarding the Enhanced Life Estate Deed, the paper that passed on ownership of 4 Fairway Lane upon the death of its title holder, Lawrence Cash, to his wife, Linda . . .

At the time of her death, the rightful owner of the Tudor Revival would become none other than the *second* born son, Thomas.

So, to put my discovery in layman's terms: Terry was the oldest twin but, for the past twenty-five years, his *younger* brother had owned the Tudor Revival.

Now I realized that, just because providence had afforded Terry first entrance, he hadn't been entitled to inherit his parents' home after their passing. This might have been the way things had been decreed in Ye Olden Tymes or in Shakespearean dramas. But this was real life. Perhaps Tom had been his father's preferred son, thereby gaining partiality over his brother and, in the end, profit?

*Although* . . .

What if Terry had felt jilted by his father's preference for his baby brother?

What if Terry, as Margot from Home FurEver had so eloquently put it, resented Tom with every fiber of his being?

What if Terry had been so against his younger brother granting my partner and me permission to renovate their parents' old house that—after twice making threats, via phone call—he headed over to 4 Fairway Lane, and in order to stop Tom from finalizing the deal . . .

He *killed* his own twin?

Lunch that Saturday consisted of the usual: half turkey sandwich, accompanied by a blended concoction of baby spinach, fresh ginger, frozen banana, and strawberries. I swallowed the last sip of my green shake as the doorbell rang.

Loading my dirty dishes into the washer, I wondered who I'd find on my front porch once I peeked through the curtains. Lo and behold, I discovered none other than our neighbor from next door, Mr. Kravitz, aka Fairway Bob.

"Come in!" I cried, eager for some human communication after spending the past few hours alone, talking to myself.

"I won't stay long," Bob promised. "I know you guys are busy with the new fur baby." He presented me with a soft, wrapped package. "I just wanted to say hi and see the little cutie-patootie for myself."

"That's very kind." I tore off the paper to reveal a stuffed bone, striped in red, green, and white, that would later earn the moniker *The Italian Job*. "But we aren't bringing Clyde home until the morning. JP's not even back from his film shoot."

Bob visibly blanched, embarrassed by his blunder. "The

adoption isn't happening till Sunday? I feel so silly!" He reached for the gift I held in my hands. "I can take that back and bring it by after you've brought Clyde home, if you want."

"Don't beat yourself up," I insisted. "Knowing me, I didn't specify which day we were adopting Clyde. I've had a lot on my mind, what with . . ."

Here, I hesitated.

I'd been about to finish my statement with the words: *finding out our new business partner, Terry Cash, is a suspect in the death of his own brother.* But, with Bob being a close friend of the twins—he'd been the one to first introduce them to us, what felt like a lifetime ago—I didn't want to say too much. My fear was that Bob might run off and reiterate to Terry what I'd revealed.

"Really, I can come back tomorrow," he assured me.

"No, please stay. There's something I wanted to ask you about."

After I fixed us a couple iced coffees, Bob followed me out the kitchen door onto the sun porch, where we made ourselves comfortable on the sectional.

"I love what you guys have done back here!" Bob gestured flamboyantly, reminding me why most people thought him to be gay upon first meeting. "This couch is so comfy!"

"You like it?" I asked, proud of the deal we'd gotten at Art Van.

Bob lifted his iced coffee cup, like he was about to make a toast. "If you boys need to do any staging for your show, my shop is available twenty-four seven."

"I'll definitely keep that in mind," I replied. "While we're on the subject . . ." I filled him in about the box I'd found in the bedroom closet at 4 Fairway Lane.

Bob's reaction came as quite a surprise. "I never knew Tommy owned the house outright after Larry and Linda died! Why didn't he tell me, I wonder?" He sounded more hurt than offended by learning that his best friend had harbored a secret.

"Well, did you realize Tom was younger than Terry by twelve minutes?"

"That much I knew," Bob answered, as if the detail were no big deal. "Like I said, there was never any love lost between those two. Even before I met Terry, Tommy told me how jealous his twin brother had always been of him."

I watched as Bob slurped his iced coffee through a metal straw, draining half the glass in a few seconds, before he continued speaking.

"Tommy was always his daddy's favorite. Growing up, he got better grades in school. He played almost every sport. He had a steady girlfriend. Terry—as much as I like the guy—from what I heard, he was always a bit of a screwup."

"That would explain why Tom inherited the Tudor after his parents both passed," I deduced, playing back porch detective.

"Well, it's Terry's house now," Bob sang. "He got everything Tommy owned when he died. The house across Woodward, the house over here, Tommy's SUV, Shout!" He paused momentarily as he polished off his cold drink. "And a sizable chunk of change, as the only beneficiary of Tommy's life insurance policy."

While I was curious by nature, my mother hadn't raised me to be rude. I wasn't about to ask how much money, exactly, Terry had received upon the death of his baby brother. But based on the gesture Bob had made after making his statement, accompanied by the words *ka-ching, ka-ching!*, I assumed that Terry Cash would be living high on the hog for the rest of his days, maybe longer.

This brought me to my next question for Fairway Bob: "Is there any chance you think Terry might have killed Tom, in order to collect the insurance money?"

Bob's hand fell to his heart. Either he was having an attack, or I'd deeply offended him with my comment. "No! Terry can be a real pill. But he would never hurt Tommy."

"I'm sorry for suggesting such a thing. It's just . . ." I told Bob all about the cell phone records that Nick Paczki had pulled, proving that Terry had spoken to Tom on *two* separate occasions on the morning he died—after earlier stating to the police detective that he had *not*.

I told him about the witnesses—Kyle Young and Campbell Sellers—both of whom had partially overheard the phone conversations in which Terry had blatantly threatened his brother's life.

Lastly, I revealed the way Terry Cash had raised his temper, after Cam and I had casually suggested that he might have played some part in the death of his brother.

"He grabbed me, right on the street in front of Shout!" I explained. "You should've seen the look in his eyes, Bob. He got really angry."

"Well, can you blame him, PJ? Tommy is dead. They weren't just brothers, they were *twins*. Cut from the same cloth. They shared a home together, from womb to tomb." Bob stopped to reconsider the words he'd just spoken. "Well, they *will* share a tomb when Terry's time is up, you know what I'm saying?"

I did.

But, based on the evidence that had been piling up, I couldn't shake the suspicion that Terry Cash was a killer.

# Chapter 27

My phone rang at six-fifteen.

For the second time in less than twenty-four hours, the caller ID displayed: *Unknown Number.*

I knew this time it couldn't be my partner calling from some loaner phone, since I'd just heard from JP an hour ago. He'd officially been wrapped and would already be making the four-hour drive back to Pleasant Woods. His estimated time of arrival, he'd determined, was somewhere close to nine o'clock. Hopefully, he would get home sooner, if he broke the law a little by exceeding the speed limit on I-75.

Under usual circumstances, I'd send the mystery caller to voice mail. But these were *unusual* times. Something compelled me to pick up . . . and so I did. "This is PJ."

It was a stupid move. I shouldn't have answered the phone in the first place. What if the person on the other end of the line was a telemarketer—or, worse yet, a *murderer*?

Thankfully, I'd taken the risk.

"Hey, it's Danny. Murphy. From Shout!"

I'd almost forgotten that I'd given the bartender my number the night before, after we'd chatted about his no-longer-secret one-night stand with Terry Cash. While I recognized his deep voice, I also appreciated his identifying himself, had I not been so certain.

"Danny, what's up?" I casually inquired, following my question with: "Is everything okay?"

"Actually, no. I need to tell you something."

I didn't like the sound of this. Still, I kept it cool. "Okay. Well, I can come up to the bar in a bit. We can chat while you're working, if that's all right."

"I'm not at work. I quit."

I didn't like the sound of that, either. This time, my apprehension was harder to conceal. "You quit your job? Okay. Well, where are you now?"

"Outside." For a former bartender with the gift of the gab, Danny Murphy was suddenly a man of few words.

Putting a hand over my phone, I instructed our smart speaker to lower the volume on the satellite radio channel I'd been rocking out to—Alt Universe, on Polaris XM—before I'd received Danny's call. "Outside what?"

"Your house."

I stood up at my mammoth desk: a solid wood, double-sided partners-style period piece, circa 1920s, that I found online for less than five hundred dollars. Picked it up from a woman in western Michigan, just south of Battle Creek. I'd been trying to get some writing done on an outline I'd been developing for a *Murder High* sequel. Tentatively, I'd titled it *Murder U*, at the suggestion of my editor, Sabrina, who found the play on words whimsical.

After walking the distance from our home office on the second floor, down the staircase, and into the living room, I peeked out the front windows. Sure enough, I could see Danny standing on the sidewalk across the street. A slight delay occurred when he spoke, between the words I heard in my ear and the ones I could read on his lips.

"You see me?" he said, waving his free hand. He wasn't

wearing his work uniform: black jeans and T-shirt, with the Shout! logo displayed across the chest, which is how I'd only ever seen him dressed before. Instead, Danny sported shorts and a tank top, revealing a slight sunburn on the tops of his smooth shoulders.

"It's sweltering out there. Come in," I instructed the former bartender through the phone, before promptly ending the call.

For the past week, Pleasant Woods had seen a streak of temperate weather. Much to my chagrin, overnight the heat and humidity had taken a turn for the higher. The stickiness suffocated me, like a strong pair of hands wrapped tight around my throat. On days like this, I couldn't wait for the conclusion of summer. It made me want to kill Ursula for ever suggesting we tape season two of our TV show starting the first week of August.

About to pull open the heavy front door, I took a brief moment to admire the refinishing job that JP had done on season one, episode six of *Domestic Partners*. He used a chemical-free orange stripper to remove the original varnish, then sanded down the oak veneer, applied some walnut stain, three coats of water-based poly . . . and presto! The portal into our home looked like new—and we saved close to a thousand dollars on buying a replacement.

"After what I did for him . . ." Danny took on a biting tone as he stomped up the limestone steps onto our front porch. "The way I lied to protect him . . . then he just up and tells me I mean nothing."

I ushered Danny into the foyer and shoved the solid wood door shut behind him. The cool rush of central air was a welcome relief as we stepped into the living room beyond. I gestured for my unexpected guest to help himself to a seat on the sofa. He continued to stand, arms folded tightly across his torso. He shook his head, mumbling to himself as he stared at a spot on the wall above the fireplace.

"Danny, I'm not following you. What did you lie about to protect whom?"

"Who else?" he spat, running his hands through his thick dark hair, frustrated. "Terry Cash! He totally blew me off last night. So, I told him he could take his job and . . . well, I won't repeat where I told him he could stick it."

Since it was far too hot for iced coffee out on the sun porch, we continued our conversation seated on the dining room window seat, overlooking Woodward. In a few short weeks, a day-long deluge of classic cars would take over the avenue, in what was known as the Dream Cruise. From what we'd been told, folks either loved it or abhorred it.

According to Cam, the majority of Pleasant Woods gays fell into the latter camp, hitting the highway and getting the heck out of Dodge come the third Saturday in August. It seemed that the small resort town of Saugatuck, located on Lake Michigan, was the place to see and be seen. I, personally, looked forward to taking in the parade of antique autos for the first time. My father, the proud owner of a 1981 copper-colored AMC Concord "woody" wagon that he'd tricked out himself as part of his midlife crisis, had been boasting about it all summer. He couldn't wait for me and JP to hop in and go cruising with him, showing off his ride for the several hundred spectators who lined up annually along the route.

"Tell me what, exactly, you lied about," I told Danny.

"'Member when I said Terry left my apartment close to eleven?" he answered, eyes cast downward. "Well, it was actually closer to ten-thirty."

While I wasn't thrilled to learn that Danny had lied to us, there had to be a reason he'd done so. I sat back on the custom-made cushion and waited for it. "Okay."

"I figured you guys suspected Terry killed Tom, so I fudged the time frame to give him an alibi."

"Why would you do that? If Terry's found guilty of murder, you could get in trouble for obstruction."

"I know!" Danny hung his head. "I just wanted to protect him. He might seem a little strange. But deep down he's a good guy. That night we spent together, Terry didn't say much. But we had a connection. I haven't felt this way since . . ." He intentionally allowed his sentence to trail off.

"Since Tom?"

Danny looked up at me, his eyes filled with fear. "I didn't mean to lie. I just didn't wanna risk losing Terry. So much for that!" He got up from the window seat and began pacing on the Arts and Crafts carpet. "I invited him to stay over my apartment again last night, after we closed the bar. He told me what we did was a one-time thing. It was a mistake and it wouldn't happen again. *Ever.*"

"Well, that sucks," I said, not meaning to be snarky but sincere. "Did Terry say why it was a mistake?"

"Not in so many words. Just the typical things a guy says when he has no interest. It's not me, it's him . . . I shouldn't waste my time . . . he can't be trusted."

This last excuse I found to be of intrigue.

"Why can't Terry be trusted, I wonder?" I asked, just in case Danny had an idea as to what the doorman might have meant.

He had none.

"I don't know. Maybe he did kill his brother? Once it comes out, there's no way we could have a relationship, if Terry's in prison for murder."

I told Danny how sorry I was to hear that things had gone south with Terry Cash, resulting in him giving up his job. But, if he could possibly think of *anything* else that could help me and JP prove that Terry had committed this heinous crime, Danny would be doing his civic duty.

"And I'd be happy to talk to Detective Paczki on your behalf," I proposed, regarding his earlier fudging of facts. "Nick's an old family friend. He'll understand how your feelings clouded your judgment, I'm sure."

"Anything else, like what?" Danny said, after racking his brain a moment and failing to come up with further evidence.

"What about the phone calls?" I said, offering a suggestion.

"What phone calls?"

I explained how, when we'd first spoken to Danny, he hadn't mentioned anything about hearing Terry talking to anyone—around either 9:26 or 10:32, the times we'd later learned that Terry Cash had telephoned his brother.

"Ah," Danny said, realizing that he'd been caught telling another untruth. "Okay, so I did overhear Terry on the phone, just before nine-thirty. 'Member, I said I woke up and he wasn't in bed? I checked the time on my phone, thinking maybe he'd snuck out on me."

"Uh-huh . . ." Again, I didn't appreciate the lying on Danny's part. But better late than never in learning the truth, I supposed.

"Well, the reason I woke up," he confessed, "was because I heard shouting. In the hallway, outside my bedroom door."

"Terry was shouting?" I said, trying to envision the scenario as it might have played out.

"I could see him—he left the bedroom door slightly cracked. He was on the phone arguing with somebody."

"Could you hear what he was saying?"

"Well, yeah. He was super mad, so he was being super loud. Which is why I woke up."

*Now we were getting somewhere!*

"And what did you hear Terry say?"

"He said: 'You made a promise. I won't let you get away

with this.' Then he snapped his flip phone shut and came back to bed with me."

Based on the cell phone records obtained by Nick Paczki, this was obviously the first call that Terry Cash had made to his twin brother on the morning he died—the one that Kyle had overheard at The Depot Diner, when Tom had refused to acknowledge their breakup in the middle of breakfast, in favor of answering Terry's call.

What was it that Tom Cash had said in response to his brother's threatening comment?

*You don't like what I'm doing? Kill me!*

But then there was the issue of the second phone call— the one that Cam had overheard a little over an hour later, at precisely 10:32.

"Not sure," Danny said sullenly. "By that point, Terry had already left my place. If he called Tom again, maybe he did it on his way to wherever he went next?"

In his conversation with Nick Paczki on the morning his brother died, I could recall Terry Cash stating that he'd been moving rather slowly, so he showed up tardy for brunch with Fairway Bob.

*A little after eleven, maybe eleven-fifteen?*

In my mind's eye, I could see the two men dining together in Chianti, across the room from where JP and I had been seated . . .

Bob looked super summery in his floral print button-down, khaki shorts, and sandals. Terry wore his usual athletic attire and hoodie, Michigan State ball cap perched atop his head. As Terry took his seat, Bob had been sipping coffee—an indicator that Bob had already been waiting a while by the time that Terry had arrived.

I couldn't recall, however, whether or not Terry Cash looked as if he'd recently showered. If he'd taken the time that morning to leave Danny's apartment and go home to freshen up, it could easily explain the reason why he'd been late meeting Bob for brunch.

*Or . . .*

Terry could have taken a detour en route to the wine pub, stopping by his family's former home down the block, where his identical twin brother, Tom, had been busying himself cleaning up the overgrown yard.

What if, at precisely 10:32 a.m., on a Saturday morning in mid-July, Terry Cash had placed a phone call to his brother, during which he'd made an idle threat that he, shortly thereafter, carried out?

He could have easily followed Tom into the Tudor Revival and upstairs to the second floor, arguing as they went along. Upon reaching the summit, in a fit of rage, Terry could have unleashed his fury in the form of a firm push. The wind knocked out of him by the sheer force of the blow, Tom would have most likely fallen backward and tumbled down the rickety old staircase . . . to his *death*.

What if that had been the way in which the events of that fatal morning had actually played out?

What would it mean?

Why, that Terry Cash had indeed killed his brother, of course.

# Chapter 28

My phone rang again, right before eight o'clock.

Three calls in less than twenty-four hours! I had thought, in this modern age, most people communicated via text message. Even my sixty-six-year-old mother had taken to only reaching out this way. I couldn't remember the last time we'd actually spoken, other than in person, over dinner with my dad.

However, the caller ID at present did *not* inform me of an unrecognized number.

Still, it was with reluctance that I placed the phone to my ear. "This is Peter."

"We need to talk." The voice heard through the speaker sounded troubled and tense.

My pulse quickened as I immediately imagined the worst. Being the accommodating person that I was, I would willingly agree to a meeting. We'd get together, under the auspice of discussing the situation, somewhere out of the way and without any witnesses. I'd be confronted for my lack of discretion, blamed for my annoying accusations and, in the end, permanently silenced.

Terry Cash was going to make me his next victim, I just knew it.

What could I possibly do to ward off my would-be murderer? I certainly couldn't arouse his suspicions by refusing his invite . . . *could I?*

"I'm waiting for JP to get home from his film shoot," I said, stalling. "He might be a while. We could meet you down at the bar later, maybe?"

"This can't wait," Terry urgently informed me. "I need to talk to you *now*. And I need to talk to you *alone*."

A lump lodged in my throat. I coughed, attempting to clear it. "If this is about the renovation, we should really wait for JP and discuss it with him. I could also refer you to our producer, Ursula, if you have specific questions or concerns that we can't answer."

My hope was to ward off Terry until my partner had returned to Pleasant Woods, so he could accompany me to the meeting. Or at least until I could get hold of Detective Paczki and alert him to what I'd recently learned from Danny Murphy. Unfortunately, when I'd tried Nick earlier on his personal number, I'd gotten a voice mail message stating that he was off on a day trip with wife Nora and daughter Nikki. But, in the case of an emergency, I should feel free to contact the PW Police Department.

Had I known I would soon receive a call from the prime suspect in an unofficial murder investigation, I'd have followed the detective's sage advice.

"We start taping in less than two days, don't we?" Terry said, even though he'd been in possession of the schedule since we'd first brought him on board the project.

"That's right," I replied cheerfully, not wanting to offend the homeowner since, technically, we worked for him.

"Sure would hate to see the deal fall through, last minute."

I sank down into a mission oak dining chair. The freshly

padded, and newly re-covered, seat cushion gave slightly beneath my weary body. "Well, why would it?"

After Danny had stopped by unannounced and dropped
his bombshell, I could no longer concentrate on my creative
writing. Sitting on my side of the partners desk with my open
laptop, I kept staring at the blank page, hoping the words
would pluck themselves out of the ether and plop into my
brain. But how could I plot out the unfortunate accidents
that would befall a group of fictitious coeds at Carnegie Mel-
lon University—JP's alma mater—when a real-life neighbor
whom I'd known had died, most likely at the hands of his
own brother?

Worst yet, the probable assailant now demanded a private
conference with me, one from which I was certain not to
return alive. All I could think to do was keep him talking,
until I could come up with a surefire way to avoid having to
comply.

"We have a signed contract," I reminded our new partner in renovation. "We're all set to roll cameras on Monday
morning. You can't back out now."

Terry Cash laid everything on the line, in no uncertain
terms. "You want my house on your TV show? Then meet
me. We got some things we need to discuss before we can
move forward."

As much as I wanted to convince myself that I had no
clue, deep in my soul I sensed what Terry wanted to talk
about: the fact that he knew that *I* knew that he had committed fratricide . . . and now he had to stop me from proving it.

Still, I played off my fear, hoping that if I just ignored the
uneasiness, it would all evaporate. "Like I said," I told Terry
sternly, "if this is about the show, we need to wait for JP."

"This ain't about the show," he assured me. "It's about my
brother." A brief silence lingered in the air between us. Until
Terry said, with finality: "I know how he died."

"If that's true," I stated confidently, "we should probably give Nick Paczki a call. He's the detective assigned to the case. He'll for sure wanna hear what you have to say."

"Let's leave Nick outta this for now," Terry suggested. "When the moment is right, he'll know everything."

"Seriously. I don't feel comfortable with this," I said forcefully. "If Tom's death wasn't accidental, this is a criminal investigation we're dealing with. The police—"

Terry cut me off, raising his volume and increasing his intensity. "*I said no cops!* You wanna know what happened to my brother? Meet me at the Tudor . . . and meet me there by yourself. Got it?"

*Every word.*

Fifteen minutes later, I waited on the sidewalk in front of 4 Fairway Lane. One of the good things about growing up in Michigan stemmed from the Great Lakes State finding itself on the western edge of the Eastern Time Zone. In occupying this particular spot on the map, Detroiters were afforded with almost an hour of additional daylight, compared to cities like New York, Philadelphia, and Washington, DC. During the summer months, kids could play outdoor games until close to 10 p.m., before the pale blue sky dissolved into dark navy.

Deep in thought, I found it odd the way in which the Cash twin whom I'd spoken with on the phone had worded his statement, regarding his deceased brother: *I know how he died.*

He hadn't said *I know who* killed *him*, so maybe the dead man hadn't been murdered as we'd originally suspected?

Was it possible that JP and I could have been wrong in our initial assessment of the crime scene? After all, Detective Paczki had insisted that people in Pleasant Woods don't die under mysterious circumstances. Perhaps my own mystery novel writing, along with JP's stint as a TV cop, had swayed our sense of reason?

A new model SUV pulled up on the street, startling me out of my one-sided debate. I recognized the vehicle belonging to Tom Cash. Behind the wheel sat his mirror image.

The handsome older man stepped out of the car and strolled over to where I stood. "Dude, thanks for coming." He flashed a smile, showing off the prominent space between his two front teeth. He wore his usual athletic attire, having recently finished a workout. His massive muscles were particularly pumped, the veins in his vascular forearms freshly engorged with blood. Under a white baseball cap adorned with a green *S*, perspiration beaded on his prominent brow.

"No problem," I replied, thinking how he hadn't given me much choice. "So, what did you wanna talk about?"

Mr. Cash looked around for lingering eyes and listening ears. "Not here. Let's go inside."

This was the last thing I wanted to do.

It was bad enough to be standing in the presence of a man I'd suspected of murdering his own brother. I had no intention of setting foot in the abandoned home where the alleged killing had surely taken place . . .

But what other option had he given me?

"By the way, I heard from JP," I lied, ascending the steps of the wide front porch. "He should be home soon. I told him to meet us over here."

The man opposite me stopped dead. "And I told you . . . I don't want anybody else around when we do this. Just you and me."

Because he seemed set on whatever was about to happen happening in a safe environment, I worried that he'd change his mind if he felt threatened. So I quickly changed my tune, along with my story. "I'm sure it'll take JP longer to get back from Up North than he's expecting. It always does. You know how it is, I'm sure?"

The man opposite me unlocked the storybook entrance and motioned for me to enter. "We'll make this fast, just in case . . ."

Like TJ Inkster, my literary teenage sleuth, I kept a close watch on my host as we maneuvered our way through the old house. Based on facts gathered over the past fortnight, the man couldn't be trusted as far as he could be thrown. Judging by his height, weight, and overall size, the degree of trajectory wasn't that great.

He stopped near the bottom of the rickety old staircase. With twilight upon us, the room in which we'd found our-selves had begun to grow dark.

I reached for the nearby wall sconce, ready to flip the switch. "We should probably turn on some lights."

"Leave 'em off," he ordered. Then he softened his tone. "Please. I don't want you seeing my face."

Sensing the man's pain, I felt the need to dig deeper. "Wanna tell me what's wrong? Take your time," I said, pro-longing the inevitable moment when he would make an attempt on my life, same as he did his own brother's. "I'm listening."

A colossal shadow danced across the cracked plaster as Mr. Cash slowly moved about the room. "What *isn't* wrong?" he asked rhetorically. "Let's see . . . first my parents get them-selves killed. Then my brother up and dies on me. Looks like I'm next to go, if I don't come up with five hundred grand."

Parts one and two of his statement, I totally understood. It was the third item he'd listed that I couldn't quite place my finger on. I had a hunch it had something to do with the loan that Tom Cash had recently received in order to upgrade his business.

So I asked him, point blank.

To which the handsome older man replied with relief: "I'll be cool once the life insurance comes through. You know my lawyer, Rana Vakeel?"

While I wouldn't consider her a close personal acquaintance, Cam had introduced me to the lovely attorney a few different times. Most recently, we'd chatted at last month's Ice Cream Social, held beneath the newly installed pavilion at Gainsford Park. Rana had attended the citywide event along with her fiancé, Naveen. From what I'd gathered in our brief interaction, Dr. Vaidya practiced pediatric medicine at his own Royal Heights clinic. The engaged couple's wedding nuptials, slated for November, would take place in the groom's native Mumbai, with a local ceremony to follow here in Michigan in the spring.

"I've met Rana, yes," I answered, so as to keep the handsome older man talking, as opposed to *killing* me, like I feared he surely would.

"She says it takes between thirty and sixty days. We filed the claim right after the funeral. I told 'em they just gotta be patient. They'll get their money, so just leave me alone already!"

"Well, it sounds like you've got it all figured out," I said, not wanting to pry further. "You'll pay back the money you owe, eventually, and move on."

"Easier said than done," he sighed sadly. "Especially when you did what I did."

I could sense his remorse. Any second, he'd make his official confession. The crime we'd suspected he'd committed, he was at last ready to lay claim . . .

In this very house, fourteen days prior, he'd murdered his own twin.

"You wanted to tell me something," I gently reminded him. "Go ahead . . . *Tom*."

Yes, it turned out that Terrence, elder of the Cash brothers, was in fact the younger, Thomas.

Tom turned toward me, an astonished expression gracing his handsome face. "How did you know?"

"I didn't," I admitted, feeling a bit of a fraud as a best-selling mystery writer. "Not at first, at least. I mean, there were clues I picked up . . ."

"Such as?"

"Well, the Terry I'd known briefly didn't smoke or drink or use the word *dude* when he talked to people."

"Old habits die hard, huh?" Tom laughed softly. "So, when did you finally figure it out?"

Before I'd left my house for our meeting, I took another peek inside the old cardboard box, filled with the Cash twins' childhood belongings. In doing so, I discovered an additional piece of ancient evidence, in the form of the Fernridge High School yearbook, buried at the bottom.

On page 223, sandwiched between Irina Carr and Xavier Castillo, the eighteen-year-old Cash boys smiled happily for the camera. But only *one* of the fresh-faced young men possessed the dental imperfection that, years later, I'd find oddly attractive.

I believed that Cash brother to be the unknown assailant who had entered the Tudor Revival two weeks ago . . . and, like the Biblical assassin Cain, had taken his own brother's life.

Tom stepped toward me. Instinctually, I moved back. He'd all but confessed to the cold-blooded murder of his only sibling. I needed to keep my distance, in case he'd felt the urge to strike again.

"What you're thinking, PJ . . ." He put up his hands in a show of innocence. "You're wrong. I didn't kill my brother."

I wanted to believe him, for the sake of my own safety, if nothing else. "No?"

An expression of sorrow fell across the handsome older man's face. "But I did watch him die."

As I listened intently, Tom Cash explained the events as they had occurred, on that Saturday morning in mid-July . . .

# Chapter 29

*The morning of the murder . . .*

Doorbells jingled across the diner.

At the sound, Tom Cash glanced up in time to see his young lover disappear into the daylight. He knew that he'd made a mistake in letting the guy go. But he also knew that by taking his brother's call, in the long run, it would spare Kyle's life.

Tom took a deep breath, cell phone to his ear. "You don't like what I'm doing? *Kill* me!"

"Don't tempt me, Tommy," his twin warned from the other end of the line. "You made a promise when Mom and Dad left you the house."

Tom wanted Terry to understand. More than anything, he wanted his brother's approval. But he couldn't risk losing Kyle. He needed to put aside the disagreement, if only momentarily. "Ter, I can't do this right now. I gotta get over to the Tudor and clean up the yard before Mr. Hank reports me. I can't afford a fine, okay?"

"Should've thought of that when you borrowed the money to fix up the bar."

His brother couldn't resist taking a stab when Tom was at

his most vulnerable. It was the way Terry had always operated, all their lives. Why should Tom expect anything less
from him now? Why should he expect his twin to show him
any sympathy when, in the fifty years they'd spent as brothers, Terry had never lauded Tom with anything but resentment?

"Hit me up later, okay? We can talk more about this."
Tom ended the call with Terry and immediately dialed Kyle's
number.

After three rings, he heard his young lover's voice over
the outgoing message: *You've reached Kyle. If this is important,
text me.*

Normally, Tom would have reached out to his millennial boyfriend by his preferred method of contact. But he'd
wanted to personally apologize for his behavior. Despite his
half century, Tom Cash had always been a cool dude. Keeping up with the latest trends was how he'd kept up with the
younger guys . . . and got them into his bed.

But those days were behind him now. Tom wanted only
one man in his life: Kyle. Their over twenty-year age difference had no ill effect on their relationship. Physically, the
connection between the couple couldn't have been greater.
Emotionally, the bond between them couldn't have been
stronger. Tom realized, most of all, what Kyle Young represented: his one shot at true happiness.

He had to win Kyle back, at whatever cost.

At the tone, Tom pleaded his case for forgiveness, as best
as he knew how. "Hey, Kiddo. Sorry about what happened at
breakfast. I hope you didn't mean what you said about breaking up. It's not what I want, okay? Listen, I'm heading over
to the Tudor right now. I'll give you a call when I'm done
cleaning up. There's something I wanna ask you." He paused
a moment, choking back tears as he envisioned the marriage
proposal he had planned. "I love you."

A sense of melancholy washed over the handsome older man as he walked the few blocks to his boyhood home. In the moment, Tom Cash couldn't have known the extent to which his life would soon change.

Forty minutes later, he shut off the lawn mower.

Tom popped a piece of spearmint gum into his mouth, taking a pause to admire his handiwork. Admittedly, he hadn't spent much time at his family's former home since gaining possession. The Tudor held too many memories.

Unlike his twin brother, Tom wanted to forget the life they'd led at 4 Fairway Lane, before the terrible accident that claimed both their parents. It had been Terry's desire to keep everything as it had appeared on the day Mom and Dad died. And while Tom had originally vowed to do so, the time had come for him to finally move on.

For Tom Cash, at age fifty, life was only just beginning. Once he worked out the deal with the New York City guys to renovate the Tudor on their TV show, his real estate connection, Cheri Maison, could sell it. Then Tom could use the profit to pay back the loan he'd borrowed . . . before anyone he loved got hurt.

He'd have to receive Terry's blessing, of course. It didn't matter if Tom, on paper, solely owned the property. He'd always felt it unfair that his father had willed the house to him alone. Above all—and in spite of their differences—Tom loved his brother and wanted Terry to be happy.

He pushed the mower down the driveway and across the front lawn, where he resumed his yard work. But first, he'd left Kyle another voice mail, the third such message in the past sixty minutes, in which he'd reiterated his earlier regrets. Tom hoped to high heaven that the guy would forgive him and, above all, take him back.

He didn't blame Kyle for fearing he'd be dropped once

he'd reached his thirtieth birthday. Tom had used the same lame excuse for breaking up with his other younger boyfriends. With Kyle, Tom didn't worry over how old the boy would one day become. Because he truly loved the young man, unlike those before him. As a matter of fact, Tom looked forward to witnessing Kyle Young grow older, all the while remaining by his side.

In the distance, he heard someone call his name.

Tom glanced up to find Campbell Sellers standing on the sidewalk, dressed for yet another Saturday morning house-selling open house.

Cam shouted over the roar of the mowing machine: "Can I talk to you?"

Tom released the safety shut-off lever, and the engine sputtered to a stop. After their recent argument, seeing his ex surprised him. While he completely understood where Cam had come from, he couldn't let the egocentric real estate agent off the hook without a little ribbing. "You here to murder me? *Stop! Please! Don't!*"

At the Cape Cod next door, Tom caught a glimpse of Hank and Hennie Richards on their front porch, both sporting Tigers baseball gear. Mr. Hank cried out, complimenting Tom's good work on cleaning up the yard. His wife waved and blew a kiss before following her husband inside.

Tom turned his attention back to Cam.

His former boyfriend informed him that he'd left his brand-new cell phone inside the Tudor, after their late-night visit with the couple from HDTV's *Domestic Partners*. He gave Tom an excuse that involved tripping down the stairs, at which point the device must've fallen out of Cam's pocket.

Tom led them through the Tudor's arched doorway, stopping just inside the living room when his own mobile began to ring. Disappointment overtook him as he noticed his brother's name on the display—and not Kyle's.

Ignoring Cam's growing impatience, Tom picked up, irritated himself. *"What?"*

"Tommy, you busy?"

"Yes, I'm busy!" he yelled at his twin. "If you listened
when I talk, I wouldn't have to tell you twice."

"Don't do this. You can't sign that contract with them TV
guys."

Tom didn't have time for his brother's demands. He
needed to deal with Campbell Sellers and get his work done,
so he could get home and make amends with his future husband. He'd already told Terry they would discuss things later.
What part of that statement hadn't his brother understood?

Tom shouted into the phone, firmly putting his foot down:
"I'm *not* changing my mind about the house!" He quickly
ended the call, longing for the old days when slamming the
phone down on someone was physically satisfying.

When Tom turned around, ready to help Cam in the hunt
for his missing cell phone, he discovered the Realtor had mysteriously disappeared.

Ten minutes later, Terry showed up at the Tudor, much to
his brother's dismay. He jumped out of his old car and began
verbally attacking his twin. "Tommy, I won't let you do it.
This is my house, too!"

For a moment, Tom considered contradicting Terry's
claim, but he preferred not to cause a scene. He could just
picture Bob, across the street, peeking through the curtains,
ready to give a full report to everyone on Fairway Lane.

"I'm not gonna fight with you," Tom said softly, abandon-
ing the lawn mower. "Not here."

Terry, taking his cue, followed his brother inside the
Tudor.

They stood together near the bottom of the staircase, arguing over the piece of property that had been a part of their
family for over fifty years. Tom tried to explain where he was

coming from, in wanting to hire the partners to renovate the old house. Not only did the home need to be updated, the exposure from being featured on a national TV show would help drive up the selling price. Without the money he'd make from the sale, Tom wouldn't be able to return the five hundred thousand dollars he'd borrowed to fix up his bar. And, if he failed to make good on his agreement . . .

He'd find himself with a far worse debt to pay.

"Ter, I got a call this morning," Tom said. "If I don't pay back the money in the next three months, they're gonna hurt Kyle." He regretted lying to the boy, saying he'd gotten the cash from his brother when, in all actuality, he'd borrowed it from a so-called business associate. Truth be told, Terry didn't have a dime to his name.

Ranting and raving like a madman, Terry refused to listen to what his twin had to say. "It's your fault you got yourself into trouble, Tommy. I told you not to take on that loan from them mafia guys. But you didn't listen. They can kill *you*, for all I care!"

Hearing these words from his brother did not surprise him. Growing up, Tom had given it his best shot, but he could never gain Terry's approval. No matter how hard he tried, no matter what he did, Terry had always been jealous.

Tom was the one who'd gotten good grades in school, while Terry had barely passed his courses. Tom attended University of Michigan; Terry couldn't even get into State. Tom started his own business; Terry could never find a job. When their parents passed, Tom made a promise to take care of his brother. He put Terry to work at his bar. He gave him a place to live in a beautiful big house. Terry never once thanked Tom for anything. Instead, he acted as if his identical twin owed him, all because they were born on the exact same day.

Still, Terry was his brother . . . and he loved the guy, no strings attached.

Tom told Terry to shut up. He needed to get outside and finish the yard work. If only Terry would let him pass by. He was a big dude, for sure. Tom could take him down, physically, if he had to. Instead, he headed up the staircase to the second floor . . .

Before he did something he might later regret.

Terry charged up the steps, grabbing for his twin. Tom pulled his arm away, flinging his brother off him.

That's when it happened.

Terry's foot caught hold of the loose stair board near the top, causing him to stumble.

Like in a slow-motion movie, Tom watched his brother fall backward. Terry reached out his hand, grasping for the railing. Tom reached out for Terry, but he couldn't make contact.

In an instant, it was all over. Terry landed at the bottom of the steps with a *snap*.

In that awful moment, as he silently stared down from atop the rickety old staircase, Tom Cash knew that his brother was gone forever.

Terry lay lifeless and broken, facedown on the hardwood floor. The dark fabric of his hoodie partially covered the back of his head. But it was perfectly clear: The handsome older man had broken his neck.

For his brother, it was like seeing his own reflection. Except for the baseball caps they wore, Tom realized just how identical he and his twin appeared to the outside world.

Slowly, he descended the stairs. Tom picked up Terry's hat from where it had landed, a few feet away from his brother's body. Tenderly, he touched the capital *S* embroidered on the front. About to replace the cap atop Terry's salt-and-pepper head—*out of respect?*—Tom stopped to reconsider.

Sometimes he would forget that, scientifically speaking, he and his brother were the same person, due to their DNA.

Sure, there were subtle differences, like the slight space between Tom's two front teeth that Terry did not possess. But for the most part, most people couldn't distinguish between the Cash brothers. Growing up, they used to fool their parents, teachers, and friends. With Terry gone, Tom knew that he could convince everyone else into thinking what he needed them to: He was Terry . . . and Terry was him.

He removed his blue and gold cap and replaced it with his dead brother's white and green. Reaching a hand into Terry's pocket, Tom swiped the ancient flip phone. Then he stepped through the Tudor Revival's arched doorway—along with his brand-new identity.

Outside, the man now known as *Terry* Cash dropped a fancy new smartphone onto the freshly cut front lawn. He ran over it with the mowing machine, the first step in destroying any trace of his former self.

Now, two weeks later, Tom stared at the spot where he'd last seen his twin alive, near the top of the rickety old staircase. Beside him, near the bottom, best-selling YA mystery author-turned amateur detective, Peter "PJ" Penwell, stood listening to Tom's full confession.

"I should've never took advantage of my brother dying like I did," he lamented. "I panicked, I guess. I saw a way out of the trouble I got myself into. Maybe, as Terry, I could collect the money from my own life insurance policy and pay back the loan shark? Once I was finally in the clear, I could come forward and turn myself in."

"You do realize it would be considered fraud, if you did that?"

"Dude, only if I got caught. And the people I owe the money wouldn't tell anyone they took it from me." Tom lit a cigarette. "But I couldn't do it. I can't live with all the guilt." He inhaled deeply, slowly circling the room's perimeter. "When I found out about Terry and Danny . . . it broke my heart learning my brother finally had a shot at finding love. But then he lost it."

For the first time that evening, Tom Cash spoke directly to his witness, daring to look him in the eyes. "You know I loved Danny? He's a real good guy. I didn't deserve him. But Terry did."

He sucked hard on the cigarette, the cherry embers burning brightly, like hot coals. "Ter deserves the dignity of people knowing *he's* the one who died here in this house . . . and I deserve to do my time for what I did to him."

Tom reached into his pocket for his newly purchased mobile device. With a tap of a finger against the glass, he called up the keypad and dialed . . .

"9-1-1, what is your emergency?"

"This is Tom Cash," he said stoically, "over in Pleasant Woods. I wanna report a crime."

Within the half hour, a police vehicle pulled up in front of the Tudor Revival located at 4 Fairway Lane. Detective Nick Paczki stepped out of the car and met the self-proclaimed culprit on the wide front porch.

The handsome older man held out his hands, wrists together.

# Epilogue

We pulled into the parking lot just before ten o'clock.

This time, I drove, and JP sat shotgun. We'd been awake for several hours, both of us unable to get much sleep the night before.

Truth be told, we were total nervous wrecks.

Earlier, we'd scurried about the house, attempting not to collide into each other, as we prepped for our morning appointment. JP kept searching for his phone, which I, of course, kept reminding him he'd lost during his film shoot Up North. Thankfully, he'd made it home in time to witness Nick Paczki as he whisked Tom Cash away in his squad car. I still couldn't fathom the events of the past twenty-four hours.

After standing inside the Tudor listening to Tom's personal confession, it took me a moment to process. I'd felt both confused and confounded. But it had all made perfect sense: Tom Cash didn't die on that summer Saturday morning, two weeks prior. All along, the person who'd taken a tumble down a rickety old staircase, only to meet his demise at the bottom, had been none other than . . .

*Tom's twin, Terry.*

The sudden plot twist, I certainly hadn't anticipated. For

sure I'd have to borrow it for my next novel, if I ever got around to writing one.

Back at the pet store in Madison Park, JP jumped out of the car and darted toward the building. Trailing behind, I locked the doors with a press of the key fob and kicked it into high gear.

My partner came to a sudden stop just outside the entrance. His sun-kissed face drained of all color as he gazed at me in a panic.

Pulling JP into a warm embrace, I did my best to quell his irrational fear that Margot might change her mind. All we needed to do was sign the adoption papers . . . and Clyde would officially be ours.

That's exactly what we did.

We brought him home.

Well, first we took a family selfie in the Pet Supplies Plus parking lot, and promptly posted it to our newly created social media page: @TheDailyClyde. Here, we planned to update friends and followers as to the goings-on in the life of our little beagle-bull—without being obnoxious about it.

JP held our boy in his arms the entire car ride back to Pleasant Woods. We hadn't thought to buy a harness with a tether to clip to the backseat seat belt. We weren't experienced dog parents . . . yet.

Once inside the house, Clyde sniffed around, checking out every nook and cranny of his new domain. We couldn't tell if he was excited or anxious to have at last found his Furever Home. But watching the tiny seven-month-old beagle-bull puppy take everything in, his cold black nose absorbing each and every new scent, our hearts felt full.

We couldn't have asked for anything more.

JP looked at me, completely lost. I felt the same way, unsure as to how we should proceed. With Clyde now officially ours, the last thing we wanted to do was scar him forever.

Thankfully, my phone rang, allowing us a brief reprieve from having to make any rash decisions. Consulting the screen, I discovered the caller to be the mayor's wife, Vicky Marshall.

It seemed that she'd read my play script, which she admitted to thoroughly enjoying, the ending in particular. She confessed to having no idea as to where the plot had been progressing and, upon arriving at the climax, her breath had been taken away.

Always flattered to receive praise for my creative talents—no matter from whom—I thanked Mrs. Marshall for her thoughtful compliments.

She declared that, with my permission, she would be honored to direct the premiere production, in the spring slot of the Royal Heights Players' upcoming season.

The one and only JP Broadway would star, of course.

A part of me stopped to consider the gracious offer. As much as I'd hoped to one day see the piece produced, the venue of my *Blue Tuesday* dreams had always been a Broadway show palace, not some suburban community theatre. But, as a writer who'd experienced his fair share of rejection, it felt nice to finally have someone's sincere approval.

Besides, a man had just mysteriously died in our sleepy little town of Pleasant Woods, and both JP and I had weathered the storm unscathed.

*What else could possibly go wrong?*

# Home Renovation Rules for DIY-ers

When my partner Craig and I purchased our Forever Home, we had the super fun experience of sharing the process on HGTV's hit show *House Hunters*. The house we ended up choosing is a 1924 Craftsman Colonial, located in a Detroit suburb much like the fictitious Pleasant Woods featured in this book. Fortunately, because we're only the third family to ever live in the home, there hadn't been a lot of updates to the property over the past almost-100 years, which is part of what attracted us to it.

While I wouldn't call it a fixer-upper, there were indeed some projects that needed to be tackled once we moved in. If you're like Craig and me (read: house poor, since most of our money went toward the down payment), and you need to complete your own renovations out of a financial necessity— or maybe you're just handy and you enjoy the headaches that come with home improvement—here are a few so-called rules that we've learned, and that we constantly remind ourselves of, whenever we set out to work on a renovation project.

Rule 1: *If you're going to do something, do it right.* Don't just rush through a job in order to get it done. Take your time. When painting or refinishing woodwork, do all of the prep— tape off moldings or the already-painted walls, and cover anything that you don't want to ruin with a plastic tarp or an old sheet, including the floor—because you *will* drip paint onto your baseboards or fling citrus-based stripper onto your new Pottery Barn end table, leaving a mark that you'll never get off. You'll also knock over the container of mineral spirits at some point, causing the polyurethane on your hardwood floor to turn all gooey and then re-harden, leaving a big splotchy mess . . . no matter how careful you think you're capable of being.

Rule 2: *If you can do a project yourself, don't pay someone else to do it for you.* Yes, it saved Craig and me some money by doing (most of) the renovation work on our house by ourselves. But this is *our* home. By patching and painting the walls, and painstakingly stripping and refinishing the woodwork in our four bedrooms, living, dining, and mudroom, and returning them to their natural dark-stained state, a process that personally taught us both Rule 1 and Rule 2, we've developed a deeper appreciation for the craftsmanship that went into building the house, back in the early twentieth century. We've also gotten to know our home on a personal level—every square inch of plaster, every piece of wood trim—as we've labored with love in order to restore the house to its original splendor.

Rule 3: *Every project takes longer than you think it's going to.* You might tell yourself: "Oh, I'll just do this [insert project here] really quickly . . ." But, three hours later, after banging your head against the wall and cussing loud enough for the neighbors down the block to hear you through your closed windows, you will still be working on whatever that so-called quick project was that you planned on tackling in ten minutes. However, as per Rule 1 . . . there's no rush to finish anything. Not if you want to do it correctly. *Which you do.* Especially when it comes to owning a home, especially an historic one. Any improvement you make is only going to extend the life of the house, and add more value to the property, when it comes time to pass it along to the next family. Hopefully, these new owners will take as much pride in caring for the home as you and your family once did—and will *not* paint over the woodwork that you spent more hours painstakingly refinishing than you can possibly count.

# Acknowledgments

A big thanks to my editor, John Scognamiglio, for reaching out in the early days of the pandemic and offering me the opportunity to pen my first cozy mystery. Growing up, I was a big *Encyclopedia Brown* fan, so taking a stab at this genre has been super fun.

For her knowledge of police procedures and law enforcement—and answering all my questions about police procedures and law enforcement—I'd like to thank my old pal, Officer Suzanne Wisnewski-Strautz of the Hazel Park PD.

To everyone at Kensington Publishing, past and present: Thank you for everything you've done for me, past and present . . . and future.

To my family, friends, and neighbors in Pleasant Ridge and Huntington Woods, whom I'm counting on to buy this book and come to my book party: Thanks, guys!

As always, love to Craig Bentley, my real-life Domestic Partner in Crime.

And to Marilyn, Karin, Jeannine, Raegan, and the many volunteers at Home FurEver: Much thanks for all you do for the rescue dogs of Detroit . . . and for blessing Craig and me with our dear, sweet Clydie Boy. ☺

Visit us online at
**KensingtonBooks.com**
to read more from your favorite authors,
see books by series, view reading
group guides, and more!

**BOOK** **CLUB**
**BETWEEN THE CHAPTERS**

Visit us online for sneak peeks, exclusive
giveaways, special discounts, author content,
and engaging discussions with your fellow readers.

Betweenthechapters.net

Sign up for our newsletters and be the first
to get exciting news and announcements about
your favorite authors!
**Kensingtonbooks.com/newsletter**